LOVING SYLVIE

LOVING SYLVIE

ELIZABETH SMITHER

ALLEN&UNWIN
SYDNEY · MELBOURNE · AUCKLAND · LONDON

First published in 2019

Allen & Unwin
Level 3, 228 Queen Street
Auckland 1010, New Zealand
Phone: (64 9) 377 3800
Email: info@allenandunwin.com
Web: www.allenandunwin.co.nz

83 Alexander Street
Crows Nest NSW 2065, Australia
Phone: (61 2) 8425 0100

A catalogue record for this book is available from the National Library of New Zealand.

ISBN 978 1 98854 711 4

Cover artwork and design by Keely O'Shannessy
Internal design by Cat Taylor
Set in 11.5/17 pt Sabon LT Pro
Printed and bound in Australia by Griffin Press
10 9 8 7 6 5 4 3

for Sarah

CONTENTS

If nothing is going well, call your grandmother.

Italian proverb

Why was the genuine tenderness of a loving
grandmother any less satisfying than the tenderness
of a mother?

Philip Roth: *Nemesis*

Because death always seemed a mother—
or a grandmother, someone
familiar—now I come near
the time of greying hair, I fear
the mask more than the skull itself.

Ruth Fainlight: 'Divination by Hair'

PART ONE:

LOVE & BOOKS

On the morning of her wedding Sylvie Lehmann was rowed across a lake. Her grandfather, Kit Lehmann, who pulled at the oars, felt constricted by his lightweight suit that was tight at the shoulders. Old muscles, he chided himself, as a bead of sweat slid under his collar. Then he eased both his stroke and his muscles; there was no need to hurry at a marriage.

On the little dock stood Isobel, Sylvie's grandmother, the bridal bouquet self-consciously in her hands like a spring cabbage.

Sylvie Lehmann had been rehearsing her new name as her grandfather rowed. *Sylvie Grace Taverner*. It went with the slow dipping of the oars and the drops from the blades falling back into the grey-green water. A black swan was gliding beside the far bank. Trailing Sylvie's left hand, which hung over the side, was a flotilla of ducks. Had she thought to bring bread her progress might have resembled that of a flower girl, archly turning to scatter rose petals. Still, queens did not condescend to ducks. The boat rocked a little; she could tell her grandfather was tiring. But she knew it was important not to say anything. Instead she caught his eye and winked.

Isobel was joined on the dock by a small boy who began to ask her catechism-like questions. 'Why are you standing here?' 'Why are you holding those flowers?' She turned her head to look at him—she had always admired the catechism—and gave her answers in sequence. 'I'm waiting for my granddaughter. It's her wedding bouquet.' 'Is the boat going to sink?' came next, and Isobel glanced again at the lake. Kit did seem to be making heavy weather of it and the black swan had got dangerously close. She could see Sylvie leaning forward, saying something.

In the slatted light of the boatshed, the rowboat had had some water in the bottom, as well as a handful of dried leaves. Kit was infuriated that something had gone wrong with the arrangements, that it wasn't better prepared. Later it would be revealed they had the wrong boat, number seven instead of number eight, and number eight, freshly painted and swept out, was already hired and out on the lake. The staff member, whom nobody had briefed, pleaded ignorance. Kit, groaning inwardly, had taken up the oars and essayed a few tentative strokes before digging deeper and turning the prow towards the centre of the lake. And Sylvie, exaggerating her gesture to soothe her grandfather, lay languidly back, despite possible damage to her dress. Her mood was heightened by the short time on the lake, the tribute of her grandfather's rowing; she had watched his chest rise and fall, and had moved his jacket alongside her. She thought nothing in the day would bring her so much satisfaction as her hand dipping below the surface and seeing it foreshortened and pale. The black swan that had threatened to come close had recognised a bolder creature and moved off, averting its black head and baleful red eye.

Meanwhile, for this part of the planning was on time, Ben Taverner and James Marbeck, the best man, were strolling through the lower reaches of the park. Both wore hired lounge suits with jackets unbuttoned. Ben could feel the air moving under the lining as he gesticulated, and looked down admiringly at his cuffs. They climbed a wide path towards the lake and Ben complained to James that he had been promised a jilting if he so much as gazed at Sylvie in her boat.

'Not like you to avoid a challenge,' was James's response. They were passing a giant ficus that could have concealed an elephant. But when Ben caught sight of Sylvie he felt his restraint had been wise. She was peering into a pink scallop-shaped mirror and her grandmother was dabbing at her cheek. Her grandfather was holding the bouquet. He looked as if the day had begun badly and would end that way. Under his arm was a flat box that held the veil.

They were absorbed in their preparations but then Sylvie turned her head and smiled at Ben. A sweet disorder in the dress, he thought, and the idea pleased him: he had seen so much of Sylvie already. A motion of Sylvie's hand indicated he should wait. Then, in her veil borrowed from a friend who would shortly divorce and her ball gown from an op-shop, Sylvie, with her retinue of four—the celebrant made five—made her entrance.

An hour later their little party was seated at a round table in an alcove overlooking the garden. Sylvie's veil was rolled and back in its box at her grandfather's feet. She thought being bare-headed might take care of the glances that were sent in her direction. Her grandmother was pulling petals from the peonies, white and pink, that lay on the tablecloth. In the centre was the despoiled cake stand on which only a few samples remained: a tiny custard tart, one curling cucumber and cress sandwich, the crimped crust of a savoury. The fine bone china cups had been filled and refilled to exhaustion. The napkins were crumpled on the plates and there was a ring on the cloth where the ice bucket had sat.

'Are you happy?' Kit asked Sylvie as his hand fumbled to push a white rosebud through a buttonhole. He should have thought of this when they sat down, but the whole day, from the moment he stepped into the rocking boat, had felt out of his control. Instantly he blamed himself for asking.

Sylvie to whom the tempo of the day was entirely different, turned to face her grandfather. Intently she held his gaze. He was reminded for a moment of a painter and a sitter, the first compelling look that passed between them.

'Isn't it obvious?' she said.

'And this was enough? An afternoon tea?'

'Dear Kitcat,' she said. 'When will you learn there are things you can't supply that are free for the taking.'

When he still looked unconvinced, she moved her head and kissed him lightly on the cheek. He remembered the large cheque he had deposited in her account and guessed it made up for the littleness of everything else.

'A walk?' said Sylvie, pushing back her chair. 'To walk off the cake?'

She walked between Ben and James, Isobel and Kit behind. Ben had his arm about her waist—why did men's arms and hands have this stringent code of seeming not to touch, of lying open and visible for all to see when . . . but she didn't finish the thought because she almost stumbled over a stone and Ben caught her wrist. She felt the pressure of his fingers before his palm resumed its position and lay flat.

Slowly they descended through the park. It was man-made, traces of its early planning evident in the deep bowl of the lake, the symmetry of linking paths or the placing of a fountain or a plaque. At the band rotunda Sylvie, Ben and James went one way and Isobel and Kit the other: its octagonal shape suggested a division. If the stage had been full of bandsmen blowing cornets and tubas, they would have been blocked by lines of metal chairs with backs like staves; now they could wade on the lower steps and join up again where the track recommenced.

The gate was nearby, a square sombre affair with a turnstile, but Sylvie negotiated it with ease and they followed in a line. They waited in a knot while Kit went to bring the car around. The hem of Sylvie's dress was damp and a few blades of grass clung. Isobel was thinking that it should be a dress for a day only. Now she ran her fingers through her hair and disentangled a small twig. At that instant a flock of Canada geese passed above a stand of pines. Then the car was there and the symbolism—even if none had been desired or even observed—fell off and they were on the mundane streets again.

'Relax,' Isobel longed to say to Sylvie as they set them down outside the Majestic Hotel, part of the largesse of the cheque, but she knew it was ridiculous and it was herself she was counselling. So often now this seemed the case: an instruction given to herself through an intermediary. Anyone would do and the advice was as suspect as talking to herself.

Thinking was more and more appealing, though she seemed to have jettisoned some ability to reason. The park had been almost unbearable. Kit, flushed, in the wrong boat, the sparse ceremony, the ruined table—all these things she would like to sift and arrange in some sort of order, not of chronology or importance, but into a pattern like the strokes of a painting. And she hoped, in the abandoning of fixed patterns, she would find something for herself.

At the hotel, in the suite Kit had booked—he had brusquely declined 'The Bridal Suite', fearing a bed scattered with rose petals and the nudges and winks of the staff—a suite commendably plain, apart from a bottle of champagne that looked as if it had been sweating for hours since the sides of the silver bucket were dry, Sylvie put one hand on Ben's shoulder, the other about his waist, under the lining of his jacket, and indicated with a nudge that she wanted to dance.

'Wait,' he said and flung the jacket off onto the quilt.

'Music,' Sylvie said. 'I'll hum.'

The only tune that came to mind was 'Beautiful Dreamer' and she began to sing the words softly as they turned on the grey carpet with the thin red stripe.

'Beautiful dreamer
Wake unto me.'

'Are you a beautiful dreamer?' she asked into his chest, and his words of affirmation came back as if they were deep within a sounding box which vibrated before the word was formed.

'What shall we do?' she asked. She meant, since there had already been a lot of bed—not as comfortable as this one but bed nonetheless—that she wanted something different for the late afternoon.

'A long bath? A walk?' It was clear which he preferred.

Outside it had begun to rain, a soft misty rain with amazing powers of dampness. A few hours and everything would be soaked.

'A walk first. And then a bath. I expect there is bubble bath.'

So the jacket went back on and Sylvie's half-coat which left a swathe of very stained satin showing. There were raised eyebrows at reception and the offer of an umbrella, which Ben accepted. Two streets brought them to the beach and a grey sea with a curious hint of brown. The brown was river mud, Sylvie told herself, pleased that facts remained. She slipped off her shoes and put one in each pocket—she would have liked to throw them in the waves to see if they would float. Ben tried to grab her and drag her under the umbrella but she broke free. She threw her head back in the soft rain until her face was drenched, and her hair, and a tiny pool formed in the small of her back.

The call Isobel made to the keeper of the boats went smoothly. Her comments were accepted—he intimated all the boats might be painted the following spring, and she wondered if there might be another occasion to hire one. Recalling Kit, she thought it was unlikely. She refused a refund.

She went to the art gallery, she changed her books, she went for long walks. She walked past the gates of the school Sylvie had attended until she was expelled, and saw again the line of cars with young men behind the wheels. She stopped and stood under the same spreading sycamore where she had witnessed a flash of blue like a kingfisher as her granddaughter glided by inside one of the cars. Frozen to the spot, Isobel had hardly dared breathe. The blue car eased into the traffic, then the motor revved and it was heading over a small bridge.

Sylvie's mother, Madeleine Lehmann, was in Paris. A note had arrived with the promise of a wedding gift and a hope that a meeting would take place soon. Isobel knew she could depend on her daughter's good taste. As a child she had been given a jewellery box and it had replaced more common toys as her greatest treasure. Madeleine was classically good-looking; her expression was both sympathetic and serene. She had a gift of stillness that was very appealing. Over the years a good many jewels had been added to her box.

When she was fifteen, the same age as 'Claudine', Isobel had bought her the Colette novels. They were barely touched, the pale blue, mauve, almond green and melting pink covers stayed glowing in her bookcase, and yet something must have been absorbed. Madeleine had gone on holiday to France with a girlfriend, quarrelled with her, and stayed. At first she had remained with the Lévêque family she was billeted with and later, with their intervention, for they considered her inexperienced and perhaps romantic, a Lévêque cousin. Cautiously she memorised a few streets, a few cafés. Her pale hair and hopeful expression—even when she knew she was lost—often brought someone to the rescue.

She found a job in an English-language bookshop, Le Livre Bleu, not because she was knowledgeable but because of her resemblance to Grace Kelly. She had seen the card in the window, *On recherche une vendeuse*, and pushed open the blue-black door. A severe woman, with hair so tightly pulled back from her forehead it seemed to be scalping her, regarded her from behind a desk whose artful clutter Madeleine would learn, when it was her job to dust it, was carefully contrived. In her second week Madeleine placed a shiny red apple there and received a nod of approval. The salary was tiny, risible, but Madeleine was content. When she needed new lodgings, Madame Récamier offered her a room above the shop. She had access to a tiny bathroom and the gas ring on which coffee was made. Cooking was not permitted, but Madeleine could buy a *croque-monsieur* in a paper bag or stroll along the rue du Dragon taking small bites from a sugary lemon crêpe. The number of young men visiting Le Livre Bleu increased, as Madame Récamier anticipated. Every afternoon she saw to it that Madeleine spent some time rearranging the window, placing the latest Joyce Carol Oates or Philip Roth in a prominent position. Sometimes Madeleine made a spiral staircase of the books or leaned them against one another like dominoes about to topple. In the store room at the rear of the shop were crammed a few authors' busts, remnants of a set: Dickens, Edgar Allan Poe, Mark Twain.

Howard, an American postgraduate student, took Madeleine to the Louvre to view the Victory of Samothrace. She was impressed by the number of students sketching in each room, the whispered conversations, the soigné appearance of the dark-suited assistants at the desks. Afterwards they sat in the Jardin des Tuileries and Howard told her that the isolated and dramatically placed Victory was once commonplace and could have been ordered from a catalogue.

'You could phone and order one?' Madeleine asked.

'Well, there wouldn't have been any phones. Probably despatch a servant to the stonemason.'

She sat puzzling, enjoying the faint sun. Howard, looking at her sideways, was admiring her profile, thinking she was worth asking out again.

There was a series of Howards and Jerrys and Scott Jnrs before Madeleine became aware of the interest of an older man, Bertrand Gosselin, who was often in the poetry section, reading Robert Lowell or Randall Jarrell. Once she wrapped *The Dream Songs* by John Berryman for him; on another occasion he waylaid her with a poem about a dead girl who had chased geese. Madeleine had not known what to say, any more than she had known what to say in the Louvre; she waited for a sign, and when none was forthcoming—a poem must stand on its own feet, he would tell her later—she smiled. Soon Bertrand began seeking things for her to read. Madame Récamier did not seem to mind if she sat beside him for a few minutes on an old sunken green sofa while he recited a few lines of E.E. Cummings or Ogden Nash. 'He is a good buyer,' she said to Madeleine one afternoon after he had departed carrying a parcel of books, including the latest Joan Didion.

It was always expected by Isobel and Kit that Madeleine would eventually tire of France and come home. When she did, shortly before her twenty-third birthday, it was discovered she was pregnant. She refused to name the father or answer questions. Already in the second trimester, though hardly showing, she seemed as serene as any of the Madonnas in the

Louvre. Only when Sylvie was born, after a prolonged and complicated labour, did her confidence fail her. Isobel saw that Madeleine had not thought ahead, and that this was now to be her role. In a strange way she was grateful: her daughter's character was so puzzling, she welcomed an occupation as a distraction. Overthinking had always been a problem: turning a subject over and over, looking for a chink of light. Madeleine still spoke of the bookshop in the rue du Dragon and of Madame Récamier whose arthritis had advanced and who now walked with a stick.

Madeleine was entirely unaware she was considered 'easy'. One afternoon she had allowed Bertrand Gosselin to undress her in his fusty old apartment where parcels of books from the shop lay unopened on the floor. She lay on his bed, in the hollow formed by his body, and he stroked her from head to foot. She couldn't hear what he was murmuring. It might have been lines from one of the poems he had shown her—perhaps not the goose girl, though her own head was propped by a pillow bearing the scent of pomade. She felt his dry lips on her forehead, then her breasts which were speckled by the slanting and mote-laden light. Afterwards she got up and used his tiny bathroom with its floral hand basin and damp towel. He offered to walk her back to the shop but she declined. She went carefully down the stone stairs and then to an outdoor café.

While she had made her toilette in the cramped and grimy bathroom—the piece of green soap had a dark crack like dirty fingernails—a memory of something in Colette had come to her. It was *Gigi* where the mother returns from singing in the opera chorus and, though exhausted, attends to a minimal toilette before falling into bed. Madeleine saw again the line of books her mother had added to each birthday—only the Claudines and *Gigi and the Cat* had been read. Out of the blue another title came to her: *The Pure and the Impure.*

Back at Le Livre Bleu she washed her hands in the carefully scrubbed basin and brushed and rebraided her hair. Madame Récamier gave her a sharp look and turned aside her head.

Grandmotherhood was handed to Isobel in the dawn Sylvie was born. She checked her watch and, to make sure the time would always be engraved on her mind, she wrote 3.17:22 in Biro on the back of her hand. Hours later, when she was home again, almost too tired to stand, she wrote it in lipstick on the mirror, and finally into a notebook she carried in her purse. She had read that children wanted this time to be remembered and felt betrayed if it was forgotten. Never had Isobel slept so deeply. When she woke she expected the mattress to be hollowed out or scorched. An amazing light seemed to fill the room, the light her mother, a practising Catholic, had told her was the light of forgiveness. No one in the family had taken Geraldine Foley's churchgoing seriously, though she was often in a good mood when she came home.

At the same time as the light filled the room and touched the lipstick scrawl of the night before, Isobel felt the burden of her own helplessness, as if her flesh too had given birth and was now light and soft, triumphant and deprived. The day's chores awaited—she got up and rubbed at the lipstick with her finger, smearing it.

But the half-hearted chores could not compete with the tiny

child who slept securely swaddled in a plastic crib. Isobel tried to imagine that breathing, rehearsed in the womb and yet so new in the unfamiliar open air. Perhaps the mind did not think yet; it only felt. The eyes gazed at the ceiling or walls, at the whiteness which was the body of a nurse. The first murmurings would enter the ears, the clatter of instruments, or a piece of gauze or cotton wool would approach, dipped in a warm saline liquid.

Isobel sat with Kit at the breakfast table, her hands wrapped around a mug of coffee. She felt light-headed and at the same time heavy-limbed.

'What sort of mother will she be?' she asked him.

'We must hope,' he said, touching her hand with warm fingers.

Ben Taverner who had married Sylvie at the kiosk on the lake had seen from the first a sober core in her. He was aware—not fully aware, no man could ever be—of the attention the opposite sex paid to surfaces. On their honeymoon—a word they both derided—Sylvie had insisted on one ritual: before she would go to bed with him they must stand under the stars together and recite 'The Owl and the Pussycat'. It was her favourite poem from childhood, and saying the words

> *'Dear Pig, are you willing to sell for one shilling*
> *Your ring?' Said the Piggy 'I will.'*

brought back all the comfort she had known and more. She started to explain to Ben the wonderful run-on line about the ring and the fast and fervent response of the pig before Ben put his arms around her and tried to draw her inside the room. He forgot about cares and surfaces until the next morning when Sylvie was in the bathroom and he could hear running water and the energetic sound of teeth-brushing. Her hair was damp as if she had towelled it lightly and then run a brush through it. Tendrils dried first and made a floating frame around her face.

Of course on the surface Sylvie could be exceedingly annoying. Her anger flowed freely; her kindness, in contrast, had to gnaw its way to the surface as if scouts were required. It began in a trickle like one of those tiny streams that rise in a water meadow, curving and twisting from the moment they begin to flow as if some attack is expected and camouflage is necessary. Ben could not foresee, because no one knows the future or how it will be diverted by things invisible, how his patience would be tried and have to fortify itself like someone or something in training: a triathlete or a bulked-up muscle.

His body was strong, and stronger after the night, though only a small proportion had been devoted to sleep. Now he was fully relaxed, ready to refill with energy. He could feel his heart beating steadily. He thought they could play nurses and doctors—Sylvie could wear her white slip. There was something about nurses' uniforms and what they wore underneath. But even this, as comforting as 'The Owl and the Pussycat', which he was going to memorise, paled beside the reality of a new day.

They had lived together for six months before he proposed. That was the current mode: the male came to a decision, after a period in which the partner was checked out, and to compensate for the trial period—for it was nothing less, however sugar-coated the terms—something secret was arranged. The beloved, which was now the correct term, was surprised by her suitor dropping to his knees in a public park or a banner attached to a tree. In extreme cases there might be a public announcement at a sports ground or following the final blessing at church. This had happened to one of his friends: the vicar had cleared his throat while the altar boys lined up behind him and raised his hand as if beginning the sign of the cross. In the pew his friend's fiancée let out a scream. Ben thought there was something ugly about the bargain, like a child being deprived of a reward. What if, on the day the reward was finally earned, a frightful quarrel broke out and it was too late to cancel the musicians or the restaurant booking during which the ring was to be slipped into a champagne flute? He tried to think of something Sylvie would not sneer at, spontaneous enough to be abandoned without causing a ripple if the time was not ripe. She was naturally suspicious; in fact she reminded him of a cat, one of those enigmatic animals whose purpose is to train its owner into suitable routines.

In the end he settled on a walk by the sea, the ring tucked into his pocket and, for extra security, tied in a square of red silk. He had tied it so tight that when the time came to present it the knot could not be undone and they had both worked on it together and Sylvie had used her teeth. He thought he might take that for an omen. Then they had walked in the shallows, holding hands. The grey-green water was cold and swirled around their ankles; their heels sank in the sand as suction pulled the waves back. It's all one piece, Ben thought. The harmless little waves into which even the suicidal must wade, pulled by the breaking waves and caps beyond, and then the great moving ocean itself. He pressed his toes in as well and, glad his proposal had worked—he had rehearsed only one sentence: now said, he dismissed it from his mind forever, as if the words would never be required again—gripped Sylvie's hand until she exclaimed at the pressure.

Now he was prepared for more and more of Sylvie to be revealed. He had never considered her vain, so the unscrubbed look had not deterred him; in fact he thought he preferred it: her skin slightly buffed as if by wind, nose shiny, cheeks flushed or pale. Why did women prefer opaqueness, he wondered whenever she began dabbing something out of a squat container under her eye sockets as if she was building up to an approved expression stroke by stroke? He had learned there were several possibilities: bare face, boldly revealed to his gaze; the face for going to the dairy for milk or bread which paid attention to the cheekbones in case the swarthy Italian who ran it caused her to blush; lipstick and perfume for her grandmother. If a party was in the offing he knew to withdraw and fuss with his shirts, of which there were only four, or pick up a magazine. On her wedding morning Sylvie had perched on a high stool surrounded by makeup artists wearing pouches and wielding brushes: she had described it to him, but reserved the sense of comfort she felt as the fine powder fell on her skin like scales on a moth's wing. She had left it on, all this handiwork, and invited him to despoil it. There was makeup on the sheets and pillows, lipstick stains on his face as if something clenched in a fist had been passed, as if they had bitten one another. She assured him that no one would blink at the sheets. Each afternoon when they returned, the bed was pristinely made up, the top sheet turned down like a freshly addressed envelope.

Sylvie seized a pillow and flung it at his head and then, when it came flying back, she replaced it among the others that formed a portcullis against the padded headboard. Ben caught sight of the maid in the corridor, wrestling with a laden cart, and wondered, since he was a cause of her labour, if he should offer to push it. Her skin was dark and her eyes, when she looked up, fathomless. On the second to last morning a chance arose and he helped push it into the service lift.

On the last morning he went down early to pay the bill, own up to drinking two sauvignon blancs, a Napoleon brandy and a Hennessy from the mini-bar.

'Nothing to nibble?' the clerk asked.

'Nothing to nibble,' he replied, and his face was split by a wide grin.

'You know absolutely nothing of this Sylvie,' Cora Taverner had said. She had looked up the girl's grandmother's address in the phone book. One Sunday she took a drive past the house, parked opposite and pretended to be consulting a map taken from the glove box. This enabled her to raise her eyes and scan the house. The upper storey was clearly visible over the box hedge. A wrought-iron gate and a white path dividing a flower bed. At least there was order here. She drove away, slightly restored, until the following week one of her friends produced a potted biography of Sylvie Lehmann.

Expulsion from two schools or more, promiscuity, an affair with a married man—as the punishing sentences unfurled in Marcia Temple's unctuous voice, Cora concentrated on controlling her face. She pretended Sylvie was not the girl her son had told her he would marry over her living or dead body— he would prefer her living, at least he conceded her that, but any sabotage on her part would be a waste of breath.

'I've always considered heredity important,' Cora told Marcia, as if her attention was just returning. 'But how far back should we go? Or can we go?' She meant how little any of us, or indeed the gossip that issued from a single mouth, counted. Though her heart pained and she longed for Marcia to go, she was pleased that the abstract turn the conversation had taken had won back some ground. A little hope returned, and the thought that if Ben was intractable she had detective work to do, an inventory to fill.

Back at home, she placed her hands under the cold tap and then held them out to check if they were shaking. It was too soon, and she was too fearful to begin comforting herself with images of Benjamin as a baby. He was two and they were on the window seat together. She had pushed one of the windows open and latched it. A yellow rose was close to the glass, and she reached out a hand to touch the petals. Luckily it was thornless so if he copied her there was no danger. This was her role: identifying danger, second by second, until he lay safely in his cot, soothed by a story about animals who lived in burrows and helped one another. When the story finished, she tucked the covers in and touched her lips to his forehead, pushing the soft baby hair aside. 'Kiss,' he would demand, and she would feel her heart lurch and the quick response of control. On the window-seat squab he had advanced towards her, confident her outstretched hand was there for him, and put his arms around her neck. 'You can marry me, Mummy.'

She could never raise the memory without embarrassment. How could he be responsible for a gesture in which there was such an imbalance of power? For a moment Cora allowed her mind to return to the past and the embrace of a cherub. Were they really light to carry, those rounded dimpled angel-babies? Benjamin had felt weightless that day. Or had his gesture so claimed her heart he weighed nothing at all?

Three days after the wedding a large box arrived from Paris. It was slightly water-damaged and crushed in one corner. Isobel put it in the spare room, after inspecting it and removing the stamps for the local kindergarten. With typical extravagance Madeleine had affixed quantities of tape which might account for the delay: the parcel might have attracted the attention of Customs. A sort of certificate was enclosed inside a flap, and on a declaration she could read the contents and values in Madeleine's handwriting. *Antique linens and damask, candlesticks (2), napkin rings, ivory (2), silk pillowcases (2).* Isobel imagined Madeleine sorting through the linens in a poky little shop in the Marais, feeling the quality with her fingers, trying to imagine what Sylvie would like. The one time Isobel had frequented such a shop there had been a great deal of discussion. It seemed important not to reveal that the heavy linen she was intent on would be used for curtains. Instead she went through the pretence of having a large bed, and they discussed thread counts and how deep the turn-down should be. For all that, Isobel felt the woman looked at her suspiciously as if her perfidy was showing.

Sylvie and Ben would not return for a further week—'a secret,' Sylvie had said when Isobel had enquired about the destination.

'And if I need to contact you?' Isobel had pressed, though she was longing for a week to herself as well.

'If anything happens there are the police and the coastguard, helicopters and ambulances . . .'

As always her granddaughter said too much. Still Isobel did not let her irritation show. Perhaps 'coastguard' meant they were going on water. 'I'll call out the guard,' she said, and the faintly threatening moment resolved into a smile.

For a moment Isobel wondered if the parcel should be opened—she could use the excuse of damage, the linens might need airing or pressing—then she remembered that opening could be the best part.

Unknown to Isobel her thoughts of water and coastguards were perspicacious. In a small seaside village Sylvie and Ben were talking to a fisherman. Sylvie, more moral than she sometimes appeared, was thinking of *Captains Courageous*. The fisherman, in his twenties—there was an older man in the galley, glaring—wore huge rubber gloves and his face was burnt and weathered.

'Do you ever take passengers?' she called down to him.

'Never women,' he said, and she pulled a face.

'Then could we buy a fish?' she asked. She was in a good humour, thinking she must read the book again. Probably it would bore. Her grandfather had given it to her in one of her most difficult years. Little did he know what was in store. She had rejoiced when the rich spoilt boy had succumbed to labour and the sea.

'I'll give you a fish,' the young man said. The face had disappeared from the galley. There might be a quarrel later. He handed up a red cod, and Sylvie squeezed his hand and gave him her most extended smile.

Cora Taverner would have boycotted the wedding had she not been called away at the last minute—she blessed the fates for her delivery—to her daughter Anne's bedside. An ambulance in the middle of the night, a distraught son-in-law and a small grandchild. Into this chaos she gratefully stepped, consigning the wedding to a lesser sphere. Her son seemed to have no knowledge of what was going on; Sylvie was arranging it all.

Had Cora been present she might have consoled herself with the appearance of the woman she was spying on standing on a little jetty, clutching a bridal bouquet. Isobel's face had been pained that day; she had fought and raised it to neutral and then solicitous; she felt Kit's aching shoulders and splashed jacket more than the sight of the rowboat lumbering through the water. Sylvie's voice drifted to her as a vibration. She raised her hand to wave, and again when she touched Kit's shoulder, probably to the very spot that required massage.

Ben had explained his mother's absence—her apologies had been fulsome and insincere; a card containing a generous cheque 'to spend as they wished' had been forwarded.

'Do you think your mother would cover this fish?' Sylvie

had asked when Ben was fumbling for coins. Should they keep an inventory?

As for Sylvie's own mother, years of retelling had produced an accepted story, despite no father's name appearing on her birth certificate. On this alone Madeleine had proved adamant. For the short time Sylvie lived with her there had been a series of rented houses where Sylvie sometimes had a room of her own. But then letters had come from France, a relationship had resumed or been offered; Madeleine's longstanding depression had been recognised, and she had gone. Her agonising over linen in La Maison Ivre would go unacknowledged, though Sylvie would add initialled and lace-edged sheets to an ongoing notion of love.

But the absence of both mothers on her wedding day had been a relief. The day was perfectly balanced, with Kit straining his muscles at the oars, Isobel on the jetty, the bouquet against her tussah silk, and Ben and James strolling through the lower grounds.

Isobel had an idea of her granddaughter's attachment to rooms, or a single room, when the final arrangements were made and Sylvie came to live with her and Kit. Madeleine would return to France for a period of six months, returning to the Lévêque family she had stayed with on her first visit. This too was negotiated; one of the daughters, Céline, had left home and there was a room available. Madeleine's curious passivity, which remained unchallenged, made her an accommodating guest. She made few demands, joined in dinner parties and visits to the cinema; within a short time she had resumed her role as one of the Lévêques.

That another family was preferred, that she had in some way failed, was something Isobel did not allow herself to examine. Occasionally she pulled a thread and an insight, fleeting and inconsequential, came with it. Loving letters came eventually, describing the room in the Lévêques' house in Neuilly. The walls were pale yellow.

Sylvie possessed the same sense of colour. Almost any room she occupied was plain and uninviting but in the final house she had shared with her mother there was a diamond-shaped window with coloured panes. Her room had been converted from a passage and was just wide enough for a single bed and a dresser. Her clothes hung on a doweling pole Kit had fixed at an angle. When this house too was to be vacated, Sylvie's grief had been extreme. She was four and the window was her consolation. She stood on a stool and pressed her face against the glass. Kit had found her there one afternoon, sobbing. The stool toppled over as he lifted her, and the wails increased. The head, pressed against his neck, was hard, and her cries, until they died away in a series of stops and restarts, gulps and hiccups, reverberated inside his skull. He thought he knew the cause: stability was required.

There was no way he could replace the window but, suddenly inspired, he bought a glass brick. In the weeks following he repainted the smallest of the bedrooms and Isobel bought a striped cotton rug. Kit tied a cutting ribbon across the bedroom door and Isobel carried the not-too-sharp kitchen scissors on an old sofa cushion. Behind them trailed Sylvie, her face in what, for a four-year-old, passes for neutrality, which simply means the next expression has not yet arrived and the smooth skin rests. Both her grandparents watched as the scissors made a small then a larger cut in the pink ribbon and the porcelain door handle was turned. Isobel had drawn the curtains so the room was dim, the glass brick on a tea trolley at the foot of the bed. It was to this that Sylvie moved, exclaiming and lifting it in both hands. The surface of her eyes came alive then; the light entered and the surface flickered. That night Isobel, climbing the stairs to begin what would become a nightly ritual—no more than ten pages of a book, a tucking-in and a kiss—found she was too late, and Sylvie's sleeping head, book, bear and glass brick were in a line on the pillow.

The honeymooners returned and the parcel from Paris was duly opened. Layers of tissue and expertly tied ribbons were undone, and out came sheets from another century, edged in fine and faintly yellowed embroidery.

'I wonder who slept in them?' Kit asked. He was thinking, incongruously, of cheese wrapped in vine leaves or dusted with what looked like fine ash.

'Someone very proper,' Sylvie said. 'Someone brought up in a world of linen.'

Linen to cover everything, was Isobel's thought. As if the body was a temple and when it was unveiled the sheets remained to cover front and back. Rolled in the sheets were two silver candlesticks that 'might have come from a nunnery', Madeleine had written on a card with scalloped edges. She had neglected to ask for a certificate of authenticity. Under the sheets were two fine large table napkins and two napkin rings. Inside were entwined initials: *B* and *D*.

'Beatrice and Dante?' said Kit, holding one up to the light.

'More likely Brigitte and Didier, humble residents of the suburbs, too poor to own a carriage,' said Sylvie. Anything to cover the knowledge that her mother had stayed away. Still the sheets would be good to slide between, naked. In any case, almost everything outlasted a human being. Upstairs she must find her glass brick and take it with her.

She could hardly wait to take possession of the flat above a shop she had stumbled on and which the Chinese family of greengrocers, after years of cramped living, were vacating for a house they had bought in Mt Eden.

'It smells of noodles and cabbages,' Ben complained when they were alone in the tiny back room. An ancient toilet was crammed into a space the size of a cupboard. But the upstairs rooms, that had overflowed with beds, had windows that could be forced open once the paint had been scraped and the hinges oiled. After a day among citrus scents and cabbage stalks, unwashed potatoes with earth clinging to them, the family must have consoled themselves by sleeping in a fug.

On the sill, against the middle pane that didn't open, the glass brick instantly reflected the shivering leaves of a plane tree.

Sylvie had been walking along K Road after her anthropology lecture. Ben had agreed she should go back to university for a year and see how she progressed. The degree path, disordered as it so often was at first, and Sylvie was no exception, needed to be smoothed. He was sceptical about the relevance of the great apes. He could admit there were many parallels in the boardroom or in politics, even at Meier Olson where one leg, in his one and only suit, was raised to touch the bottom rung. Sylvie was passing a fruit shop and slowed to look at a pyramid of persimmons. She went in, drawn by the earthy scent that early morning hosing had failed to erase from the concrete floor. She could smell newsprint as well and the mingled scents of flowers drinking deep. She bought a red apple, lifting it from its nest of green tissue and then taking the tissue as well. The young Chinese man rubbed the apple on his apron, rewrapped the tissue around it, and handed it to her.

'Bag?' he asked.

'Thank you. No,' she replied, catching, though he had said only one word, a different order of language. An old Chinese woman had materialised at the back of the shop. In her black dress and apron she was almost invisible.

Sylvie walked along the street, biting into her apple. She had read something, but couldn't remember the source, about a male bite and a female one. The male, who had the more powerful jaws, took a deeper bite, practically one whole side of the fruit, before offering it to the female. This was just like the apes, she decided, turning the apple so a channel was made. Then she bit deeper and the core was revealed like a keyhole.

A schism was opening in her mind: her basic disapproval of anthropoid behaviour, and her need to make Ben see that this behaviour was deeply embedded in the human race and therefore useful, though he undermined her theory by behaving like one of the more intellectual apes, content to be lower in the male dominance hierarchy.

Still she felt the ape's imperative to find a nest. It amused her to think that a creature so inclined to theatrics and mock rages had such a desire for freshness in its nightly nest. The long arms could reach into the trees and pull down low branches with springy fresh-smelling leaves. Apes had a superior sense of smell, so a used nest might be doubly offensive. After the night's sleep and before the elaborate grooming that occupied several daylight hours, the nest was kicked over and all traces removed.

'It is natural for the apes, it is natural for me,' Sylvie thought, walking unheedingly along and bumping into a man who swore at her. He had an angry glaring face, so she turned and went back to the fruit shop. She walked quickly towards the rear where the tiny grandmother was standing, her hands folded over her apron. She saw the man walk past without glancing in. This time Sylvie inspected the boxes and partitioned sections slowly before she crossed the road and walked on the other side. It was from there that she looked up and saw the sign: 'Flat to Rent. Apply Within'.

She almost went back; then she reflected she needed to bring Ben. And like an alpha ape she needed to attend to her grooming: no ticks in her hair, no lice eggs on the thick fur that covered her shoulders. On the department noticeboard was the famous photograph from *National Geographic*: the sloping shoulders of the huge silverback resembled the fringe of a great forest. A blue-black mist seemed to rise from the fur, a beauty both poignant and powerful. So all the grooming paid off.

In his tidy casual clothes Ben stood in the upstairs rooms that would become their first proper home. He towered over Ma Xingjuan, Ma Shen, Ma Cheung.

'Shop open 6 a.m.,' Ma Xingjuan explained.

'No problem,' he replied. He liked the idea of slipping down to buy a peach or a bunch of red grapes, leaving the money beside the big silver till for Cheung to ring up. In the evenings, if they left the door open, scents of fruit would drift up the stairs.

They could just afford it, with a little help from Kit.

Sylvie did eventually meet Ben's mother at the University Women's Club. It was an awkward meeting punctuated by silences that were a test of will. Cora Taverner sat in a club chair while Sylvie was perched on a deep and disadvantaging sofa in slippery leather—whatever animal it came from would have had raindrops sliding from it at speed. She clenched her back and wiggled her hips to ease herself. Then she thought this might look provocative and she suppressed a smile. Cora, of course, noticed. The words that passed between them seemed to lie on the air like wafers.

Cora was careful at first to avoid references to Ben or to test Sylvie's newfound knowledge of him. This untested knowledge floated between them, but after a suitable length of time had passed it could no longer be avoided. There were childhood illnesses to be mentioned and the lingering effects they can have, even in adulthood. This led naturally to sensitivities. Only a mother could broach these since from the earliest stages of her child's development she had become their sole keeper. Benjamin might not have gone to boarding school but he had entered a male world, and doors, starting with the bathroom door, had been shut on her.

For a moment, sensing this, and seeing it might apply in her future, Sylvie felt a moment's sympathy. But it could not last and soon, aware her face was being minutely scrutinised, her look became glazed and she found herself examining the furniture.

'Your mother . . .' Cora was saying. 'She too was missing.' The implication was this was an absence of a different kind, something far more sinister than tending an ailing daughter.

'I believe you travelled by water,' she went on, when no information about Sylvie's mother was forthcoming.

'I've heard stories of her,' Cora said, when the tea things were gathered up and Sylvie, taking advantage of a temporary absence, had shoved a cushion behind her back. A sinking posture, she sensed, put her at a disadvantage. 'Was she rather vain?' It was as far as she dared to go.

'No more than half the human race,' Sylvie said, meeting her eye.

If she had heard about Madeleine's treasure box, Cora's lips would no doubt have curved in a sneer. It sounded babyish, almost retarded. Yet Sylvie knew her mother's love for jewellery was no more blameworthy than a magpie's liking for shiny things. Why should a child not reach for one thing instead of another? The treasure box, as Isobel explained it, had been in the window of an antique shop, sitting on the seat of a red velvet chair. Isobel had gone in, looking for a plate to replace one she had broken. She turned around and Madeleine had vanished. She ran to the door and looked up and down the street, then back into the shop. Madeleine was crouched in the window, pulling out the fake beads from the box which she had lowered to the floor. As Isobel watched, catching her breath, she saw her daughter stroke the gem-encrusted lid and then kiss it.

Isobel had felt she could not deny such a longing. It was as mysterious to her as it was to Kit. The silver and gold beads—from Mardi Gras in New Orleans—were included. When the auctioneer lifted out a handful, Madeleine began to cry. He smiled but his eyes were judging as he looked at the avid little girl.

'It will be your Christmas present,' Isobel said firmly to Madeleine, and Madeleine had nodded vigorously. She was three and it was only July: Isobel knew her edict would be overridden.

Clearly Cora knew nothing of this. She was probing about diet, meaning Ben's, the lethargy women failed to notice in men who worked with their brains.

'You needn't fret about fruit and vegetables,' Sylvie said. 'A band of gorillas would find it hard to keep up with Ma's Fruit & Veg.'

The face that looked back at her had none of the philosophical mien of a great ape. Suddenly apes seemed very appealing: an ape that might unseat Cora with a swing of its heavy forearm; an ape unpeeling a banana with delicate black fingers as if each segment of skin was a long yellow petal.

Looking back, Sylvie could see the boat on the lake was easy. Whole days now required such attentiveness. It began in the early morning when she needed to be up and presentable in case

Cheung came and knocked on their door. She heard the shop door open and the bell's first chime even before the light in the room had fully revealed their few pieces of furniture: a dresser with round handles like buttons and an old tapestry chair. Sylvie would open the door and Cheung would bow, holding out a gift of fruit from the market. It might be a pear or an apple. One morning it was an aubergine with a miraculously glowing skin. However Sylvie tried, Cheung could not be dissuaded.

She still remembered the first morning Cheung had caught her in her dressing gown, hastily and properly belted, and averted his eyes. That morning his bow was deeper as if a god had vouchsafed a secret. Surely he would see it was inappropriate. There were offerings of fruit on the windowsill, a line of tangerines. Ben had thrown one to her as she stood on the far side of the bed. 'Oh hell,' she cried, pulling her arms through the sleeves of the old robe that was as soft and comforting as a bath towel, the moment she heard the soft footfall on the stairs.

'The God of Hunger,' she said to Ben when she had unloaded three perfect lemons onto the bed. If she kept adding to the tangerines she could make a train. It was too late to pretend they were shunners of fruit. The only solution was fruit salad for breakfast and dinner.

It was not merely her dressing gown that seemed slothful. Other resolutions were coming undone. At first, remembering Lea the courtesan in the Colette novels her mother had left behind, Sylvie had tried to attend to her appearance before Ben woke. This was difficult because he slept heavily and woke first. He lay with his arms folded under his head, looking at the ceiling, as if the tasks of the day were written there. He swivelled his head and caught all the things Sylvie wished were invisible: her sleeping face with its uncontrolled expression and the movement he said he could see behind her eyelids—the twitching of a dream—her crushed hair, her night breath. The body had to close down, as far as it could, she understood that, but she hated her dry mouth before swallowing recommenced, the grainy feel of her eyelashes. And then would come the knock on the door on mornings when her ears had closed down as well and the steps went unheeded.

'Can't you go?' she said to Ben, nudging him in the ribs.

'The household god brings fruit only to the mistress of the house.' He slid the pillow over his face to stifle his laughter.

'I might give up the great apes,' Sylvie said to Ben one evening when they were dining at the Mexican Cafe. They went early because Ben was convinced the cooks were fresher, the service faster than later when the air was full of wine fumes, raised voices and the occasional spectacular quarrel.

'Why stop now?' Ben asked. Surely she was trying to get to the bottom of something? Normally he found her doggedness endearing, though it could be intensely irritating. He thought ape spoor and deconstructed nests should lead somewhere.

'I suppose in some ways it could be useful,' Sylvie said. As usual she began with a bold statement and then backed away. 'I could never be on a committee without thinking of apes and giving people roles.'

'Reducing someone to an alpha ape. I don't see how that could help.'

'That shows how little you know,' she said, kicking him under the table and making their plates wobble. 'You can never reduce an alpha ape.'

Nonetheless he felt he might try. At the drafting office there were manoeuvres that might be diverted. There were ways of withholding praise or puncturing something, the strategic use of silence. He had held out in this fashion at a meeting during the week. In truth he had been distracted but the poker face he prided himself on, his cheekbones that he deliberately visualised as frozen, had come to his aid, and when he responded it had sounded mature. Sylvie, he thought, was too absolute. She saw a flaw and instantly it swelled and flooded everything. Then he reflected he hadn't been abandoned, if this is what Sylvie's mother had done. Perhaps he should suggest a trip to Paris. Then the thought of their finances intervened and he looked down at his plate where the Devil's Nachos were beginning to congeal. Sylvie had ordered a milder version so he must be the alpha ape. The napkin she had tucked into her blouse was spattered with the rich red sauce.

Isobel, in the room that had been Madeleine's and then Sylvie's, was dusting the bookcase. The Colettes occupied most of one shelf. Only *Claudine* and *Claudine at School* were slightly worn. Possibly *The Ripening Seed*. The others had that sealed look of the new book, held with gossamer cords. She lifted one to her nose and sniffed, and the paper smell was still there, sealed inside the creamy pages. It was herself she had bought them for, thinking she lacked some kind of primitive knowledge and might gain it from this woman who liked to scrabble bare-fingered in the earth with a cat and dog by her side. Whatever this knowledge was—instinctual, amoral, relying on feelings, the reading of signs—she had wanted to pass it on to Madeleine. She had seen the books as manuals, since her own nature made her an observer. Madeleine might be vain and easily duped but she was not divided. After each defeat she returned to her plan: she was like Gigi, who preferred her old plaid dress and cotton stockings.

When the Colettes were in two piles, Isobel emptied the other shelves. She would ask Sylvie if there was a special book. Those on the top shelf were tiny, designed for little hands; some had thick cardboard pages, easy to grasp and turn. Little fingers grasped the edge and lifted it and the image of a striped ball and a single bold word reared up and fell down on the other side. Madeleine had shrieked with pleasure when this happened. Now the paper that overlapped the cardboard was peeling at the corners.

Outside, in the garden, the pungent scent of the tall gum was wafting its cat-piss smell. Over the years Isobel had grown used to it: a sudden burst that smelled like tomcats. She thought again of Colette and her animals, her eyes darkened with kohl so she looked like a cat. The secret was never to apologise. Animals might feel shame—their old spaniel, Gatsby, when he had an accident, hung his head—but it might be the shortest way to a biscuit. In the novels Isobel had identified with the blundering less-sophisticated characters, the uncertain English girl thrown off balance while she was being taught innocence was no protection.

Sylvie confronted Professor Woolf while he was standing in the doorway of his office, talking to the Dean. She stepped back, mock-modestly, and surreptitiously rubbed at the corner of one eye. In her hand she held a balled-up tissue. The professor was inordinately disturbed by tears, particularly when they issued from a pretty woman. Stocky or unprepossessing students— naturally no male would think of trying it—had to fall back on reason, doctors' certificates, or makeup applied to look like spots. Sylvie's hair was freshly washed and the shampoo scent still clung to it; she had dabbed perfume on her wrists and sprayed her throat. The two top buttons of her blouse were undone and the professor's eyes would naturally follow.

'Aren't you ashamed of yourself?' Ben had asked, watching her preparations. The air shimmered as she savagely brushed her hair. Then she scooped the loose hairs from the brush, rolled them into a ball and threw them out the window.

That morning Cheung had brought the first white peach and bowed lower than ever.

'What is knowledge if it is not applied?' Sylvie had responded.

Then she had blown Ben a kiss and run down the stairs. Cheung turned and received her best professional smile.

Animals have a very good notion of space and the perils or implications of invading the space possessed by another. Humans are not so sensitive. They are far more likely to be cornered. The Dean moved away, and boldly Sylvie took the vacated space, which was too intimate, and therefore embarrassing for the professor, but admirable for her purpose.

'This is not the first extension,' Professor Woolf began

47

firmly, but his neck had turned a promising red. And Sylvie had not backed away; if anything she was fractionally closer. One hand touched her hair.

'I know,' she said. 'And it's not a very good excuse. It's just that he will keep bringing fruit and I will keep overeating. The consequences . . .'

He raised his hand to show that no elaboration was required.

'I could bring you some,' Sylvie offered. 'This morning he brought a very exotic peach.'

Visions of a troop of apes feasting on ripe peaches hung between them.

'Self-control. I wish you'd lecture on that,' Sylvie said. 'In the primate sense, naturally.'

The merest offering of flattery, a tiny branch held out with a single tender leaf at the end of it, and she knew she had won. The balled-up tissue was unnecessary.

Self-control, self-control, she thought to herself as she walked away along the corridor. Who needed self-control when there were such strategies?

Isobel was mistaken in thinking Madeleine had taken nothing from the Colettes. It was true she had closed *Claudine* and *Claudine at School* after a few chapters. But she had sensed the power of Monsieur Willy who had locked Colette in a room to write. Howard, after informing her of a fiancée in Connecticut, had returned to America. Madeleine was left with the age-old female balancing act: were lingering looks, embraces and lovemaking equal to the anguish of being removed from someone's life? Madame Récamier, who had warned her about students, remarked on rings under her eyes and suggested a night cream.

Gradually weeks when Madeleine could barely summon up an interest in John Dos Passos or George Santayana passed and something stirred again. The plane trees, so brutal-looking in winter, like a comment on human behaviour, showed hints of green. Religiously she applied Madame's under-eye cream. Soon she was clambering up the rolling ladder to fetch down a copy of William Empson's *Seven Types of Ambiguity*. She wiped dust from its top edge and ran her fingers down her skirt. By the time the trees were in full leaf and their clenched truncated knuckles invisible, Madeleine was herself again. But she had made a decision: in future she would love older men. There had been an imbalance between herself and Howard. Sometimes he had laughed at a gesture, even during lovemaking, and she had felt offended; she wanted her naïvety, if that was what it was, to be a charm.

The man into whose hands she pressed the Empson noted her trim ankles as she descended the ladder and the way her skirt lifted when she put her foot to the floor.

Madeleine had broken off her Alliance Française lessons when she was involved with Howard; now she resumed them. In the shop they spoke mostly English: it was where English and American novels were purchased and also a place to practise a few halting sentences after the traditional greetings. Madame Récamier could often be overheard discussing whether Joyce Carol Oates was too prolific or if Jack Kerouac was braver on paper than in real life.

Slowly, surrounded by novels and plays, poems and

memoirs, and overlooked by serious-looking posters of Barthes and Hemingway, Bellow and Eudora Welty, Madeleine felt her confidence return. Madame Récamier protected her, though outwardly her manner was stern, even faintly disapproving. The next man Madeleine allowed to take her to dinner was scrutinised by both, and Madame gave a faint, barely perceptible nod as they set off.

'You must always give the impression of a full life,' Madame Récamier instructed her. 'A woman or a young girl must always have an air of being engaged in many things. She should be faintly distracted, so when she looks at a man he sees her attention turn towards him and receives it as a reward.' Privately she thought Madeleine's life must be dreary, with little to entertain her outside the shop. She suggested visits to galleries and exhibitions. No matter if she was unaccompanied, she told Madeleine. An unaccompanied woman, if she walks confidently, will always attract notice. She should look as if she has just finished an entrancing novel whose mysteries continue long after the book is closed.

Madeleine attempted to carry out Madame's instructions on the following Sunday. She sat, in one of the hard little chairs, through Mass at Notre Dame and watched bishops and priests and altar boys swinging thuribles. When she came out, doubting she looked engaged or mysterious, she glanced up and saw the gargoyles looking down, their expressions vicious and calculating in the grey air.

The next weekend she tackled the Louvre by herself. At first it was a struggle to keep her composure among the crowds, the queues that seemed to know where they were going; she had attached herself to the wrong one and was redirected. She felt herself blushing, and when her ticket was purchased she went to the sculpture court. Slowly a calm descended on her: the layout was spacious and the sculptures themselves with their super-human proportions, their stone or marble surfaces, made her think of time travel. Just that week she had had an interesting discussion about H.G. Wells with a strange bearded man who had informed her he read nothing written after 1946.

Madeleine stayed in the sculpture court for nearly an hour, until she almost felt she lived there, slept on one of the benches, bathed in a small pool and was surrounded by stone guardians whose blank eyes were kindly. She saw the beauty in clumsy heavy limbs and erotic embraces that became gentle when they were carved from stone.

When, with aching feet, she climbed the stairs to her room, Madeleine felt pleased with herself. She had visited not only the sculptures but the *Mona Lisa*. She had stood back as the crowd pressed forward, straining to see the mysterious smile. Then, in her new swing coat, Madeleine had turned away and threaded her way back against the tide of bodies. She drank an espresso in one of the cafés. No one had accosted her, though she had been noticed. In her handbag she had the notebook in which she had written the names of the sculptors she had particularly liked.

Two months later—even the Mona Lisa could not have predicted this—Madeleine was pregnant. Her period was late but she thought little of it. In Le Livre Bleu they were stocktaking and one afternoon she slipped from the rolling ladder and banged her hip against the desk. That evening a large black bruise was developing and her side ached. Still she could not be spared: there was hardly an inch of uncovered floor in the shop, and despite the *Fermée* sign on the door faces were pressed against the glass almost every hour of the day while the phone rang incessantly. But Madame Récamier was adamant. In three days the work was done and Madeleine climbed up the ladder, replacing the stock. When Le Livre Bleu reopened there would be canapés and glasses of champagne for the regular patrons.

Another month passed and Madeleine grew listless and dreamy; she felt she would go to sleep on her feet. She had forgotten the party she had gone to with Alain, one of the visiting book salesmen. He introduced each new season's title with an amusing anecdote, usually something scandalous about the author. They had gone out for supper and then to a bar where Madeleine had tried absinthe for the first time. She leaned over the glass, watching the milky colour rise. In the street Alain took her arm. Soon they were climbing stairs, five flights. On each landing Madeleine leaned against him. She laughed and hiccupped. She put her hand over her mouth and apologised. Then she laughed again. After that—there were other people in the apartment, it was not his—she remembered only a velvet eiderdown on an enormous bed and sinking into it as if she had found a nest.

Ben knew about some of Sylvie's exploits before they were married. Cora, starting later, soon discovered more. Isobel's role was known to a small circle; the absent mother, subject of wilder speculation, remained mysterious. The difference between son and mother was that Ben expected to find light in the unrevealed corners, Cora only an increase of darkness. It was like chiaroscuro: which was the more important, light under a chin revealing tender flesh or shade deepening where a candle flame could not reach? All the advantages lay with the light. Cora found her carefully aimed barbs thwarted by Ben's determination to be charitable, and the charity included herself.

Isobel, in an earlier time and place, had attempted to hold the world, as it affected Sylvie, at arm's length. She considered it the worst feature of grandmothering. That everything should be under her command: dangers foreseen and warded off, from the largest to the most minute, from kidnapping to a fall on steps. The years when Sylvie was a child and these dangers were small and manageable, spreading out from her child's bed, were replaced by something resembling vistas and howling winds. An added burden was that her care must be hidden; her warnings, if she dared issue one, oblique. How simple childhood now seemed. Isobel's own grandmother had talked of heartache replacing aching arms as the child grew. At the very time when Isobel's mind wanted to relax, an intense concentration was required. Wasn't physical tiredness better, even broken nights?

Sylvie was four when her mother returned to France to stay with the Lévêques. Isobel was forewarned about the tantrums that could occur at four-and-a-half, but Sylvie was remarkably subdued. The house her mother had rented had been sold the week before the decision was taken, almost as if the world was sending a message.

Isobel thought she might be able to relax now that Sylvie was in Ben's care; she could not know the role Cora Taverner had taken up. And if she had, would she have intervened? If they found a common subject it could have been how they overlapped like intersecting circles or the sunlit and shadowed portions of the moon.

But Cora Taverner would not approach Isobel Lehmann. It had begun badly. She had not been invited to ride on the lake. Perhaps she had been expected to skulk in the trees. The very idea of a second boat and perhaps the oars colliding was ridiculous; she shuddered at the idea of polluted lake water on her shantung suit. Her daughter's illness had arrived just in time.

Sylvie, oblivious, had handed in her overdue primate essay and, lightened by what she felt was her exposure of the weaknesses of the rigid patriarchal society, was walking through the park that bordered the university. It was Isobel who had propelled her there and it was the anthropologists, one dressed in a gorilla suit, others wearing bone necklaces, who had snagged her on Open Day as she walked from stall to stall. Some disciplines, like philosophy or English, threatened by falling rolls, had set nets to catch the unwary. The third-year male student in the gorilla suit had grabbed her arm, then knelt and bestowed a kiss on her palm. The memory still made her laugh. Doubts she had chosen the right subject had lasted for a week—the lecturers, too, wore primitive necklaces or amulets, but by then she had convinced herself that beginning at the beginning, like Alice in Wonderland, was a prerequisite to understanding anything. Her own emotions, no matter how much Isobel delved and dug into them, were primitive too and if she had been abandoned in a forest she would have had to make a nest from tree fronds or a palisade fort like the one in a glass case in Professor Woolf's office. Now, walking easily through the park with its fountain and palm trees, she felt how far behind she had left the apes with their repressive society. The tedium of it must increase the importance of power: a fight over females or food would break up the day. She put aside images of allogrooming, the delicate sifting through fur with those surprising fingers, moments when even power was forgotten in the simple pleasure of being alive.

At the edge of the park where there were various routes around tree trunks and gnarled roots, steps or paths, Sylvie sat for a quarter of an hour on the grass. In front of her passed groups of students. Others also came to a halt and put down their satchels and backpacks. For some it was a chance to embrace or lie, full-length, pressed together. One couple nearby, of equal height, could have been mistaken for a fallen tree.

She was thinking of Ben. Even in the ape community there was a sub-set of males that did not conform. They were dreamier, content to be lieutenants. But such is ape and human nature, they took compensation elsewhere. Without threatening the hierarchy they offered prospects of peace and negotiation. Sylvie smiled to herself, thinking of apes responsible for town halls, opera houses and libraries. They would be good comforters.

She had met Ben Taverner on a day when she was sitting on a low stone wall that separated the university from the street. She was eating a chicken sandwich, half-inside and half-outside a brown paper bag. Behind her, in the driveway leading to the Biological Sciences Department, was a trailer piled high with dead white chickens. The breeze was fluttering some of the feathers. The way the carcasses were flung down caught her eye. Suddenly the connection was too much; she felt she might vomit. Hastily she shoved the half-sandwich back into the bag and crushed the top. Now she felt she really was going to be sick. She pressed one hand to her mouth and dropped the bag at her feet. She fumbled for a tissue. There were rhododendron bushes in the driveway; she might put her head in one of those. But from there she would be able to see the chickens.

Ben stopped in front of her and picked up the sandwich.

'No,' she cried. 'Not that.'

Then she had turned her head, preparing to run, and she had bumped his shoulder. He put out his arm to steady her and the bile rose in her throat. She told herself it was nothing, it was clear as water, it was not green, there was no chicken in it. Somehow she choked it down, though the next heave could not be far off.

He should be back at the office. She simply looked too sick to leave. There were people passing by and roaring buses; someone in a white coat came and wheeled away the chickens. In a little recess he found a seat and a handy rubbish bin. He could see that she was suggestible: he hoped the bin seemed tactful, not an omen. Her eyes were running with tears.

'Call me and tell me you're all right,' he said when the last minute he could spare arrived. He gave her his card.

··ॐ ॐ··

How strange these encounters are. That afternoon as Ben Taverner bent over his drafting board and later worked on costings he felt something significant had happened. Normally he would have been on the other side of the street but someone had recommended a new place that sold Turkish kebabs. He had pressed two buzzers to get across, waiting at a traffic island for the lights to change. The man who had recommended the Turkish place had heavy garlic breath; he was half-tempted to turn back. And then there was the girl with the bag. He wondered what was in it and why she had suddenly, with panicked eyes, convulsively screwed it up. Her hair, not quite shoulder length, was lightly curled and tendrils from the centre parting floated away from her forehead. If she had not been agitated and her mouth covered by the bag he would have guessed she was normally serene.

Then she dropped the bag and her hand went up to her mouth. He guessed what was happening. A few quickened steps would take him past. Instead he bent and picked up the bag. Mustering the last of her strength, she had stopped herself. It was a kind of heroism, he thought, though anyone with medical knowledge—a friend who was a house surgeon had told him the body was basically a simple mechanism—would have disagreed.

The afternoon wore on and there was no phone call. On his way home he walked past the wall and down into the little sunken garden but there was nobody there. He even lifted the lid of the bin to see if there was a brown paper bag with a half-eaten chicken sandwich inside.

A week passed. Then on Friday as Ben came down the steps to the street—Meier Olson was on the first floor, most of its view blocked by a spreading alder tree—he noticed Sylvie standing beside the entrance. She was looking straight ahead, but as he came level she turned her head. In her hand she held a book, wrapped and tied with a red ribbon.

'I thought you might like this,' she said.

He smiled as he thought of the method in it: he could lean against the building and open it, but the ribbon suggested something more ceremonious. A wind was blowing and the paper and ribbon might fly off. All this without a direction being given: his respect for books increased. There was a workman's café nearby, as neutral and downtrodden as the book might be special: he felt he was setting it a challenge.

They looked at one another over a Formica table scarred with cigarette burns. Sylvie sipped a glass of water, Ben stirred two twists of raw sugar into the unspeakable coffee. For some odd reason he felt angry. In an hour or two his stomach would ache.

Quickly he untied the ribbon and pushed it towards her, then he tore at the paper. He couldn't imagine why he was so tense. What expression should he wear? The paper parted and he was looking at *The Professor's House* by Willa Cather.

'The professor's house,' he said aloud. He couldn't think of anything to say.

'It's about a professor who doesn't want to move house.'

Now he had totally dried up. He turned the book over and read a summary. He needed to go to a class where people gave books and other people opened them—one of those sessions where the participants swapped roles.

'Thanks,' he said. 'Thanks very much. I promise to read it.' He thought it was very unlikely. A house and a reluctant professor. He wished he had never met the young woman opposite him. Then his gaze rested on the parting dividing her hair. Even in the steamy heat of the café, tendrils of hair were floating. The parting made wings that on a man would have been a moustache.

A week later and he had still not opened *The Professor's House*. On its top edge it was stamped *Jason Books* and he thought he knew the shop it had come from. He concentrated on his work; he half-admitted to himself that it might be the most certain thing in his life; he felt resolute and hollow at the same time. He turned his head to look at his colleagues, imagining their hair grey and lines deepening on their foreheads like the grey clerks in Dickens. Would Heidi still be wearing her pinstriped shirt with its choir-boy collar or Russell still affect a pencil behind his ear? The alder tree was shivering against the window, the very opposite of the neat and controlled trees airily parachuted onto plans for public squares. From time to time he got himself a coffee or went downstairs to breathe in the air from the street. A building further along Symonds Street had been closed because of Legionnaire's disease. Ben's preference was for slightly lower temperatures and sash windows.

He scanned the opposite side of the street where the university buildings rose in clusters. He tried to imagine them as an estate, the holding of a single powerful family. They were not uniform enough for that. Paths ran between them, small insignificant areas of garden, but there was no grand design. There were bicycle racks and rubbish bins and a security booth with a yellow and black striped barrier.

A few more days and he was ready to acknowledge his own misery. He had met a deadline by working late and coming downstairs when a street light was shining inside the alder tree. He thought of something Sylvie had said about the professor:

that he had designed a house he did not want to move into. Eventually he found the book under a pile of folders. He opened it and read: *The moving was over and done. Professor St. Peter was alone in the dismantled house where he had lived ever since his marriage, where he had worked out his career and brought up his two daughters. It was almost as ugly as it is possible for a house to be . . .*

·∘⤳ ⤲∘·

Isobel had decided for the sake of future harmony or no harmony at all she must persist with Cora Taverner. Through the years Sylvie was growing up, alternately attending school or being expelled, Isobel had attempted to teach her to turn a situation about and play the opposite role. Only rarely had it worked and rarely, Isobel had to admit, did it work for herself.

She could not tell if she would have liked another woman standing beside her on the jetty. A woman who might have pushed her into the lake. Ben Taverner had been good-humouredly evasive about his mother but Isobel, covertly observing him during the day, thought he looked relieved. Still there must be pain; it would be unnatural if some words had not been exchanged. It was Sylvie she was concerned for, that she should not be undermined or defeated by stealth. It might take years, Isobel told herself, checking her appearance in the mirror, settling the largest pearl in her necklace in the hollow of her throat. She had swallowed a teaspoon of brandy before she phoned. A cold voice had answered, and when she issued her invitation it had said, 'Why?' 'Why not?' Isobel had replied but she had said it gaily. The voice had relented a little when Isobel suggested they could at least see one another, gain an impression. Even war criminals were enclosed behind glass.

The conversation had not lasted very long. Isobel had proposed somewhere neutral and they had agreed on a hotel lobby where they could have coffee. There were bound to be little nests of chairs surrounding low tables. Both might have been thinking of the civilising presence of waiters bringing trays and extra hot water.

Isobel had always loved hotels. When she and Kit stayed in one she often opened doors marked STAFF ONLY and pretended she was lost. She loved the exteriors, the foyers and dining rooms, the small and large conference rooms with their skirted tables for buffets, the huge food warmers and the staff behind them wielding tongs or solicitously carving a giant ham. She loved imagining someone on duty on the concierge's desk or reception coming off, swinging through a door, panelled in dark wood on one side and plain and scuffed on the other, someone loosening a cap or undoing a silver uniform button as their feet sped over what a second before had been plush carpet and was now linoleum. If Isobel found herself in a kitchen she would ask for a glass of water. A headache was extremely useful and she crossed her fingers behind her back in case a real one should eventuate.

Now, on the day they had agreed to meet, Isobel was there early, to foyer watch. A busload of tourists was being bowed through the big front doors and she thought the commissionaire was not bowing as low as usual or else his bows were graded: a group could not warrant the deference shown to an individual. A flat box of flowers was delivered and whisked up in the lift in gloved hands. Luggage carts with gleaming brass handles moved like small trains.

Cora obviously felt she was being watched as she came through the door and up the stairs to the reception area. Isobel signalled by waving her fingers and then rose as the plump determined-looking woman approached. Her voice on the phone had suggested someone tall and stately, and for a moment Isobel was confused. She got half to her feet and then sank back in her chair, unwilling to use her height to advantage. For a moment she remembered the title of one of Kit's books: *The Art of War* by Machiavelli.

Only a few seconds had passed and Isobel saw the meeting was a mistake. She, who had called it, had no agenda beyond sitting together, sizing one another up, and rising at the end to a handshake or a touch on the shoulder. In unlikelier scenarios a hand touching the other's waist, a peck of lips to a cheek. And then walking away, with or without a backward glance, already making an inventory: a blush on the neck or tearing a small cake to pieces as if it were bread.

Cora sat forward so her legs were planted on the carpet, exactly in the centre of a heraldic shape that could have been a phoenix or a crown. Isobel hunched herself back into the overstuffed cushions. Nonetheless she tried to look expansive, as if she was taking her cue from the heavy chandelier or the claw-legged table with its absurdly large floral arrangement. But Cora's look cut through all that: it seemed to be saying, 'What have you got to say for yourself?' And Isobel, who had vowed as she came through the big glass doors and received the commissionaire's bow not to utter the word 'sorry' under any circumstance or any provocation, had begun with it. 'I'm sorry not to have met you earlier.'

There was no response other than a cool examining look. The waiter now arrived with the tea. It mightn't have been the Japanese tea ceremony, Isobel thought, but there was still a good deal of lifting and placing. She wondered, wildly, what waiters, intruding at this moment when intimacy should have been established, heard. Then he was gone and she offered to pour.

'Was there a reason for this?' Cora said when sips were being taken with the solemnity of a tea-taster. Isobel half-expected her to signal the waiter for a spittoon.

'None,' Isobel replied. She set the clock again on the word 'sorry'. 'To meet, to see one another.' To take your measure, to see what I must do in future, to see what I should expect.

'I can't ease your conscience,' Cora replied, and now Isobel felt the tell-tale heat in her own neck. She put her cup down and it made a tiny sound like a bell.

'My conscience over what?' she asked, but there was no reply until another sip had been taken.

'Why, your conscience over allowing it. Your granddaughter and my son. What were you thinking of?'

'That I could have prevented it?' Isobel asked. 'That it was my doing?' There seemed to be a pulse in her throat now. Despite the tea her mouth was hideously dry.

'I have played the role of Sylvie's grandmother,' Isobel said.

The passion rising in her was shaking her. Perhaps treaties were composed in this rush of feeling, clause after clause going down the parchment with no loss of nobility, the language flowing to the pen. The evenings stroking Sylvie's hair, the storms and the silences, the quiet hours, usually when Sylvie was not there, that were so hard-won and precious. Isobel's relearning, if she needed to relearn, that beauty and effort were intricately connected. How changed she had been by it all. And then, on the jetty, fearful Kit would have a heart attack through not having a practice the day before, the cool breeze touching her spine through her light clothing, and the odd warmth of the bouquet she was holding to herself.

'I hope the role may come to you,' she continued, meeting the inimical gaze. 'If it does, if you are fortunate enough to receive it, it will be through Sylvie. It will be through her agency.'

Isobel, without making a proper farewell, walked fuming up the street. At first she hardly saw anything; bodies moved around her or she moved around them; she felt it was miraculous she didn't collide with someone. But there was an old pattern at work and she flowed with it. Then she realised she was going in the wrong direction. It hardly mattered. When eventually she felt calmer she found a coffee shop and went in. She was not thirsty but she thought a second drink might take away the taste of the tea she had drunk at the hotel. Only half Isobel's cup had been emptied before she understood the woman facing her was determined on enmity. Sylvie would not stand a chance. Instantly Isobel saw herself in armour, resuming her guard, scanning the horizon or looking at the sky or even the entrails of animals.

That Isobel should have prevented the marriage! That her role should have been nothing more than a steady discouragement directed at Sylvie and Cora's son; that even without a meeting they should have been in cahoots. No wonder Ben had been evasive about an introduction. She saw again his face as he appeared on the path, walking with his best man. Slightly dishevelled, flushed, but undoubtedly happy. Kit had had a friend from a poisonous family, a cold withdrawn father and a mother who had bound her son to her until he resisted. The years of resistance had been hideous; time and again Joaquin fell back into what he described as a bear trap. It was the presence in his life of Kit and their friendship from primary school that had enabled him to climb out. Kit was amazed and denied any credit. 'I saw there was sanity,' Joaquin said. 'I saw I could choose it.' It had meant a complete severance. Only years later had Kit been told; then he recollected years in which his friend had been particularly close, when he had stayed with their family at weekends and once even for Christmas.

So it was possible, Isobel thought, as she pushed her chair back and got up. Ties could be cut, there could be choice—even savage choice—if there was enough will.

'I was surprised you asked to meet,' Cora had remarked. 'What could you expect to achieve?'

To this Isobel had not replied, concentrating on the golden stream that was issuing from the teapot. A little softness, she might have said. A little grace. Clearly she was dealing with a primitive. An egotist whose demands were paramount. Any graciousness would simply be for obedience.

After her coffee Isobel felt re-energised. She couldn't wait to get home and talk to Kit. She would talk about Joaquin as well; she knew he still wrote to Kit, long old-fashioned letters on monogrammed paper from his London club.

The long walk restored her. At first, shocked and dismayed,

she had almost limped, but now she strode and her breathing became calm. Kit would know what to do. Something that had rubbed off on Joaquin would rub off on her.

·◦⧽ ⧼◦·

After the wedding gift, it was several months before Sylvie heard again from Madeleine. That had been the pattern through her childhood. Carefully chosen postcards from a stand in a tabac: the Eiffel Tower, Les Invalides. A line of tiny kisses, which Madeleine felt might cause offence, below her signature. For herself, she knew she would not have survived without the help of the Lévêque family.

Her return to them when Sylvie was four had come at a time suitable to both parties. Madame Lévêque loved to cook, to reign over a household of which she was the centre. Monsieur Lévêque was anxious that the domestic arrangements which had kept him happy for over forty years should not be jeopardised, something there had been a hint of when their youngest daughter left home to study and then marry. Madeleine had arrived at just the right moment. Besides, she was sad and undernourished; Madame Lévêque could nurse her back to health. Genevieve Lévêque and Madeleine Lehmann had restored themselves together. After six months Madeleine took a job as a private secretary to an Englishman. A big florid man, he reminded her of the Scarlet Pimpernel. His cheeks would flush in the most un-French way; she could gauge not just his mood but the slightest shift in his feelings. It seemed a desirable quality.

Arranging Hugo Brudenell-Bruce's diary, remembering his

wife's birthday and ordering roses, Madeleine thought she had found her vocation. Like Genevieve Lévêque she loved to serve, to anticipate the smallest thing. In Madeleine's case it was the arrangement of mail in piles of priority; in Genevieve's the gleam on freshly polished brass. Hugo was an importer of fine English men's suiting. As an advertisement he dressed in tweeds and fine wools; his large frame enabled him to carry off *le style Anglais*. Every lunch hour he went to the same restaurant, a small family affair, where porcelain roosters of every description formed the décor. Hugo was inordinately devoted to rugby. With the proprietor of La Cambuse he could endlessly discuss the merits of a prop from Toulouse or the roots of the English game in public schools.

Madeleine found him perfect. Unlike the French men she met on the street, his eyes never appraised her figure or her clothes, the shoes and handbag that matched, the artful knotting of a scarf. She still visited the Lévêques occasionally for Sunday lunch. Best of all, emboldened by the protectiveness she felt Hugo would offer if she requested it, she had several love affairs.

One, Laurent, she saw in the late afternoon before he went home to his family. She went to a small hotel, took the key from reception if it was not already gone, and climbed two flights of stairs. The lift, frequently broken, was too daunting. Laurent had taught her quickly and clinically to undress and lie on the bed; he made up for this by a repertoire of caresses and positions that were unfamiliar to her. Sometimes she thought of a French exercise book in which school children wrote letters inside tiny squares. Then she dressed again and hurried back to Hugo's office for another two hours' work. He had usually left by this time to take an apéritif or a single malt whisky with colleagues.

On the walk back from seeing Laurent, Madeleine considered her position. She had a daughter and yet she was still dating, still searching. Only the search was false. If only she could combine Hugo with someone like Laurent. The lovely tweeds and Laurent's knowledge of what to do in bed. Sometimes he kissed her hair and dabbed at her forehead with a corner of the sheet. He watched her dress, as if she was now rewarded for his indifference when she arrived. On the cobblestones Madeleine's toes had learned to curl slightly. It was something Sylvie had shown her. The toes of children endlessly moved and felt their way across the ground.

Isobel had never said to Madeleine that she could not manage Sylvie. But not saying a thing did not mean it was not felt. The bigger concern of Madeleine's breakdown had pushed it aside. Some part of Isobel, whose own life felt uncertain at this stage, had welcomed the tiredness she knew would come with the demands of being older and caring for a child. She felt a need to impart something, though she had no idea what this might be. The day Sylvie had come to Isobel one of her closest friends, Ann Scott, had died, and one of her sharpest regrets was that she would never again be able to enter her friend's house. It was in this house that Isobel had confided a good many secrets and had even slept for an afternoon in a small sunroom which Ann kept for guests. When she woke she looked out at the massive trees in the garden, their trunks smothered with ivy. A light breeze lifted some of the leaves and not others: a delicate singling out. She had watched for hours, wondering if there was a human analogy. Then Ann had appeared in the doorway with a cup of coffee.

Still, if Isobel could have seen Madeleine as she worked for Hugo she might have been reassured. Here at least was a father figure with no hidden agenda. Or not until the day Madeleine caught sight of him under an arcade in a side street, pressing an envelope into the hands of a young man. She had walked on, without turning her head, hardly faltering. The next day she was as carefully dressed as ever and he was in his superlative tweeds. Luckily it was not his wife's birthday—Madeleine did not think she could have managed that. And when it did come around, three months later, she ordered yellow roses as usual and he signed the card.

By now Madeleine's French was passable. Still with a trace of something foreign, but it was apparent to even the most casual listener that she had taken pains, and this was the most important thing. At first she was mortified when the response to one of her tentative sentences was a volley of words she had no hope of understanding. One lunch hour she had gone into a bookshop to thank an elderly man who had helped her the day before, coming out onto the pavement and pointing in the direction she should go. She had the first words ready, 'Monsieur, je veux vous remercier pour l'aide que vous m'avez donnée hier . . .' But then she faltered; the bookseller, peering at her through his half-spectacles, had clearly failed to recognise her. She had fled the shop, followed by the stares of other customers, some of whom were waiting impatiently by the till.

Now, between seeing her married man—it was Laurent who suggested she use the term *petite amie*—and sheltering under the protection of Hugo, Madeleine hoped she might find someone who was free. The offices of Brudenell-Bruce were in the 6th arrondissement and Madeleine, avoiding the bookseller and hoping she did not see him in front of his shop, could imagine she was strolling among professors and scholars as gentle and protective as her father. But it was mainly students who moved around her, arguing and gesticulating, stepping into the gutters. They crowded into cafés and Madeleine marvelled at the way a debate continued even while the menu was being consulted. A long communal table would be commandeered and Madeleine, from her modest seat by the window, could observe the elaborate structure of a critique of a movie director or a politician, embellished by gestures and smoke rising from individual cigarettes. Outside was an important intersection, controlled by a traffic policeman. A girl on a bicycle with books in a wicker basket wobbled past, almost brushing the sides of cars. When her café crème had been lingered over for the requisite time, Madeleine got up and walked slowly towards the office. There had been no further sightings of Hugo under the arches and she banished the image from her mind. The young man might have been a beggar: the contrast between Hugo's worsted and the other's black shabby clothes was so great.

She tried not to think of Isobel and Sylvie. Her failure, after Sylvie's birth, had been so spectacular the doctor had suggested a private nursing home. Madeleine knew he meant counselling and therapy, possibly a regimen of drugs. She had begged Isobel to let her stay at home. In those strange weeks she had slept in her old room and Sylvie had been brought to her for feeding, which had also failed. Isobel had attempted to explain that she should not grieve over this, and Madeleine had tried not to show her mother that she did not grieve at all.

·❧·❧··

Isobel had discussed the meeting with Cora Taverner with Kit;
then she decided to let it rest. She loved turning something
around and becoming the other person, the other party.
Inventing stories for strangers was like flavouring food. The
moment she met someone she began to delve beneath what she
imagined was the surface, however carefully it was contrived.
In Cora Taverner's case she could imagine the layers as clothing.
The undergarments would be superior; she could imagine
Cora sitting on the edge of her bed to pull on sheer stockings,
easing them up over her thighs, perhaps tugging at the calves
to release more fabric. There was something warlike in the way
women dressed to face one another. Finally there was the face.
Isobel thought there were familiar mirrors in which, because
they were befriended, her face looked back at her almost
flirtatiously, whereas mirrors in powder rooms and dressing
cubicles seemed inimical because they were not yet conquered.

As the weeks passed and there was no further contact,
Isobel constructed a kind of biography. Ben was an only boy:
it was natural that his mother's feelings should be intense.
Possessiveness, jealousy, rivalry. Cora was not a woman to veil
her character no matter how carefully she dressed. A woman
who would check a colour against her skin, since it might no
longer flatter. Isobel could imagine a great row of creams and
lotions as Cora sat in front of her mirror. Isobel considered
it the most important part of dressing and one that Kit, who
had often watched her from his station on the bed, could not
understand. Once her face was in place it didn't matter if a
tradesman called and she ran to the front door in her dressing

71

gown. Without it, both sides would register shock as if the woman had taken on the appearance of a ghost.

Sylvie had said something about Cora, and Isobel tried to remember what it was. There had been a second attempt at a meeting, with Ben present. His mother had declared her enmity in the way her fingers dug into Sylvie's shoulders as she kissed her cheek, in the spilling of a few hot drops of coffee onto her lap as she sat in an uncomfortable chair, in the dry little almond cakes that made her gag after the first mouthful. But mostly—'tank-like' had been the word—it had been in the steady and unvarying gaze by which Sylvie was examined. It began at her shoes, travelled inch by inch up her bare legs to her waist, her breasts, her neck, until it reached her face. Sylvie wore practically no makeup: a little lipstick and a dab of concealer. Now she wished she had underlined her eyes to draw attention to them, like the eyes of a lemur.

The hour the visit had lasted had seemed like three, but eventually Sylvie and Ben were on their feet again, they were at the door, the clawing of strong fingers with sharp nails was at her shoulders. This time the breath was faintly almond-scented, with an older scent behind it. Ben noticed nothing: he kept using the word 'Mother' as if it was a private joke. He and Sylvie went down the path together and the gaze was still on Sylvie's back. For a moment she was an archer in battle, braced for the arrow that might at any second strike; she felt her muscles scoop towards her spine in anticipation. For protection she shot out her hand and grasped Ben's so tightly he winced. Then they went back to Meier Olson and, since it was late Sunday afternoon and no one was there, made love in the drafting room.

·⸙ ⸙·

The moon was shining in the window when Sylvie woke at 3 a.m. Two large figs, Cheung's offering from the previous day, were resting on the windowsill. At first Sylvie couldn't think what they were; then she remembered Cheung had offered to demonstrate how to peel one and she had taken them from his hands as if she ate figs every day. The moon was passing through clouds, its great disc moving like a coin being pushed forwards and the clouds representing hesitancy, a kind of celestial courtesy. The strangest thoughts came to Sylvie when she woke at night. She thought of the buildings in the city, bathed in moonlight, and later, before dawn, brushed by the rising wind. Then would come the calming consoling sun. The calm that came then, whatever the day held, turned her thoughts to Isobel. Her grandmother reminded her of a guard, high on battlements, scanning the horizon for the first sign of a threat. The hardest thing to ward off must be sleep, though Sylvie herself was now wide awake.

She slid to the edge of the mattress and got up. Her hand reached out for one of the figs. But before she took it back to bed to peel and eat she looked out at the street. In the distance a neon sign was flashing. A few leaves were lifting in the rising breeze; the plane tree outside the window rustled as if it too had got out of bed and shivered. Its roots went down under a grille and then spread. Sylvie had read that roots could scent water and dive towards it. She held the fig in her hand and moved the pillow behind her back. Then she carefully peeled back its outer leaves to reveal the startling pink centre. By now her fingers were sticky so she wiped them on the edge of the sheet. A real feast required greediness and she felt she possessed that. And Isobel, sensing few friends at school, had sometimes prepared her a midnight feast. Tiny cubes of processed cheese and raisins. An iced biscuit and a small bottle of lemonade. If Sylvie woke in the night she reached out her hand for it, sat up and feasted in the dark.

'You're still a fool,' Madame Récamier said to Madeleine when a burglary at Le Livre Bleu meant a thorough inventory for the insurers and Madeleine had offered to help. It had been five years since she had worked there as an assistant, trying her halting French on customers who all seemed to have read the same instruction: that a greeting must be made upon entering, otherwise good service could not be expected. Now that Madame was almost eighty, smaller and shorter of breath, she had dispensed with the careful manners she had rigorously maintained. Her opinions of writers had always been firm and freely shared; in return she mostly listened courteously to an alternative point of view.

Madeleine had walked past, almost as if her feet were leading her there, on a week when Hugo was in London and she could safely take a longer lunch hour. He trusted her and she would never take advantage but this week the management of her time was up to her. There was something different about Le Livre Bleu. The blue-black door was no longer propped open by a brick and the easel with the latest arrivals written in Madame's distinctive spiky hand was not in its central place in the window. *Vient d'arriver. Le nouveau Donald Barthelme.*

Nor was Madame in her customary elegant black, her hair pulled severely back and secured with a silver clasp in the shape of a quill, sighted through the bay window.

'Alors,' she said, giving Madeleine her quick severe look. 'Your dress sense has improved.'

Madeleine said nothing. Madame's ability to disconcert remained unchanged.

'I don't expect you've come back to gloat over the loss,' Madame went on when the riposte she was hoping for—even a reference to her straggling hair would have been welcomed— was not forthcoming.

'I heard about the burglary,' Madeleine said, lowering her head. The bust of Sappho at the back of the shop had gone, along with the carved sandalwood box where poems were posted in her honour.

'Stolen,' said Madame, following her gaze. 'Someone got in through the roof. The complete Larousse went as well.'

'Can I help?' Madeleine asked. She knew better than to commiserate. She imagined Sappho being rushed down the rue du Dragon in the early hours of the morning.

'Do you have time? After attending that fatuous Englishman? Perhaps an hour or two in the evening.'

'I can do better than that. I can give you all of Saturday.'

'You always could, you poor fool. All of a day others put to better use. Well, the help of a fool is better than nothing.'

'Is there a proverb for that?' Madeleine asked, and there was an answering flicker in Madame's eyes.

'I might make something of you—endeavour to, it's perilously late—while we count the rest of the American fiction.'

On Saturday Madeleine presented herself. The door was

ajar, the brick in place, but there was no sign of Madame Récamier. Madeleine squeezed past the boxes that took up most of the floor space and the half-emptied shelves. Some sections—History, Biography, Atlases—were severely depleted and Le Livre Bleu looked like a person with a wasting disease. In places the bare walls showed through, flaking and dabbed with many colours. Then a small sound came from the back room with its faux Bayeux tapestry curtain, the section in which Harold receives the arrow in his eye. Gently Madeleine pulled the curtain aside. Madame Récamier was sitting with her head in her hands, a tisane faintly steaming in front of her.

In a second Madame was on her feet, straightening her black dress.

'Lock the door,' she snapped.

For the first hour they worked in silence. There were still boxes to unpack, since deliveries had not ceased. When Madame's back was turned Madeleine lifted some of the new books to her nose and sniffed the pages. At midday Madame disappeared into the back room and the smell of coffee drifted over the scents of dust and old plaster, the anguish of stolen words.

'Well,' began Madame, setting her cup down on a chair on which elderly gentlemen had sat fingering the pages of Proust or Thoreau or Conrad. 'What do you imagine is to become of you? Haven't you learnt anything from working in a bookshop, from me?'

Madame had sent many such questions towards Madeleine in the years they had worked together. Madeleine had been goaded and chided but her character had remained placid, Anglo-Saxon dull. The block-headed English. To defend herself

Madeleine had thought of women working in fields or washing clothes in streams, kneading bread. Their French equivalents would have been very different. No stodgy food or brutish tumbles in ditches with bits of straw sticking to clothes or hair. Yet she could see that books, carefully and lovingly chosen, as if each single book was a companion to another, and an equal, was Madame's equivalent to the treasure box that had set her dreaming as a child.

'I should have taken you in hand,' Madame Récamier was saying. Madeleine had missed part of her speech. 'A creature so naïve, so willing to receive someone else's opinion as a judgement from on high, a creature of so little spirit. And stubborn, that's the worst of it. What good is literature if the heart is not open? If the heart cannot learn.'

By mid-afternoon Madame had analysed and dismissed the type of Englishman represented by Hugo Brudenell-Bruce—perverse, indolent, like a fat white mushroom growing in the dark—and Madeleine's attraction for working for one: more naïvety, inertia. Another cup of coffee was produced and Madeleine's headache increased. Luckily Madame caught the pain behind the eyes, the way Madeleine's forehead wrinkled, and the lecture on men and how to behave towards them was curtailed. Madeleine must visit her once a week for lessons. Madeleine had just enough perception left to realise it was an honour and she had never been inside Madame's home.

The shutters were closed and a taxi ordered. At the last moment a slim novel was pressed into her hands. *The Optimist's Daughter* by Eudora Welty, one of the few American novelists of whom Madame Récamier genuinely approved.

Sylvie and Ben lay side by side, listening to the sounds of Cheung unpacking boxes. The shop was closed and the *Sorry, We are Closed* sign swung on the door handle while to Cheung *Yes, We are Open* acted like a goad. His grandparents had instilled in him that every cent was worth having. His grandfather had been serving in the shop the day he died; a tight pain had gripped his chest and there was just time to push himself through the bead curtain and fall down, still clutching the coins he was about to return to the customer. Cheung would not follow his grandparents in their desire for money. He polished a Pacific Rose apple slowly and held its shiny skin against his cheek. In the mirror he could see his face, the apple glowing alongside. And he listened for the sounds of Sylvie and Ben.

They must be lying down, he thought. Sometimes they went to bed at 8 p.m. to catch up for all the nights they were out, the nights when Sylvie drank too many cocktails and Ben too many whiskies and chasers. When they climbed the stairs giggling, almost falling against the walls. Once they had stopped halfway up and made love, propped against the wall. 'Where's Cheung?' Sylvie had whispered. He had turned out the light in the shop barely a second before he heard their key at the door and he, too, was pressed against the wall between the eggplant and the bok choy. 'They make love in China,' Ben had replied, and in the dark Cheung grinned. A little groan—she was curiously silent, this Sylvie—drifted down the stairs and a long groaning sigh from Ben. Then they must have climbed the remaining stairs, dishevelled and out of breath, and fallen through the door. Cheung stayed silently in the shop for quarter of an hour before he let himself out. The bell tinkled softly but Sylvie was filling the jug for tea and Ben was sitting on the toilet, wondering if he would have to put his head in it. He contemplated sticking two fingers down his throat, something he had never tried. Then he remembered the pleasure they had taken on the stairs and thought being sick would be an insult to Sylvie. He kept very still for ten minutes and the clammy sweat dried on his brow.

Now they were side by side on their mattress on the floor, their cups beside them. Hot sugary tea, what couldn't it solve? Or if not exactly solve, ease with its wonderful syrupy sweetness. The back of Ben's throat was warm and he ran his tongue over his top teeth to taste the sugar again. Under the cover his hand reached for Sylvie's but it was tucked into her armpit. She had turned on her side, her knees pulled up. So he placed it on her hip instead, marvelling at flesh and bone and how they were entwined. The flesh held the bone and would have no shape without it. Something to do with purpose. He imagined the hip bone rose and fell under his hand. But the thought was too complicated; he concentrated on the sugar taste instead and fell asleep.

Isobel, lying beside Kit, was also awake but it was a wakefulness that would last at least another hour. Something—a sound, a thought from the day that was over—had woken her and now each passing moment would wake her further as she examined it. The light in the bedroom was dark and heavy, velvety. Moving through it would be like swimming in a cold lake. The difference between sea water and lake water had impressed itself on her mind when she was a child. She and her brother had swum in a lake on a private property in the early morning or late afternoon. Once her brother had strapped a candle onto a wide-brimmed stockman's hat and swum ahead of her. The flame had flickered and at the lake's edge candlelight had run up the blades of flax. But that was not what had woken Isobel: siblings often try to provide light for one another, however misguided. She was thinking of a quality, an attitude, so deeply embedded in herself it could no longer be lifted out, surgically or by any other method. And it was to do with a book.

Kit, beside her, stirred and flung out an arm towards the edge of the mattress. She knew his palm would be open, like a cup. The palm that was most prized by cannibals because it shrivelled up when cooked, like crackling. Once she had picked this palm up while he slept on, and kissed it.

The book. Think of the book. And then, out of the dark, it came to her. It was one of the Milly-Molly-Mandy stories. How Isobel had disliked Milly-Molly-Mandy and her family. How stifling, even though she was very young—not more than five—when it had been given to her. She had bridled and shivered at the perfect complacent family with their beady self-satisfied eyes. And at Milly-Molly-Mandy's straight black hair. How ominous then that one of the stories, about a birthday party, had struck as surely into her heart as a surgically aimed dagger. Milly-Molly-Mandy had wanted something no one else at the party had wanted: a rabbit with a crooked eye, a lop ear. She had wanted it so much she had won the fairy doll. But because she had been carefully raised she had been able to exchange it: the spoilt child who cried over the doll got first prize and

Milly-Molly-Mandy got her ruined, peculiar, underloved one. And ever after . . .

But here Isobel turned on her side and pressed her spine against Kit. Their two spines moved closer, as if bone was the instigator and not flesh.

That wretched book, she thought. But it was the attitude she blamed, and something that was receptive in her. For surely, for some kind of wound, we are prepared? There is something hollowed out and waiting? She could not have been so receptive for no reason.

She loved what others didn't. Things aslant and odd, glimpsed from the corner of her eye. A design on the verge of failing, a beauty plucked from ugliness. The story had sunk in, into soil as rich as a well-mulched garden; her chest must have been hollowed out like her brother's catcher's mitt. And there had been another book as well. Isobel could feel her eyes closing and she pulled herself up a little in the bed. Kit had turned too and was now lying on his back: his closed eyelids gave his face the appearance of a stone effigy. The other book had no title: it was a comic, a small compact comic of adventures in a girls' school. It involved secret societies and crypts, figures in capes and hoods that were thrown back as they sat around a long table lit by candles. And a solitary girl, the head girl, who rescued a girl from a pond. A mysterious silent girl whose background was unknown. Isobel had fallen for her too, far more than for the aslant thing, the damaged toy.

Why, she asked herself, as finally she lay back, making the other effigy, the consort, with one arm straight by her side and the other now lightly touching her husband's hand. It was uncomfortable to sleep on her back for long but it seemed important to locate herself firmly where she was before sleep came. But the strong hold of early impressions, of the toy and the book, could never be undone. They had seized on such deep and receptive soil that she would carry them with her until her last breath. She could only be aware, alert. *Pied beauty* and *dappled things.*

One strong image came to her before she closed her eyes until morning. She could practically see the comic book, passed from hand to hand or hidden inside an exercise book. The scene of the rescue occupied a whole page. On the left-hand page the girl dived, her gym frock and stockings left on a rock. Then the rescued girl was led off with a towel over her shoulders, a weeping helpless figure. The mysterious girl, with the page to herself, put on her stockings and shoes again, and though figures watched, and probably praised, the silence that had surrounded her remained. It was as clear to Isobel as love, or moonlight, wet grass, rain, sea breezes. As clear and troubling to her heart as Sylvie.

PART TWO:

MARRIAGE & FRUIT

Rain-scented air was coming through the window when Isobel woke. It was her favourite scent, the air suddenly freshened and laden with moisture like a separate air, loosely held together. The leaves of the elm were turning towards the moisture and drops ran into the cupped leaves. Two thoughts came to her: that aging cannibals ate human flesh to restore their youth—that came from a book on the South Seas—and second that, like the tree, she had work to do. But for the moment she surreptitiously stretched her feet towards the bed end, noticing the creak in her knees, as if something was flowing and then blocked. Beside her Kit slept on, at ease, undoubtedly enjoying the soft moist air.

The day would not wait. Her old friend, Lillian Thorpe, was in hospital, and Isobel must press through the swing doors and walk with a confidence she could not feel along the polished corridor—it reflected her shoes back to her—in search of the label bearing her friend's name. She dreaded that Lillian might have been moved overnight to one of the private rooms she passed first: rooms in which could be glimpsed bodies in strange states of semi-nudity—a grossly fat man with his billowing stomach exposed, lolling as if beached; a sleeping woman with her mouth open and vacant eyes. She would need to prepare some words if that happened: the pleasure of privacy and a television high on the wall.

But Lillian was still in the ward with five other beds. One woman was sitting primly on a chair, waiting to be collected: her breast lump had turned out to be nothing more than a cyst, Lillian confided, and it seemed to Isobel that the woman's stature had diminished and she looked almost apologetic. Her friend seemed more concentrated on this little group of strangers, each in their own domain, though there were no boundaries except curtains. Some kind of common humanity was operating, and after quarter of an hour Isobel thought she was glad of it. It freed her as well as Lillian: their talk could be desultory, casual. Isobel had once taken a first-aid course where realistic-looking plastic wounds were applied to skin: gaping lips in need of suturing, a savagely torn ear that would require a complicated head bandage. Isobel had wound what seemed like yards of gauze around the head of the woman who was her partner as she lay on the floor.

Now Lillian's glance returned to the women whose biographies she already knew. The son of the woman who was being discharged arrived and a sigh of relief filled the room. But who wouldn't want to be an imposter in such a place, Isobel thought, as with a half-turn and a wave she was in the corridor again, passing through the swing door and moving close to the wall to avoid a passing trolley.

Was everything about human beings perverse? Isobel wondered as she came out into the fresh air. She knew from experience that illness erected barriers, perhaps with its last strength. Lillian could hardly fail to have noticed Isobel's surreptitious glances at her face which while her husband was alive had never been seen naked.

'Is this true?' Isobel had once asked her, astonished, as she sat on the bed behind her and watched the application of layers that led to a porcelain beauty.

'It was not exactly in the marriage contract,' Lillian replied, 'but it was something he asked for and I granted.'

Isobel's own makeup had stopped at some halfway station: a moisturising cream like the cold cream used in the theatre, a concealer around her eyes and over her cheekbones, a liquid she poured a dab of into her palm and smoothed over the rest of her face. But Lillian had gone on, like someone venturing deeper into Siberia, until her skin was entirely obliterated and an artificial but very beautiful flush rose through the layers.

They had been staying in a hotel and now they walked down the stairs to breakfast. The heads of men turned to gaze at Lillian. In the lift mirror Isobel caught a glimpse of her own unfinished face and felt diminished. If Isobel could have chosen between the naked face and the porcelain one she would have chosen the porcelain one, if she could have had the speech that went with it. For it seemed that once her friend's mask was in place her speech became uninhibited, blunt and challenging. The effort of making up her face—it took an hour and she'd set an alarm clock so she could attend to it before her husband woke (they had adjoining rooms)—made up her spirit at the same time. At the breakfast table she made notes of things to attend to while her husband buried himself in a newspaper. Or she leaned her face on one hand and gazed into the distance, knowing she was noticed and admired.

'Absurd,' Kit had said when Isobel's semi-naked face was

nestled in his shoulder and her nightgown was in a ball at the bottom of the bed.

Kit had felt affronted on Lillian's behalf. He would revoke the treaty and draw up another. The naked face, like the body he was clutching, would gradually be revealed.

Isobel got in her car and drove home from the hospital. She drove over patches of melting tar and around roadworks where a lollipop man held up a STOP sign. As she waited she wound down the window and leaned her elbow out of the car, exactly the way Lillian did when she was about to make a serious pronouncement. Now there were no serious pronouncements, all the firmer for having been issued behind a flawless mask. Now there were just murmurs behind a screen or someone calling plaintively for a bedpan. Isobel felt that Lillian, with her bare face, would never concentrate on her again.

Sylvie's term as a tutor had been renewed—her useless degree, if measured in commercial terms, had still brought her respite. The exam results had been posted and most of her students had passed; one girl had achieved excellence.

Now she was meeting Isobel for lunch. A park bench had been proposed, but Isobel preferred a table and chair, and they had settled on a little Basque restaurant close to the park where they could walk later. Sylvie was early, so she passed the time looking into the shop windows with their dresses designed by fashion students. Nothing resembling them was ever seen on the street, though plenty of young people were passing. It seemed everyone had their own style and was anxious to show it; the tartan dress she was gazing at was cut in a way that suggested anarchy: the waist was swathed in sashes and the skirt had hanging threads.

Suddenly Isobel was beside her, dressed in an old but classic suit, its long skirt deeply slit, showing a glimpse of fine hose. The pearls that Sylvie hoped one day might be hers—though such matters were never discussed—warmed her throat. But her grandmother's face was paler than usual and her breathing was shallow. She understood the need for a seat.

'Are you well?' Sylvie asked.

It was what Isobel would have said. Not 'Are you all right?' Somehow her grandmother always implied the answer mattered.

'Not very well,' she said, 'but better for seeing you.'

They sat at a table near the window where they could watch the passers-by.

When Sylvie was a child, missing her mother more for the fact of not having one, Isobel had used the word 'Darling' often. It flew around Sylvie when she was five or six, and then when she was seven it stopped. Isobel told her that seven was the age of reason and the soft caressing word had served its purpose. It would always be there, under the surface. It could be taken for granted. She thought too that if other children overheard it Sylvie could be embarrassed. Isobel had never believed in reinforcement beyond a certain point.

To mark the age of reason Isobel had taken Sylvie to her first pantomime. Afterwards they had gone backstage to meet the pantomime dame and Sylvie had found it more exciting than the play itself. Clutching Isobel's hand, which she didn't let go until they were in the daylight again, she had taken deep breaths of greasepaint, dusting powder and cold cream, which the actor was smearing liberally on his cheeks while dragging on a cigarette.

'Darling' had come a loud voice from the doorway, and one of the actresses had squeezed herself in. Isobel and Sylvie had exchanged a smile and Sylvie had understood.

Now while their orders were being brought Sylvie stole glances at her grandmother's face. Isobel must have observed her, for she said sharply, 'Just look. We're not in a spy movie.'

But Sylvie had turned away her head. Everything about her grandmother was connected with strictures. She could feel them hovering behind her chair and yet, strangely, she knew Isobel exercised an iron control: for every stricture spoken there were several delegated, sent back for revision or discarded altogether. And between them—'Look harder' was one—flowed something that could not be divided into bars or lines, an affection that was too harsh for such a soft word, that contained aches and fears and even action. As the waiter came with their tapas Sylvie remembered that Isobel had proven herself capable of writing anonymous letters, disguising her voice on the phone, investigating adding sugar (what kind of sugar, white or brown?) to a petrol tank, acquiring a Stanley knife in case she plucked up the courage to slash a tyre—though how deep would the slash need to be and where on the tyre and was length more effective than depth?

Now Isobel was looking her firmly in the eye and Sylvie was trying to take small bites of her frittata and wondering if she could manage a cake.

'Married life,' Isobel said suddenly, cutting a croquette in half and peering at the inside. 'Does it agree with you?'

'So far,' said Sylvie. She had half a black olive in her mouth and was savouring the taste. So far, she said to herself, but how could anyone tell? It was there in that tiny phrase, so *far* from comforting, so *far* to go. Already she was beginning to feel reined in, though other things were coming undone. Sometimes she wondered what Ben saw in her or whether he considered himself her rescuer. It was a view his mother might promote. In time she might measure up. Luckily, looking into Isobel's eyes calmed her. She reached out and touched the fine skin on the back of Isobel's hand.

On Sundays she and Ben stayed in bed or lounged about, or they went out, holding hands and swinging their arms, refusing to uncouple when the incoming crowds would force them apart, as if this physical message could be translated to their emotions. Sylvie wore no makeup and her damp hair from the shower dried in the sun. They chose somewhere to eat that was dark and mysterious.

Today Isobel did not feel like the park, so they went to the art gallery. There was a travelling exhibition of portraits, the winner and runners-up in a prestigious competition, but Sylvie felt bored. So few of the subjects seemed to look at the viewer. She felt she would have preferred a glare the second she stood on the threshold to the austere white room with its high ceiling and plaster rose from which hung a chandelier. A dark baleful glare that since it belonged to another century need not wait upon manners to show its distaste at being observed.

Isobel, however, was soon absorbed. She sat on a low settle and gazed at the winning portrait: a face that looked as if the artist had taken to it with a palette knife, removing layers of skin and exposing cheekbones, eye sockets. 'Before Treatment' was the title, and it was a face too desperate and self-absorbed to look at anyone. I must look at you, Isobel thought. You have nothing to offer back. Perhaps there was a style of portraiture devoted to introversion, that implied an interest in the outside world was at best a sham and real experience was always internal. She looked around for Sylvie and found her peering at a portrait of a baby in a bonnet.

'Let's go further back,' Isobel said, taking her arm.

In the doorway of the 18th Century Portrait Gallery eyes leapt at them as if a hunt was in progress and they, the portraits, were the hunters. Not a single face was pleasant: pretty and spoilt, with trappings taken from their rooms. Long satin dresses trailed on carpets, long bony hands touched a shadowy globe as though patting a child's head. Two young foxy foppish men curled their lips sardonically. Sylvie felt she would like to meet them.

Later, when they were walking down High Street again, she examined men's faces as they passed. But she saw none as confident, none with a sneer that suggested powerful connections and great wealth. One young man she looked at turned his head and looked back, but Sylvie lightly shook her head. That at least hadn't changed: the way human beings scrutinised one another, a brief summing up that might be true or false but was also quick and deadly.

In Paris Madame Récamier was ailing. Her daughter Margaux had arrived from Tours but could stay only for a week. She contacted Madeleine and asked if she could come. Her mother was being extraordinarily querulous, as if all the childhood instructions Margaux had not acted on must be repeated. The air was full of unsaid things, complaints and love that neither knew when to offer. At least Madeleine was inured to her mother's scolding.

Every afternoon Madeleine received her quota of aphorisms. A nurse came in the morning to bathe and dress, arrange Madame Récamier's hair. Some afternoons she sat in a chair, knees covered with a rug, a bolster pillow at her back. One afternoon Madeleine was surprised to find Madame's hair down, a long grey cascade reaching almost to her waist.

'My bridal hair,' Madame Récamier said. Nothing could have made her look older. Did every bride become a witch? 'It used to be a sign,' she explained. 'Your hair was taken up to signify womanhood and then on the wedding night it was let down.'

Perhaps to cover blushes, Madeleine thought. Or to give the man something to stroke.

'I want you to cut it off,' Madame Récamier said. 'I want to feel lightheaded before I die.'

Useless for Madeleine to protest she had never cut hair in her life, except for Sylvie's, and that had been only to trim an overlong fringe while she slept or to cut a curl to take with her to Paris.

Madame Récamier's will seemed to have grown stronger as death approached. 'As if I care about fashion,' she said. All the protocols of the bookshop were forgotten: the careful pyramid of books in the window, the latest John Barth or Kurt Vonnegut. Forgotten too were the feather dusters on their long handles that Madame Récamier had wielded like a Folies dancer, one in each hand. There was one old gentleman whose neck she coquettishly tickled . . . 'Well, what have you got for me, Madame?' customers would ask, and she would appraise them, considering if they were worthy of new paper and ink and marker ribbons.

One strong cut with the scissors—the same that opened parcels and sheared through tape—and the hair began to fall on the carpet. In this nearly last act Madeleine was almost as bold as Madame Récamier could wish. Soon the neck was revealed, then the ears. In the mirror Madame's eyes shone with a queer light; Madeleine took care not to meet them. Finally it was done: a boyish cut with two wings from the centre parting softening the face which had emerged.

'Stare as much as you like, child. No one is going to feast their eyes for much longer.'

But Madeleine, in order to gain the courage to inspect her handiwork, had fallen on her knees and was sweeping up the cascade of hair. Clumps and miniature tangled nests that a bird might seize on with delight. She took one of the book boxes and packed it inside. Then, because Madame insisted, they sat side by side, gazing at their two faces in the mirror.

One afternoon, not long after she first arrived in Paris, Madeleine had found herself in Saint-Sulpice, looking at plaques, testing her rudimentary French on their inscriptions, moving from altar to altar, when a funeral procession appeared. Uncertain what to do, what protocols might apply, she slunk towards the back of the church and sat in one of the hard wooden chairs. In her hand she held a pamphlet about choir practices.

The little group of mourners, elegant in black, were clustered in the Lady Chapel towards which Madeleine had been moving. The coffin was mounted on a bier surrounded by a circle of bouquets and wreaths. Directly under it was a tub of white chrysanthemums. *Choir practices every Tuesday and Sunday after High Mass*, Madeleine read. She could sing, but in French it would be impossible. That morning she had been demoralised by a small boy in a school crocodile rolling his *Rrrr*s on a pedestrian crossing. Finally the priest and the altar boys, the cross held aloft, lined up and the mourners fell in behind. Their self-assurance, for there was a sense of exclusiveness, as if death was the final elegance, increased Madeleine's loneliness. When the door was closed again and the great shaft of light gone, the undertakers came back and removed the flowers. A wreath was looped over an arm and the great tub was lifted and cradled.

It is from Saint-Sulpice that Madame Récamier will be farewelled. When the gazing in the mirror was done and Madame had patted her neck several times and examined her ears, she had instructed Madeleine to fetch a bottle of Napoleon brandy and to open her safe.

On the day of the funeral, which occurs exactly a month after the hair cutting—so little time to feel the air on her neck—at least twenty rows in the nave are filled with writers and poets, patrons of Le Livre Bleu. People bob up and down and greet one another; some cross the aisle to lay a hand on a shoulder in a dark suit. There are more hats than Madeleine has seen in one place: hats with veils and yards of tulle, lifted from ancient dusty hat boxes. The heavy perfumes worn by the women rise and compete with incense and waxed parquet.

Afterwards Madeleine stops and reads some of the inscriptions on the wreaths. *To Héloïse Gabrielle Récamier. An inestimable loss. To Madame, in memory of our long friendship.* On a card attached to a simple posy someone has scrawled *Vive le livre!* Later, at the wake, someone mentions that it was Madame Récamier who had introduced him to Proust in an English translation and had supervised him, when she feared his resolve might weaken, through the entire twelve volumes.

Le Livre Bleu is filled to bursting. Bodies are squeezed together on the narrow stairs and under them; they lean against shelves and ascend the book ladder. As Madeleine watches, a man lowers his face towards a woman who is stretched out with her feet braced against the wall, and they kiss. The lawyer, a woman almost as formidable as Madame, stands up to make an announcement. 'It is Madame Récamier's wish, before the will is read, that each person at her wake should take a book as a keepsake. But I will need an inventory and your names.' Champagne is passed around and before anyone can choose a book there is a toast. Swiftly some move towards a favourite book, one partially read as they stood thumbing its pages and wearing a pensive look as if calculating the week's budget.

But Madeleine will choose nothing. When Le Livre Bleu is empty except for one very drunk poet and a few hangers-on she asks the lawyer if she can take the jar of yellow pencils, the jar that is red and black with the drawing of a bull.

··❧ ❧··

Only once in her long marriage to Kit had Isobel to deal with infidelity. That it was she who had been unfaithful still shocked her. Since she had read about the faithfulness of swans as a child, she had appropriated that character for herself: it went without saying that she would be faithful to Kit. And Kit would be faithful to her. Years after it was over—and it was over within days—Isobel regretted the word could no longer be claimed by her. A blond word, like pale straight hair brushed until each strand glowed, a straight-spined word, a word without guile. She knew Kit was faithful by his occasional attempts at flirting with her friends, his admitting he ogled young women, his needing her to know that he loved risqué jokes.

'If I hadn't married you,' he would say, with just a hint of aggression, 'I might have been attracted to Naomi.'

'I think Naomi might have been attracted to you too,' Isobel replied, and her security ruffled him further.

At the next dinner party—a few of the group were having babies and Isobel was having fertility tests—she observed Naomi and thought if she was tempted to press a thigh or lay her hand on a trouser leg it would not be Kit's. Still she would encourage him in his illusion, for no man likes to be considered safe.

How strange then that she should fall for Paul Esser in the months after Madeleine was born, when her figure was soft and she was dazed by sleeplessness. Madeleine hardly slept at all and the family doctor recommended a clinic for a month. At Cecchetti House the babies were housed in a separate wing; the ratio of nurses to babies was high. At first the mothers saw their babies only at feeding times, with a nurse in attendance. One of Isobel's friends had been the first to insist on keeping her baby with her at a public hospital: she was regarded as a great oddity. But in the large Edwardian house with its lush lawns and flowerbeds, gravel walks and strategically placed green benches, an earlier period was evoked. First the mothers were to be rested and restored with a sound diet. Isobel found the ideas archaic. Part of her longed to be in the chaos again and have Kit hire someone, though they could hardly afford it. The face that confronted her in the mirror each morning had the wild look of Lady Macbeth in the scene just before the hand-washing. She liked the idea of near-collapse and the slow birth of coping. She would have been rewarded by that. Madeleine would sleep a quarter hour longer; Isobel's thoughts would quieten; and between them a thin thread would be woven and would hold.

At Cecchetti House, after Madeleine had been fed and returned to the nursery, Isobel walked in the grounds. Walking was suggested but not mandatory; there was also a library and a conservatory. Sometimes she tried to imagine the founder. Perhaps a frustrated Florence Nightingale with an interest in paediatrics. Someone who believed in clear colours and light and air. A rationalist, Isobel decided, as she walked towards the bench she had marked for her particular use. There was a man sitting on it and as she came closer she realised it was one of the staff, the resident specialist, Dr Esser. She herself felt far from rational and she was determined to reclaim her place. The garden sloped away—that too had been attended to, and was possibly an imitation of one of the great gardens, of someone like Gertrude Jekyll, though on a smaller scale. Dr Esser turned his head and gave her a mock grin. Husbands were allowed only on weekends: she and Kit had managed just a few long kisses.

'You're on my seat,' Isobel said. She felt there was nothing to be lost by bluntness.

'Do you want me to move?' he asked. He was edging along, anticipating her.

'Sorry,' Isobel said. There was no institution in the world, no academy with white-uniformed nurses, that could prevent women from saying sorry. Skin grafts would be required, sessions of hypnotism, possibly some kind of deep immersion bathing. And then, when the lid was raised, wouldn't that still be the first word?

Now she sat on her half of the bench, regretting it was only half, regretting that the view must be shared and that Dr Esser very likely had his own interpretation of everything, honed over years of being in residence.

'How long have you been at Cecchetti?' she asked.

'Two years,' he said. 'But it won't be forever.'

'I imagine it's well paid,' she said. Where had this strange bluntness come from? Something to do with giving birth? Everything she said sounded not only blunt but bitter. Then she looked at his face and realised he knew that young mothers, despite husbands who kissed them in the shrubbery or laid a proprietorial hand on a hip, were rudderless. That morning Kit had lifted Madeleine from her cot with the rubber castors and Isobel had thought the little figure in its gown was rising from water, and expected to see drops falling on the floor.

Already, in the last weeks before her daughter was born, Isobel had bought the Colette novels. She imagined her child turning her eyes towards them while she was still in her crib. Literature instead of floating shapes or a little carousel that turned in the breeze. If the child had been a boy, Isobel would simply have moved them to the bookcase in the hall. But the old gynaecologist she had gone to had thrown a coin into the air, caught it on his palm, and said, triumphantly, 'Heads for a girl.' She had lain on her back on the carpet with a long hair from her head looped through her wedding band and watched it swing in a circle. She had stood in front of the long hall mirror and gazed at her belly. Was she carrying high or low? She thought she was egg-shaped; the illustrations in the magazine she was consulting were unclear. And now, at Cecchetti House, something clear and controlled was opening in front of her, even if her walks were interrupted by Dr Esser who seemed to have decided one half of the bench was his.

Their following conversations were gentler. 'It's harder,' he said, 'when women are successful in another field.' He looked sideways at Isobel as he spoke, as if gauging her independence.

She had been advised by her supervisor to study for an MA in Art History. The same week she had known she was pregnant. Kit was pleased: she had the advantage of him and could observe his reaction. He had wrapped his arms around her and lifted her off her feet. Then he had set her down gently and apologised, and she had laughed. Whatever was happening inside her body was so protected nothing could disturb it, not gin, not hot baths nor falling downstairs. She thought of the first grain of sand working its way under the shell of the unsuspecting oyster. At dinner that night Kit had watched what she ate. And now this man beside her was talking of independence as if it was something women plucked off a shelf.

She got up from the seat and walked. If he wanted an example of independence he could have it. In two hours it would be time for another feed. Already Madeleine was sleeping better;

a routine was being established. It's all to do with high ceilings, she thought, as she reached the bottom of the slope and took a path that skirted a lake. Perhaps she could mention that tomorrow if Dr Esser came again. The height of a ceiling was a determinant of mood. Of happiness and clear thinking, of the love of music, of grace.

Four weeks and Isobel and Madeleine were home. Outwardly Cecchetti House had worked its spell—there were determined people behind it, for whom young women with babies were no match. Madeleine slept in a pattern that had emerged out of the broken nights: that at least held. But Isobel herself came home with a shame that would never leave her. She had slept with Dr Esser. She sat in the window seat and clenched her fists and cried. By the time Kit returned from his office everything was normal again. Each day she began again: Madeleine slept, not because of Isobel's attentive following of rules, not because of her competence, which Kit congratulated her on, but because Madeleine likely saw it as indifference and hence crying would be useless. Later Isobel would learn she was not the only woman seduced at Cecchetti House.

She thought back to their first exchange, 'You're on my seat,' 'Do you want me to move?' as if the challenge was in those few words and it had been issued by her. She was too inexperienced to see the range of emotion he could exhibit, but she remembered how he looked at her face, and eventually she had been emboldened to look back at him. One day, when the corridor was empty, he had seized her hand and pulled her into the linen store. 'These have just arrived,' he said, pulling down a tiny lambskin in a cellophane wrapper. 'You should take one and try it.' Then, before she knew it, he was kissing her, drawing her closer and closer. Her body was not fully healed after the birth: was that something he understood, that her resistance would be low? She had walked back along the corridor clutching the little lambskin underlay, trying to control her face. She met no one, which seemed a great mercy. She combed her hair and splashed her face in the hand basin. A bed vacated that morning was tightly made and a suitcase sat beside it. Under the shower Isobel scrubbed herself pink. She allowed herself to cry while the water poured over her head and shoulders. If she could have taken out her eyes she would have washed them too, and her tongue.

In half an hour a discreet chime would sound to summon anyone who might be in the garden. Madeleine would be brought to her in the arms of a nurse, lightly swaddled, tiny hands reaching for the neck of her gown or tentatively touching her cheek. Isobel looked into her daughter's eyes for a long time, trying to read an expression or even a judgement. But the surface was clear, unclouded, and the iris simply expanded to the light.

'I see you have one of the lambskins,' the nurse remarked, and Isobel tried to read something into that.

Madame Récamier's will was read and Madeleine received a jet necklace and matching earrings. In the lawyer's office she noticed a disapproving glance from one of Madame's cousins.

She wondered if she should offer the necklace to her, then decided against it. The firmness of Madame's judgements was legendary. Besides, the will was recent, dated from the previous month. There was also a letter, written in English, in case the subtleties of French should be lost on her, as they frequently were in Le Livre Bleu. Madeleine put it in her handbag and as she walked along the rue de Seine she removed the little veil she had pinned in her hair. She shook the pins free from the French twist and rubbed the back of her neck with her fingers. A few people turned their heads to look, for her skin was very fair and sunlight fell on her hair, which was the colour of bleached grass. She expected the letter to be one last lecture or a distilled warning. Maybe Madame Récamier had reached a final summary.

The letter, when she had made a cup of tea and sat down at her table by the window, contained a good many French phrases, as if Madame's last reading had been the great Russians. Though she had worked for Madame for years, Madeleine had no idea whether she was truly a great reader or not. The impression was so firmly established it was unthinkable to question it. Once Madame had swooped on the latest Thomas Pynchon, overturning Madeleine's newly decorated window to make a tower of *Gravity's Rainbow*. Madeleine had simply bowed to her judgement, allowed herself to be guided. Now, with the letter in front of her, Madeleine entertained the idea of not opening it at all, of allowing it to become lost. Then she turned it over and saw that Madame had written on the flap, in a hand that still strove to be firm, a tiny *Adieu*.

Chère Madeleine, it began. *Though I did not often call you that over the years I became fond of you and your resistance to my lectures. We were different races, different temperaments. I was too busy training you to admire. You will go on being soft and I hope that will bring you rewards for in many quarters it is admired.*

Madeleine put the letter down and got up to fetch her Larousse. She was not quite sure of the meaning of *douce*. All the afternoons she had worked for Madame seemed to have come back and were pressing into the room. Particularly the late summer afternoons when the rue du Dragon was bathed in a last stinging light and Madame was at her most snappish. Usually it was occasioned by someone leaving a pile of books on the floor and purchasing nothing. Then Madeleine, without being asked, would make tea and bring it on a tray: the teapot, Madame's cup with the gold rim and full-blown roses on the sides, a Marie biscuit.

Now, with the dictionary in front of her and the various meanings of *douce* investigated, she read on. Each word felt like lead because Madame's conversation was often leavened by spite.

I have no one to leave my last words to . . . the letter continued, and Madeleine knew she was expected to imagine Madame Récamier on her sickbed, heroically writing, husbanding her energy, which was to be felt as a compliment. She would have gone on writing if someone was visiting, forcing them to sit by her bed, fiddling while her pen was poised over a word. She was cruel, Madeleine thought, but I could never admit it. That was my English stupidity, wanting to see the best. My bland skin, my expression that infuriated and in which she saw traces of pleading. But then I would bring her tea which she would grudgingly accept and the mood would pass. I loved her, Madeleine realised, but she was careful to push me away . . . *and they are not very fine words*, the letter continued. *No one can know another person though there will be insights, glimpses, what artists call 'epiphanies', though they will never be enough. Do not trust them, little English rose. There are odd protections in being naïve but you must not depend on them. My lawyer is sitting beside the bed as I write this. How she squirms and then resumes her proper expression. I simply send you love and my black jet necklace as a safeguard.*

The signature was spiky and scrawled—perhaps the lawyer had sighed or risen to her feet. Madeleine got up and put the Larousse back on its bookshelf. Then she took it down again and inserted Madame's letter at the word she had looked up: *sweet*.

Sylvie opened the door of the flat and two peaches were nestled in a box of straw. Something must be said to Cheung. Yesterday's two green bananas were still on the windowsill. One day Sylvie expected an itemised bill. Or perhaps they would quarrel and insults like blood oranges would be flung. But not today: today she cradled the two peaches that had rested in the shade of the closed door behind which Cheung might have heard two breathing bodies, twisting in the sheets, turning towards one another and then away, for there was a subconscious text in the way the body made its feelings known.

Sylvie was discovering that marriage had a way of revealing the body that she had not anticipated. The nights were hot but the open window brought some relief as well as early morning traffic. Ben slept on his back, hardly moving once sleep claimed him. If he went through the cycles of sleep he gave no sign; there was no tossing, no rising through the shallows after a disturbing dream. A strange dream had come to Sylvie the night before. She was bodiless, a shape like Edvard Munch's *The Scream* except the shape was ectoplasm and no agony was involved. In her dream she thought it was a soul. The soul was rushing through a great warehouse, gathering up organs: a heart, lungs, spleen, kidneys. Soon it had the supplies it needed. It chose a rope of intestines which it looped over an arm. As it flew it inserted the organs into their proper places. Sylvie woke in a sweat and reached out her right hand to touch Ben's side where his left kidney would be.

Then she lay looking at the ceiling, at the plasterwork and a cobweb attached to the light fitting. The noises of the street were beginning: footsteps, weaving and unsteady, a few bars of a song and then a crash as someone collided with a rubbish bin. Soon the sanitation truck would come and all the street's detritus, like sweat on human skin, would be harried into the drains.

To avoid thinking of the dream which had something maniacal and gleeful about it, Sylvie thought of Léa, the courtesan in *Chéri*. Léa had kept a powder puff under the pillow to restore her morning appearance for a lover. Sylvie slid her hand under her pillow and found a toffee wrapping. Then she slipped out of bed and went to the window to look out. A few lights were burning; in the flat opposite a woman was cradling a baby, rocking backwards and forwards like a boxer. Sylvie picked up a plum and began to eat it. She thought she might keep a supply of soft-centred peppermints under her pillow: the whole point of Léa was secrecy.

She must have an independent life but somehow the initiative was moving away from her. Perhaps that was the meaning of her dream. Start again, shop again for a heart and lungs, choose the choicest entrails, glistening and shiny. Or say, This is just a sojourn. Get in supplies but don't take anything too seriously.

The light in the room was changing. At first it could hardly be perceived; it existed in imagination only, as an idea. Then, like snow, stroke by stroke building, the darkness thinned, became anaemic, the thick strokes were replaced by thin.

For breakfast Sylvie ate a banana, a nectarine and a few green grapes. Before she left she made the bed and closed the windows that let such refreshing air into the flat at night. No one could climb onto the roof above the shops without being observed, but she did not care to take the risk. Cheung came and went during the day and often stood in the doorway in his green apron which usually had a few damp patches from spraying the vegetables. Sometimes, descending the stairs, Sylvie felt like Eurydice going down to the underworld with its earth walls and no windows. There were three jobs to be juggled: four hours of tutorials under the supervision of Professor Woolf; two evenings of waitressing at Living Food, a student hangout where the food was copious and cheap; and two hours of half-hour sessions of walking his Cairn terrier for Mr Arlington, an elderly man whose stratagems for keeping Sylvie talking were beginning to pall. The terrier, Lovejoy, was as delighted as Mr Arlington to see her. Each time she braced herself to utter a farewell speech, he pressed another banknote into her hand.

At 10 a.m. she was sitting in a seminar room in the

Anthropology Department furnished with a long narrow table that could be augmented to form two wings. Today that would be unnecessary: only five students, three female and two male, had showed up. Sylvie kept the door propped open for a further five minutes while she marked the attendance register. A few large textbooks and folders were on the table, but nothing could turn the room into The Royal Anthropological Institute where breathless discussions were had about the discovery of a new species or a primitive tribe. A few cabinets of butterflies would help, Sylvie thought, getting up to open a window and look down on the motley students passing in the quad. The students themselves seemed to have discovered nothing and were willing only to show they could regurgitate pre-digested food. A large number of coloured markers were sticking out of one of the set texts as if, by themselves, they were enough to warrant a grade.

Nor, when the door was closed, was there any keenness to debate a point. Sylvie would begin something—a statement, a supposition, a quote from a famous anthropologist about his work in the field—and ten eyes looked back at her wonderingly, as if the room was a pen into which someone had thrown an unknown food. Which one would venture to pick it up or tear off a piece? Not curiosity but an awareness of traps seemed to be the dominant emotion. Yet surely even the great primates, between bed-making, grooming one another's coats, feeding and sleeping, had time to gaze at a distant hill or to examine a flower?

'How do you get to be a tutor?' one of the girls asked when the quote from Claude Lévi-Strauss had fallen flat and been answered mainly by Sylvie.

'You have to show initiative and a deep interest in the subject,' she replied, knowing the reply was false. Ambition and toadying were better answers. 'Tutorials can be a way of gauging that.'

Instantly five bodies straightened themselves and the owner of the stickered book searched his mind for a question.

The hour soon passed. The door was opened again and another, larger group of students hovered. I can hardly sail out with my nose in the air, Sylvie thought. Nonetheless that is what she did, as if she truly had status and was rising in the hierarchy. Then she clattered down the stairs and out into the sunlight. She skirted the building and walked through a shaded garden with the same low stone walls as the quad. Tired-looking hydrangeas and rhododendrons were growing there. She crossed the road and walked around one side of the floral clock. At the fountain her feet slowed and she sat on a green bench, easing her back against the slats. The mouths of the spouting fishes which seemed to hold little tin whistles reminded her of Isobel and her insistence, after Sylvie had gone to live with her, on water play and long baths. On summer weekends the garden hose had been left running and Isobel had applauded the holes Sylvie dug and filled with water, the dams she made with stones and pieces of wood. Isobel who was elegant had encouraged the hesitant and withdrawn Sylvie not only to muddy her hands and knees and have dirt oozing between her toes but also to wipe her hands on her dress or run her fingers through her hair. Sylvie could still remember her surprise when she first tried it: the long marks on the bodice and skirt of her cotton dress, her palm pressed against one cheek and then the other so later in the mirror she could see the drying warpaint. Isobel left her to her own devices but she came out to admire the terraces in which Sylvie had planted little twigs with their leaves on to make an avenue. Already the bath would have been run and the big jar of bath salts awaited.

What was Isobel attempting to wash off, Sylvie wondered as she gazed into the fountain, seeking for a centre or a focus. But the nature of fountains was circular, like something chasing its own tail: the source of the water, the mechanics, were lost like Sylvie's almost-overflowing bath. As much time as had been spent in the mud was spent in the water and the ochre stripes on her cheeks were replaced by pink. Probably Isobel didn't know what she was doing either, Sylvie decided. Yet like all primitive creatures she had sought order, a balance, and when one was required a counter-balance.

Twenty minutes had passed by the fountain before Sylvie got up and turned her face towards the city. She hurried under the tall palms that gave an impression of a Victorian drawing room: elephants' feet and embossed wallpaper and dried flowers under glass domes. And yet the sky above the palms was light and lively: little cumulus clouds were moving briskly; only the students, lolling on the grass, seemed sluggish. I must not imagine too much, Sylvie thought, as she ran swiftly down one of the flights of steps to the street below. Something was happening in her marriage but she couldn't tell what it was.

Madeleine's final Englishman—Madame Récamier had been right, a failed English rose deserved an Englishman—had decided they might settle in Australia. He had Melbourne in mind: a city of manageable size that could be explored and the exploration would come to an end. He assured Madeleine that the bookshops were excellent; it was what she would miss most. Freddy Rice was ready to settle down, and he had chosen Madeleine, surmising, though she was twenty years his junior, that she too had reached that stage of failure that made settling desirable. Freddy had had his disappointments: a passionate first marriage that had collapsed as rapidly as the soaring attraction that had begun it; two more had failed in slower tempo; a long period of bachelorhood with a mistress.

They were driving on the Périphérique, and Paris seemed to Freddy like a beautiful scarf pulled through a ring. The ring road kept everything undesirable, everything a tourist might not wish to see, out. He knew this was an oversimplification: there were graffiti-ridden arrondissements and groups of scowling youths even within the ring. Soon the Daimler was racing towards a turnpike and there was a curious sense of free-for-all. Only the disappointed should marry, he thought, looking sideways at Madeleine's face. Her chin was softening and soon the sides of her jaw would have two extra columns of flesh.

Two hours later they had arrived at Civray-de-Touraine where Freddy had converted a cluster of barns and outbuildings into a weekend retreat. A large outdoor table was overshadowed by an ancient mulberry tree. The outbuildings had long ago been let to local artists: a landscape painter who worked clumsily with a palette knife, and a potter whose pots and plates were glazed blue. The flag of Lorraine fluttered over the largest of the barns which was used as a sleepout.

'Don't cook anything,' he said to Madeleine as he pulled the car in beside the garage which, despite his leaving instructions with the local builder, still hadn't been fixed. 'A boiled egg will do.'

'Toast soldiers?' Madeleine said, turning her head.

'How well you understand me,' he said. 'Though I could change the order to poached.'

On this they were in perfect accord: a tiring or overwrought day did not require a stupendous culinary effort at the end of it.

'The Empire will not fall,' Freddy said as they came into the kitchen, in the dim light made by the shutters. 'Neither the French nor the English, if three courses are not served on a white tablecloth.'

That evening, under the spreading mulberry, Madeleine lit a citronella candle and they ate poached eggs (the order was countermanded) and drank a glass of cabernet franc. A grainy honey was spread on the thick slices of wholemeal toast before the eggs were placed there, wrapped in their cowls like monks. 'The best of both worlds,' Freddy said, raising his glass and with his other hand lightly touching her hair. He liked that in certain lights the fine lines on Madeleine's skin were visible. The expanses of cheek were still smooth and the appearance of youthfulness would last for a few years yet. A great deal could be forgiven if the cheeks stayed smooth.

They slept in modest single beds that reminded him of his childhood furniture. The room had nothing else except a circular rag rug, a dresser, a chair and a trunk. Freddy folded his hands over his stomach and thought he could feel the goodness of the eggs laid by contented hens.

The following evening they walked by the placid river. Occasionally a skiff passed and there were waves and shouted greetings. They took a glass of wine with the artist who brought out his latest canvases—the palette knife still in evidence—and Madeleine wondered at the brutality of the technique. In the dark they strolled through the garden. A new flower bed had been dug by the gardener who would be coming the next morning to consult. There would be elaborate enquiries about family and health, the journey, ending with an inspection in which Freddy trailed behind, cursing that he knew the names of so few plants and knowing that the wily Raoul knew this and was concealing it under extreme politeness. 'Just plant whatever you please,' he wanted to say, but the rift his impatience would cause would mean a session twice as long as an apology. As for meals, why should he not eat when he pleased, gorge himself with an animal appetite one day and a mouse's (highly unlikely) the next. In Madeleine he had recognised a similar indolence. He would wake when he pleased and wear his dressing gown to breakfast.

In the morning Freddy decided he could not face Raoul and told Madeleine to say he was indisposed. Sympathetic noises were made; Raoul preferred Madame, as he privately called her, for he had guessed which way the wind was blowing.

Now she walked beside him, agreeing that the herb bed needed refreshing or that the lime planted by Monsieur was in the wrong place. Raoul considered plants were connected to the person who planted them, indicating their character which might otherwise be hidden. He suspected Freddy had no sense of proportion and would prefer an English sweep despite the smallness of the section. Instead everything must be in scale: drifts of dried leaves against a wall before a bonfire was set; a single yew planted on the boundary to suggest a solemn avenue.

A leaf landed in Madeleine's hair as they stood admiring an espaliered apple tree.

·∙⫷ ⫸∙·

Isobel, who had embarked on a thorough house clean—though she doubted it would be either complete or thorough, her spirit was bound to fail—opened one of the long drawers in her writing desk and pulled out the Stanley knife with which she had once futilely slashed at the tyres of a car. A feeling of shame almost overcame her. It was a miracle no one had seen her, bending over, supposedly fumbling with the lace of her shoe. It had been winter and raining; she wore a hood. An umbrella would have offered better protection but been hard to hold. There was an old tyre in the garage, stacked against the wall, and she had practised on that, surprised at the hardness of the rubber, the strength it took. The tyre had been put out a few months later in the skip Kit had hired, hidden under branches and broken furniture.

Of course her act had been futile. Her heart had been beating so heavily and her hand on the knife was shaking. But she had called up some kind of buried rage—the loss of her father, the death of her childhood pet dog—for she had read that acts of violence required an increase of adrenalin, which meant that those on the receiving end were at a disadvantage: she thought she had made one successful gash.

Then, hearing footsteps or it might have been the drumming of the rain, she had straightened up, thrusting the knife deep into her pocket. She had forced herself to walk away slowly, to avoid drawing attention to herself.

The memory forced Isobel to open another window and a connecting door. The aim of spring cleaning was to let the air flood a house closed for the winter, to let dampness and mould receive the sun, for stale odours to dissipate. But her half-hearted cleaning was over for the morning. She went to the kitchen and made herself a cup of coffee. She drank it at the bench, looking out into the garden where there was a gnarled lemon tree. She could remember when it had been planted, shiny-leaved and bearing a single flawless fruit. Now its crown was like an umbrella; the trunk was twisted and misshapen and the lemons themselves covered in some kind of scaly growth.

Kit had known nothing of her behaviour, of course. She told him she was testing her ability to walk in all weathers in case they got a dog.

'Why do we need a dog?' he asked. 'Isn't Sylvie enough?'

Sylvie had taken to escaping the house at night, and neither lectures nor locked doors had prevailed. Kit's admonishments had been gentle and Isobel's more strident but the effect was the same. Isobel could pick the exact moment when Sylvie stopped listening by a slight involuntary movement of her head or the clenching of a fist. Anecdotes from her own past, recast in a language Sylvie might understand, though Isobel had a great longing to speak in the language of her own girlhood, as if she was seeking comfort—all this was to no avail. Something in a Sylvie cell had ignited, and the desire spread along her nerves, engaging her mind and limbs. She could no more stop escaping than a sleepwalker can resist rising from her bed.

So Isobel had taken to stationing herself in the garden at night and waiting. She thought Sylvie knew this, but when she appeared she gave no impression of searching or even regarding her surroundings. The sash window was eased up—it might have been oiled because it creaked less—and the figure in jeans, sneakers, jersey and anorak appeared, and Isobel in her own anorak waited in the shadow of the elm. The windows could not be locked, Kit had said, because of fire. The gate clicked open, and then Sylvie was gone.

The first night she kept guard Isobel was in time to see Sylvie's shadow pass close to the hedge that overhung the pavement. The houses in the street were large and they all had high walls. Isobel got only as far as the first corner, and watched the figure turn sharply and disappear down a lane. She hung up her anorak, undressed, and crawled into bed, pressing her spine against Kit as if by sheer will she would weld them into one entity: his sensibility, her absurd effort at shadowing. The next morning she went to the lane and walked down it. It was a shortcut, used by the local children. It came out on a broad thoroughfare. It was a perfect pickup place: either a car could pull up by the lights or there was the park with its stone walls and its great avenue of oaks whose branches were entwined in the manner of a Gothic nave.

What premonitions of defeat rushed along Isobel's nerves as she lay sleepless, a dread equal to and arising at the exact moment these night trysts began. Sometimes she tried to lighten her mood by imagining a Resistance fighter, in a trench coat and beret, blowing up railway lines and bridges. Soon she would be intercepting mail and sending coded messages. Even as she attempted to smile—not a convincing thing to do in the dark—her heart sank. She was entering a world she was totally unfamiliar with, a world the thick hedges and high walls in the street were meant to keep out.

Towards morning she heard a slight movement and sat up. She took her dressing gown from the bedpost and quietly opened the bedroom door. She would pretend she was sleepless and was going to make a cup of tea. Already the stratagems she was forced to adopt were bringing distress, self-dislike. Outside Sylvie's door she paused, not daring to turn the handle. Then she walked boldly along the corridor, hoping to salvage her dignity, hoping that her footfalls at least were heard, that Sylvie knew she was on guard. All the longing in her heart that had been reawakened, the agonies that she thought—and deserved to think—had died down. What she was intending to replace them with she did not know. She only knew it should be something calm.

Just recently she had turned down an invitation to lunch and a hint had been given—wasted but nonetheless there—that she might not be asked again or there would be some penance before she was reinstated. Her failing had been that her excuse—'I don't feel like going out at present'—was badly thought out. There was an insult in it: 'You are not worth the effort.' But when her apologies had failed Isobel had had a good day. She had sat in a bergère chair in the room she and Kit called the den, and for the first time she had seen a harmony she had not realised was there. There was a glimpse of the hall and a niche where the library ladder reclined against the shelves, its topmost rung resting against a set of Dickens that the afternoon light had turned a rosy pink. The hours that might have been spent in the preliminaries to gossip—for that is what they were—were passed instead in reading a review and then searching the shelves for a book while the points were fresh in her mind. She tried to decide if the critic had a clear palate, like a wine taster, for enmity was often disguised and obscured by initial praise. She felt sure, as she read a few paragraphs—a description of the island of Capri—that she too was being discussed, perhaps even at that very moment. And she understood why she had declined: she dreaded that the conversation might lead to Sylvie.

··৯· ৼ··

Sometimes when Cheung's dual offerings overflowed—pomegranate and green banana, grapefruit and pear, rock melon and six plump dates—Sylvie took fruit to her grandmother. The sun streaming through the window speeded up ripening, and Sylvie and Ben helped themselves morning and evening. Still somehow, like a treadmill that has developed a wobble, the supply had outstripped their consumption. Sometimes Sylvie ate squares of chocolate instead and Ben, who was an avid movie fan, made popcorn. Their consumption of wine was increasing: two glasses was becoming a whole bottle.

Now, after her tutorial and before walking Lovejoy, Sylvie put into her library bag a Black Doris plum, a nectarine, a green and a red apple and the six dates to bring the line on the windowsill under control. On top of the fruit she laid a scarf in case Cheung should peer inside. He gave her a little bow when she came downstairs and into the back of the shop, miraculously cool with the scent of soil washed from potatoes, parsnips and carrots.

'How nice it smells,' Sylvie said for what seemed the hundredth time. Sometimes she tried to vary the words, just as he varied his offerings. He smiled and his eyes took in her bag, the slight bulge the plum made against the fabric.

'Have good day,' he called, and, resisting the urge to bow in turn, she smiled back.

Isobel thought the fruit a strange selection but she smiled as well; Kit could have the plum.

'I've something to show you,' she said.

The wedding photo taken by the stranger had arrived. It had been misdirected and re-addressed; the outside was festooned with stickers and stamps. Isobel had only a vague memory of a tall thin man standing behind her as she waited on the jetty, feeling foolish, as the rowboat approached. She had not noticed when he moved to a different vantage point to include the waiting older woman in a shot that caught the prow of the boat, Sylvie's leaning to dip her hand in the water, and Kit's slightly harassed look, letting one oar rest for a second while his hand touched his hat. *This is the one I like best*, he had written on a business card with his name and address at the top. She saw he was some sort of doctor, perhaps a specialist. Isobel had replied with a brief note. There had been no response, for which she was grateful—she had exaggerated her thanks a little, suggesting a conclusion. Now she wondered if a similar photograph was on the wall of his home or even if it had appeared in an exhibition.

Sylvie squinted at it, not knowing what to say.

Something had been done to the colour, for surely the day did not have such a faded look. The lake water seemed almost grey and her hand, dipping into it, looked transparent. In the distance she could see a black swan, like a punctuation mark. Her grandfather was making one of those gestures that were like looking in a shop window ostensibly to admire the contents but in reality to catch one's breath.

'Do you like it?' Isobel was asking. 'It's not the usual . . .'

Sylvie thought that when years had passed it might become *The Wedding* or an illustration for a ghost story. Luckily she was not wearing her veil. She looked at Isobel, because the figure on the jetty with its flowers was not very flattering.

'Who was this man?' she asked.

'A perfect stranger. I expect he had pretensions.'

But later when Sylvie checked the name on the card and then on Google it seemed he was quite well known and had exhibited for years in Toronto.

That evening when she was running Lovejoy through the streets of Mt Eden Sylvie ran hard too, as if she was escaping something. Why did Isobel like everything that was odd, awry, peculiar? Lovejoy sensed something as well, for he barked joyously and joined in what he thought was a game: fierce running and then panting as they came to a lamppost. Ten lampposts had been passed before Sylvie came to a halt, clutching her side for stitch, and rolled over on the grass verge. Lovejoy placed his paw on her abdomen as if to prove, despite his sheltered life, he was one of those dogs like Greyfriars Bobby that would mourn at a tombstone or warm a child lost in snow.

Every Tuesday Ben went to his mother's for dinner and every Tuesday his mother probed. The state of his health, the broad happiness she wanted for him—something like the Lombardy Plains or the deserts of the Kalahari, an unvarying sweep—his career and how it was progressing. Underlying everything was his happiness with Sylvie and whether it could last. Only once had Sylvie been to dinner and now the invitation was not offered. She had walked out, not in a dramatic way which was her instinct, but simply after using the bathroom in the guest room's ensuite. The side door to the garden had been open and she had gone through it. There was nothing in the bathroom, except lavender-coloured tissues, to write a message on. While she was walking alongside the hedge she sent Ben a text. *Escaped. Invent something.* His phone had beeped while his mother was in the kitchen, and he grimaced and straightened his shoulders.

After that, as Sylvie had intended, there had been no more invitations and Ben went to the weekly dinner on his own. At first he had argued, sometimes violently, that Sylvie was misunderstood but soon it had become easier to eat in a semblance of harmony and leave as soon as possible. He could usually escape one dinner in four with something that had come up: indisposition was always a good standby. Soon Sylvie was enjoying her Tuesday evenings far more than he was. She met Isobel at the library or dined with Kit at his favourite Italian restaurant. Kit thought it was perfectly natural to avoid people he did not like; he had rarely seen a long-drawn-out contest between enemies end in resolution.

'You've made a feint,' he said to Sylvie the next time they were out and a black-waistcoated waiter was bending over to light a candle. As the waiter straightened up he caught Sylvie's eye and a frank look passed between them.

Kit bent his head over the menu, typewritten on an old Olympia and sealed between two sheets of plastic. After the restaurant closed the menus were wiped down. At the bottom were four desserts, long ago committed to memory.

'A feint, a sidestep,' Kit said. 'Who can tell if it was the right one?'

He knew she always acted by instinct, without reasoning. And since the deed was done, reasoning was pointless. He wondered where, in a well-governed body, it could be inserted?

Sylvie was winding linguine around her fork, plunging it in as Isobel had shown her, holding the spoon in her left hand. She leaned forward to scoop it into her mouth and Kit marvelled at the beauty of her neck. Her skin was pale and luminous; he half-expected a shrimp coated in tomato sauce to glow as it passed down.

'Don't watch,' she said.

He kicked her under the tablecloth instead and she coughed and made a choking sound. The waiter appeared with a glass of water.

'Why did you do that?' she asked when the pink in her cheeks was fading and she had wiped her smeared mouth with a paper napkin.

'Pure instinct,' he said. 'I wanted to test something.'

'To see if I could choke on a shrimp?'

She tried to remember what was left on the windowsill. Something cool that would soothe her throat. She thought there was a Nashi pear.

She looked at her grandfather severely and caught the twinkle in his eyes. Cowardly as ever—or was it wily?—he had ordered the log-like cannelloni which he was cutting into neat rounds. She could never outwit him, she realised. But could you ever learn from someone so devious?

Ben was not home when she got back. She gulped in the

earth/fruit/flowers combined with the heat-of-the-day smell before she climbed the stairs. She knew instantly that the flat would be empty. A body, even a resting one, always moved the air. Breath was enough. The small machine of breath, she thought, as she leaned against the door which was slightly stiff. On the windowsill she ran her hand over a Jonathan apple and a spotted banana before selecting the pear. She ate it standing at the window, waiting for him to come.

Ben's father, Gilbert Taverner, had died when Ben was three; his mother had been widowed when she was forty. There had been a stillborn child between him and his sister; his mother had never said whether this was a boy or girl. Tactfully he knew not to invent invisible companions. But most of his childhood was spent strengthening himself against a will that didn't know its own strength. If things had been different, if his father had not died of a rare heart condition, his mother's will might have shrunk back like some bulky creature, a hippopotamus perhaps, that lived half-submerged in mud. A great dose of good fortune would have been required. There was money enough, a house, and his mother, once he was at school, found employment in a solicitor's office. She soon commanded the other secretaries and a good few of the men. But nothing came to soften a will that had received nothing from life, apart from himself, that corresponded to what she was expecting.

She must have welcomed it, he thought, bracing himself, now they had reached the coffee, for the ever-growing catalogue of Sylvie's faults. He clenched the fist not holding the cup while keeping a smile on his face. He would seize on one fault and rebut it, but she would have another waiting. He wondered that she didn't employ a detective. Then he thought that might be for the future. She laid the faults at his feet like the bottom layers of a dry stone wall: each stone tested for its ability to withstand the elements and the equally scrutinised stones it would support. 'What have you been doing?' he could ask, futilely. 'Has it been a good week?'

One night, when he and Sylvie had been standing by the window, munching fruit, Sylvie had proposed a list of excuses be pinned by the phone. That way, importunate calls—like his mother's dinner invitations—could be thwarted. Not knowing what to say, not being fluent at the time, was a severe disadvantage.

'Some detail,' Sylvie said, biting into a Granny Smith. Ben peeled a mandarin and popped the segments in his mouth.

'Nothing anyone can check,' he said. 'Like appointments.'

'The appointments of others would be suitable. I met my friend X and accompanied him to the psychiatrist.'

'My mother would check the psychiatrist.'

'Not if he was then admitted to hospital.'

'Seriously, though,' she said, nibbling at the core, testing how close her teeth could get to the pips. Once at primary school she had swallowed a core for a dare and lived in fear that apple tree branches would sprout in her lungs.

'Let's think of one each before we go to bed. And write it on a list by the phone. In code.'

'I witnessed an assault in the street. I'm too strung out to go anywhere.'

'That has possibilities.'

'I think I'm getting a virus,' he said. Viruses were infinitely variable. They came in all strengths.

'I don't want to go to bed with you if it's infectious.'

'It's not. Not yet,' he said, taking her hand.

··❧ ☙··

If someone had asked Cora Taverner the reason for her antipathy to Sylvie no satisfactory answer would have been forthcoming. If she had been at the lake and witnessed the scene taken by the photographer, if she could have brought herself to admire the sepia-toned photograph, now enlarged in a gilded art deco frame and hanging in Isobel's hall, if Sylvie had been more amenable or made a gesture, would it have made a difference? But rumours flew, and her dislike stuck at the name and could go no further.

For her part, Isobel thought she might try again if she could think of a way forward. It irked her that Cora Taverner could make a sentimental capsule of Ben's childhood and smugly congratulate herself while she was prohibited from doing the same for Sylvie. *A child whose mother had abandoned her, rebellious and out of control, an upbringing that was touch-and-go . . .* Even if Madeleine should return, the problems would remain.

The stages Sylvie had gone through were unlike those of other children. Undoubtedly Ben was one of those. With a mother like Cora any rebellion would be snuffed out before the child even noticed. Sylvie's home life had been so uncertain that even a gently introduced routine was a palliative at best. Isobel thought back to the day the land agent had phoned and begged her to keep Sylvie away from the house Madeleine was endeavouring to sell. 'It's difficult enough,' she said, 'without a child dressed in a sheet making wailing noises.' Sylvie had got inside one of the rooms, pushed a chair under the door handle and banged on the wall. Something rattled, to imitate chains. Only quick thinking had saved the situation. When the buyer—no longer 'prospective'—had gone, the agent spoke sternly through the door. There was no answer: the chair had been moved and the window was open.

And where was Ben Taverner while this ghost was running about, disappearing into the tangled garden and a stand of native trees? Probably studying under supervision, cold milk in a glass tumbler on the table, energy chocolate broken into neat squares and nibbled as he bent over a piece of long division.

Disorder is distasteful to some people, Isobel decided, trying to make allowances, but her own ventures outside order had been among the richest in her life. The shadowing of Sylvie, the investigation she had undertaken like a Pinkerton detective. She had followed the blue car Sylvie got into, and thought she was unobserved. In films the getaway car might be boxed in by the pursuit car in a blind alley, the criminal cornered among recycling bins and pallets. Isobel slipped on her dark glasses in case her eyes should meet the eyes of the driver in the rear-vision mirror. But she was meticulous about keeping to the speed limit. If the blue car got ahead at the lights she took it as an omen and instead of spinning down side streets she turned and drove home.

Pinkerton detectives, she told herself, removing glasses and headscarf, probably get paid on results. She was wondering if she should borrow a friend's car in case the man she was shadowing mentioned something to Sylvie. Her own number plate might already have been recorded. Suddenly she remembered something from *The Cadfael Chronicles*: a man hiding in a forest behind the broad trunk of a tree blissfully unaware that an enemy had entered the forest at his back and was about to strike.

Now, years later when Sylvie was safe, it seemed the shadowing had been taken up again by a woman who feared the loss of her son beyond anything. A woman, Isobel thought, who saw the same continuity in destruction that most people find in peace. Someone who would not be content until everything was laid waste and she could begin again.

Isobel decided against meeting face to face. Instead she might try to find something out. She could listen and ask questions. What sort of woman is she? she could say casually. I'm afraid an early meeting went wrong. Very careful delicate language would be required. It would be best if the name was not introduced by her; that way she could remain innocent. There might be someone who liked Cora, found her admirable. There might be pity to add to the portrait, as there sometimes is in a full biography. But in biographies we don't usually meet the person, Isobel reflected, gathering up her books for the library. She could start by choosing a biography of someone she disliked. Not Ayn Rand, she decided. She would draw the line there.

That evening there was no answer when Sylvie knocked on Mr Arlington's door. From inside issued frantic barks, scratching of claws. Lovejoy's claws were in need of trimming, since he did not get enough exercise. Sylvie knelt down and pushed open the brass letter flap. The dog's eyes were looking up at her, his front paws clawing at the door. Any attempt to calm him increased his agitation.

'You must not mention the W word,' Mr Arlington had warned her on the evening of her interview. 'Any word starting with W seems to set him off.'

'I'll try,' Sylvie said. The word Wonderful came to mind. Wilful. Wish fulfilment. She had knelt down to offer her cupped palm to Lovejoy, and he had taken whatever visiting-card scents from it he required to make a character judgement.

It was strange that the door was locked. Then Sylvie recalled that Mr Arlington had a fear of intruders, especially during his afternoon nap. Lovejoy slept at the foot of the bed, ready to bark at the doorbell or footsteps. Slowly he was wearing down his master's prohibition to put his head on the pillow. But the back door was unlocked, and Lovejoy rushed at Sylvie as she came into the hall. Instantly she missed Ben and thought of texting him. But that seemed the wrong order of things: she should have the courage to face things first.

Mr Arlington had fallen from his bed and was lying on his side, one arm flung out, the other twisted under him. His mouth was crooked and his eye—the one she could see— half-open. Sylvie knelt down and fumbled with her phone. 'Ambulance,' she said, when the voice answered. Lovejoy was running around her in circles, barking, so she had to repeat the address. Then she ran to the front door and opened it wide. She snapped on Lovejoy's lead and held it firmly. She took the cover from the bed and laid it over Mr Arlington.

Then she stood on the porch to wait.

'Thanks for controlling the dog,' one of the officers said to her later when Mr Arlington had been carried into the ambulance.

'Which hospital?' she called, but traffic drowned the sound of her voice.

There was nothing for it but to take Lovejoy with her. She locked the house and put the back-door key in her pocket. She stopped at a dairy near the flat and bought dog biscuits and Masterpet Choc Drops. Then she led Lovejoy through the shop and up the stairs. 'Will explain later,' she said to Cheung. 'An emergency.'

It's a pity dogs don't eat fruit, she thought, once they were inside and the door key was safely in a dish on the windowsill. There were three overripe bananas at the head of the queue, and a dubious-looking avocado.

She poured water into a bowl and set down a handful of the biscuits. They were shaped like tiny bones and in different colours. When they were gone she held out three choc drops on the palm of her hand.

'Does your mother like dogs?' Sylvie asked that evening when they took Lovejoy for a walk through Myers Park. Ben, who had endured one of his mother's heavy dinners the night before, was non-committal.

'She has bridge,' he said. 'Lots of engagements.'

'And my commitments,' Sylvie said. 'What of them?' Tomorrow she had a seminar and a shift at Living Food. Giuseppe hated dogs and would probably offer to put him on the menu. He would make up absurd names for dishes: *Dog falafel with cucumber sauce; Dog with couscous and baked eggs; Dog cooked over a slow fire with lentils and spices.*

'What commitments do you have with Lovejoy?' Ben asked when they were home again, crouching beside the small animal which seemed powered by electricity. The biscuits were wolfed down, the water lapped, the muzzle shaken, the small beady eyes alert.

'He can sleep at the foot of our bed. That's what he's used to. Tomorrow I'll try to find if there are relatives.'

'We might have to put him in a boarding kennel,' Ben said.

'Not without someone's say-so. Otherwise we could be accused of dognapping.'

Then she thought of Isobel.

Lovejoy settled at the foot of the bed on a pile of blankets and apart from a few sighing noises was quiet. Ben turned on his side. Even his back seemed unwelcoming as if Sylvie had added another problem. Only Sylvie stayed awake for hours, careful not to toss and turn, thinking of Mr Arlington's face with its blueish lips. She saw now she should have touched his flesh. Felt for a pulse or held a mirror to his mouth. There was no one to relive her experience with or give it Godspeed.

Finally Sylvie tracked down which hospital Mr Arlington was in—she phoned from the seminar room as the first students were arriving, bumping their books onto the tables. She held up a hand for silence and then, as more students arrived, went out into the corridor. She leaned against the wall and answered questions about her relationship to Mr Arlington. 'Dog walker,' she said. 'I have his dog with me. I need to contact someone.'

'Mr Arlington passed away last night. I suggest you contact his lawyer.'

'And who might that be?' Sylvie asked. A fresh wave of students was passing.

'I'm sorry I can't help you with that.'

The call was terminated and Sylvie went into the tutorial room. She was fiercer than usual to the students who sat there. One who was lolling sat up, another abandoned an excuse that would have taken a dog-like expression to be convincing. She began to talk about language and the care that was necessary. It angered her to think that the sentences laboured over by Henry James at Lamb House and which so resembled the sentences of anthropologists could be lightly dismissed. Then, since they were studying death customs, she digressed to *The Wings of the Dove*. 'The Wings of the Dove is backed with death as surely as the death customs of a primitive tribe.' For a moment Sylvie had surprised herself. Every sage knew that death threw life into relief, but had it occurred to her students?

Later, walking through Albert Park, Sylvie reflected that not only was she now the possible owner of Lovejoy but her income had been greatly reduced. She would miss the banknotes Mr Arlington used to press into her hand. He had liked her to hold her hand out flat so he could lay the notes on her palm. Then he would close her fingers over them and give her a sly smile. Sometimes she found an extra twenty dollars. Once she had reproached him for overpaying but he had simply said, 'Mine to give.'

After the civil ceremony at the mairie in the rue Bonaparte, Freddy Rice lost no time in calling in the packers. He continued to be courteous, even tender to Madeleine but his mind was elsewhere. While she existed in a daze—he thought this was one of the least attractive aspects of women: that legitimacy was their true desire and everything light that preceded it was simply a game—he attended to his affairs with a ruthlessness that might have surprised her. Had she noticed, she would have seen it as protectiveness, designed for herself, whereas he had selected her after the other avenues of his life had been thoroughly explored and he was willing to settle.

In Melbourne they would stay first in a hotel—he had no desire to set up housekeeping arrangements—and in the weeks before the furniture arrived they could buy a house.

What unsettled him most were the screeching birds. They were everywhere, even in the heart of the city. In the business district, on his way to see his lawyer, a mocking caw sounded above his head. 'Who do you think you are?' it seemed to be saying. He looked up and located a black and white bird with a sharp beak and a beady eye regarding him. He thought of the pope who had had the birds in his garden shot. Other birds, sometimes in a line, laughed like women at a party. He was in a bad mood by the time he was shown into the offices of Straus, Mahon & Hollister. Coming out, after a lengthy meeting, he half-expected the bird to be waiting.

But Madeleine found the birds delightful. She took their harsh calls for wolf whistles, crude compliments.

'Aren't there some that dive on your head?' he asked, taking her arm.

The restaurants were good, however, and in inexhaustible supply. The fashion of sitting in traffic fumes was well established, though the crowds were thinner. Freddy thought he might buy a few pieces of primitive art: an exhibition of Aboriginal art was showing at the National Gallery; he found the resemblance to the Pointillists striking.

Madeleine thought sometimes of Sylvie and the contact that must be coming closer. She wondered if it could be arranged without recriminations. There would be a house and the elegance it would provide. Freddy was bound to apply his theory about civilised discourse being dependent on a certain height of ceiling. Sometimes he carried it to ridiculous lengths. At one of their dinner parties he had dragged the library ladder into the dining room and drawn lines on the wall and written *Sophisticates*, *Intellectuals*, *People of Worth* and at a lower level *Peasants*.

The next morning Madeleine had climbed the ladder and scrubbed at the wall. Freddy had come into the room and seized her around the waist and nuzzled her neck. Then they had danced a slow foxtrot. Now, whenever the theory of ceilings was mentioned, she knew to look animated.

She saw too that Freddy's European sophistication was an advantage in this city with its preponderance of brick, trams and screeching birds. While they waited for the furniture they took rides to various suburbs. In one called Middle Park the tram teetered like an old dowager down the middle of a tree-lined street with gentrified cottages.

'Here,' Madeleine said, though she knew the decision would not be hers.

In the end they settled on St Kilda. The tall apartments, the street with fabled cake shops, the trams climbing up the Esplanade, even the gaping mouth of Luna Park—it reminded Freddy of a death's head—but mostly it was the view of the great bay that made the decision for them. A narrow stuccoed house with steps leading from the street, a small but cleverly planted garden with a flowering dogwood whose topmost branches reached the window that would be their bedroom. Already Madeleine felt bolder. It was as though she had been allocated more air. Here people were spaced out, unless they were pressed into a nightclub or queuing for theatre tickets. Across the street was a bench facing the sea on which she foresaw she would like to sit. Below two roads carried a steady stream of traffic, and beyond, where the grassy edges of the beach began, there were walking paths with people crossing in different directions. Finally a strip of golden sand was just visible and the unthreatening waters of the bay.

'Will you be happy here?' Freddy asked when, after a day spent with lawyers, the purchase was finalised and they were dining at a restaurant whose French doors opened on to dune grass and patches of yellow sand.

'Very,' she replied, placing her hand over his. She knew it was the expected response, but this time it felt heartfelt. She would walk down to the street of cakes and examine the windows like a connoisseur. The cake shops were in a line, as if they expected this, and were in competition. Somehow she did not see Freddy with her on these excursions. She did not think he would like to climb the hill on the way home burdened by an apfelstrudel or a baba au rhum.

Sylvie, Isobel and the meeting they would undoubtedly have, Madeleine pushed to the back of her mind. There was furniture to unpack, rooms to dress in the way food is 'plated'. There was an upstairs room that could serve as Freddy's study. Shelves would need to be measured and made, and the desk, with banker's lamps at either end, arranged under the window. Rarely had Madeleine felt so excited, so focused. While Freddy was at another meeting—the accountant—she sat in the upstairs room, her back against the wall, feet stretched out on the polished wood, watching the movements of the dogwood. The swaying and retraction of its soft leaves made shadows on the white walls.

Something is given and something is taken back, she thought. It was not something she would have listened to from a human being, but from the graceful swaying of a tree it seemed both profound and right.

Isobel was displeased to find an excitable Cairn terrier had bounded into her kitchen in the wake of Sylvie. Now it turned in a circle, claws clacking, uncertain whether to leap up or lie on its belly on the linoleum.

'Could Lovejoy have a bowl of water?' Sylvie asked.

As Isobel bent to place an old enamel bowl on the floor she noticed the deep rings under her granddaughter's eyes. Her annoyance at the ruse—mentioning the dog by name then asking for water—deserted her and she looked at Sylvie in concern. Meanwhile the dog seemed to sense something was required of him: he slurped less noisily and became watchful.

'He can sit,' Sylvie offered and, on cue, Lovejoy sat on his haunches. It was his sole trick, besides deciphering words beginning with W.

'Two untrained creatures,' Isobel said, relenting even more. She hardly dared think what her role was to be.

'He would have been useful once,' she began and then stopped.

'When you were following me,' Sylvie said. 'He would have made you even more conspicuous.'

'I often wondered if you knew,' Isobel said. 'I'm afraid I wasn't very good at it.'

'It meant a lot to me. In the end, I mean.'

She had seen her grandmother's figure receding in the car's back window. Sometimes the engine was deliberately revved, flinging her forwards then back against the seat so Isobel's last view must have been of a head disappearing. Why had she not seen the malice in it? But everything was danger, danger. Now she shivered at the immaturity it had covered with such bold strokes.

They sat at the kitchen table with Lovejoy's lead looped over a chair. No more banknotes pressed into her hands. No more conspiratorial looks over Lovejoy's deplorable lack of training. They both admired wildness was what the look said.

'When is the funeral?' Isobel asked.

Sylvie had not thought to look.

There it was, in the column with a black border.

She would have to leave straight after to be at the university. But Isobel had not yet agreed to anything. One of the things she always insisted on was equivalent effort: spring cleaning the bookshelves together when Sylvie's hands were almost too small to lift the heavy dictionaries and the atlases. But Isobel had not relented: when Isobel's back was turned Sylvie had rubbed her wrists down the side of her skirt and tried not to sniff. And later she had been rewarded with a hug. They had looked up together at the top shelf. The smallest books were there and Sylvie had stood on the second step of the ladder to pass them up. Besides handing them up she had been responsible for dusting each top edge where the dust had fallen for a year. Still, that night she had sensed the power of an adult over a child, even when a lesson was at stake, and she had taken her mohair gloves out of her drawer and put them on. Halfway through the night she must have pulled them off again because in the morning they were at the bottom of the bed.

If Sylvie had expected Lovejoy, stationed between herself and Isobel in the front pew, to show any sign of loss or grief she was mistaken. Only twelve people were present; Lovejoy made thirteen. Sylvie thought she detected the priest in a sigh, the way someone might glance at a watch. He seemed to spread his arms wider in his white alb as if to encompass distant relatives unable to attend. In the porch, after the Mass was over, they gathered around the hearse and Sylvie tugged at Lovejoy's leash as the little dog attempted to stand on his back paws. Perhaps Lovejoy associated her with walks and not even death could take away an anticipated pleasure.

'I'll walk him,' Isobel said when they were moving towards the car. One of the mourners who had introduced himself as a business associate of Mr Arlington had given Sylvie his card.

After a bowl of water for Lovejoy and a change of clothing for Isobel, they set out. Instantly Lovejoy's spirits revived. He dived after scents and was almost swallowed by a hedge. If another dog approached he bounded forward, barking madly. An Alsatian went past on the other side of the road, plastic bag neatly knotted to his lead which was tied to a child's stroller.

The young woman in charge of the convoy wore tights and a windbreaker, track shoes with fluorescent strips on the heels.

'You look exhausted,' Kit remarked when they returned and Lovejoy had gulped another bowl of water and a small handful of biscuits. He turned in circles and collapsed on the old yellow blanket that had been found for him. A basket would have to be bought and even toys. What mental age was he? A ball or the equivalent of Lego? Isobel was too weary to think. And Sylvie, walking along Symonds Street where Isobel had dropped her, was disillusioned as well. She had expected something like Lassie. If you couldn't get lifelong devotion from a human, a dog could show you how to do it. As she passed the security booth, she thought of Lassie's long golden coat, flecked with snow.

Isobel had thought Cora Taverner's antagonism would fade, but she was wrong. There must have been occasions when minor Capulets and Montagues or Guelphs and Ghibellines did not cross to the other side of the street. Perhaps in the future there would be the birth of a child: a great-grandchild for herself, for her rival a grandchild. They might stand around a christening font together, careful to take up the farthest position from each other where their enmity would not be observed.

At her bridge club Cora Taverner met a woman who spoke slightingly of Isobel. Isobel had once taken bridge lessons given by the club president and been overheard to remark it was a game for those who wanted to waste their abilities. 'Time,' she had said, 'that could be used for organising a field hospital or rescuing orphans.' Isobel had only sat at the tables a few times before the appeal of being outdoors became irresistible. She had not resigned, simply never reappeared. Letters from the secretary went unanswered. Rena Schnackenberg, the woman who had partnered Isobel, felt let down not by amateurish play, because Isobel had made a few credible bids, but by an attitude which felt like disdain.

'I'm sorry Ben has married into that family,' Rena remarked to Cora.

'I think he was bewitched,' Cora replied. 'I'm biding my time.' There the subject was left, both knowing it could be reopened at any time. But, once opened, information seemed to fly in. Sylvie had been sighted sitting under a tree in the park, her head in her hands and a vacant look on her face. She had been seen weeping outside Meier Olson. And once in the art gallery with an elderly man, strolling between paintings, not looking very animated, though if the informant had lingered and followed Sylvie and Kit into the next room, they might have witnessed an attempt to imitate the expressions of two young foxy Regency bucks.

Ben knew his mother's prying, her need to get to the bottom of everything, came from motives of which she was unaware. At her husband's funeral she had straightened her shoulders and stretched her neck when the vicar, prone to address the bereaved, and particularly widows, personally, had talked of her new role as the head and guardian of her little family. For Anne and himself it meant a scrutiny their father, in his blandness, might have protected them from. Instinctively Ben began to keep his own counsel, to confide in his mother only in ways that would win her approval. The result was that his mother searched harder, looked for diaries, read letters, engaged women friends in her spying. Sylvie would have been amused to know how much of her life had been pieced together by a woman she was determined not to see and whom she would tolerate only at Christmas and on Ben's birthday.

She had gone with Ben to the cemetery on his father's anniversary. A white bouquet was already in place, and a card signed by his mother. For a moment Sylvie imagined the woman standing there in her winter coat, head bowed. Yet if Cora had materialised a brittle manner would have been instantly in place. 'How is your research going?' Sylvie wanted to ask. She knew questions were being asked; one or two old school friends were still in touch. 'Why the curiosity? What is there about me that you find so provocative?'

But Sylvie did not want to investigate this either. Now the first year of marriage was over, a new kind of alertness was required. Just what it was she couldn't say. It felt as subtle as the change in the light as autumn approached and the clocks were put back. Ben's career was advancing and yet she could foresee a time when it might stall and its sameness become a problem. She walked past Mr Arlington's house and noticed a land agent's sign dug into the lawn. She missed walking Lovejoy and yet, now the little dog was with Isobel and would remain there until a new owner was found, she hardly saw him. It was Isobel who took him for a walk at dusk so fresh and familiar scents could lull him to sleep.

Two Bartlett pears were just outside the door to the flat, along with a note from Cheung. *May have to vacate premises*, it read.

That evening when Ma's Best Fruit & Veg was closed, Sylvie and Ben sat at the back of the shop, drinking green tea from glass cups. The warmth of the day and the scent of the fruit seemed to concentrate behind the curtain that Cheung pulled to hide the sink. A bin of vegetable stalks and spoiled leaves awaited collection for a pig farm. It was no different from a dress shop, Sylvie was thinking nervously—anything to keep her mind off what a move would involve. No one wanted to see the unpacking and sorting and labelling: in the case of vegetables, the cutting and trimming; in dresses, the security tags and the spot cleaning gun. Cheung would not be hurried and they drank the tea companionably.

Sylvie was wondering if she should ask for a fortune cookie. Perhaps after the bad news was imparted. Though the messages were incomprehensible and often sinister.

'Is the shop not going well, Cheung?' she asked.

'Not too well,' Cheung replied. 'Not as hoped. Now landlord wants to raise rent. Take back top flat. Make into sewing repair business.'

'When?' Ben asked. A certain romance had grown up at Meier Olson when it was known he lived above a fruiterer.

'One month. Notice coming soon.'

'Where will you go?' Sylvie asked. She knew the street was changing. A new nightclub had opened two doors along, lap dancing. Businessmen were seen scuttling inside the doors, usually in camouflaging groups. She thought they should be

141

forced to buy punnets of strawberries and cherry tomatoes.

But Cheung who was so frugal, so attentive to a customer purchasing only a single apple, had another shop in the suburbs. He would go there.

Upstairs, Sylvie and Ben ate the Bartlett pears. The skin was firm but the insides soft and yielding.

'Where?' she asked. 'Where?'

Ben put his arm around her shoulder and his juice-stained fingers left a stain on her collar.

'No more fruit,' she said, and her fingers put a stain on the back of his jacket. It would be good to make love without washing their fingers. But in the end they did, standing side by side at the basin, washing their hands and brushing their teeth. Ben had read of someone dipping their lover's toothbrush in kerosene.

Sylvie woke in the early hours and thought she heard a sound in the shop. She put on her dressing gown and crept downstairs. Cheung had come early and was sitting on the low stool, his machete beside him and a box of cabbages at his feet. For a moment she thought he had his head in his hands but he got up and bowed as he always did. Then, sensing her pain, he took down a box of fortune cookies and removed the tissue wrapping. He brought two cups of green tea and they sat sipping and reading the messages. They ate the hard little crescents—a message in itself: the moon might shine but life is hard—and read aloud: *Your shoes will make you happy today. Land is on the mind of a flying bird.*

When Sylvie crept upstairs again Ben was sound asleep and the two pear cores were gleaming on the kitchen bench.

Isobel thought she should offer her house, but Kit demurred. She sensed that Cora Taverner intended harm: a house could be a fortress. Then, late one afternoon, Sylvie skipped along the hallway, eyes gleaming, and told her there had been a lawyer's letter. She scooped Lovejoy up in her arms and he responded hysterically, his whole body wriggling and shivering.

No relatives had come forward to contest Mr Arlington's estate after six months. But it seemed he had added a codicil to his will a few weeks before his death. 23 Gramercy Street was to be sold eventually, but the young woman who had walked Lovejoy and stayed on to talk to him some afternoons for as long as an hour could live in the house for a nominal rent for the remainder of Lovejoy's life. Better still, she should have first option to purchase the house if that was in her power. There had been an interview—the lawyer had a low opinion of old men and their whims—and Sylvie had endeavoured to look serious.

'How old is the animal?' the lawyer, a Simpson of Simpson, Simpson & Vale, asked, and Sylvie looked at him blankly. Did he mean a vet should look at Lovejoy's teeth and issue an affidavit?

'Let me think about it, discuss it with my husband,' she said. It had already been done: they had danced together in the upstairs flat and Cheung had come quickly up the stairs to see if they were in need of assistance.

'No assistance,' Sylvie called as she whirled around, 'though a pineapple would be nice.'

'Two slices, straight away,' said Cheung.

And then Sylvie had taken the bus to Isobel's, jumped off at the stop before because she wanted to run. And then she was dancing with Lovejoy, tempted to throw him up in the air and catch him again, the way fathers did with babies. Only now he was precious, so precious.

Sylvie and Lovejoy ran two blocks before they slowed. Lovejoy did his business behind a bush; she kicked a few leaves and grass clippings over the little mound. In ten years Lovejoy would be a geriatric dog, on as many pills as his master: uppers and downers, mood pills, pills to open bowels. Mr Arlington had drunk a brandy and soda every evening, and one evening— was it the fatal one, when the decision was made?—Sylvie had had one too. Ben had been visiting his mother, receiving another earful of poison, like Claudius from Gertrude. She had used Mr Arlington as a substitute, for in unhappiness any human being will do, and lingered long after she should have left. And if that ironic decision had produced a decision in another, to secure the life and comfort of his little dog, the sole warmth that pressed against him in the night, what did it matter that every decision was ambiguous?

As she slowed and turned back, Lovejoy and herself both tired now, she thought they had talked about a book but she couldn't remember its title. It would come back to her when her mind had quietened. She might even remember whole sentences, because it seemed important to go over and over that evening, looking for clues.

In Melbourne life had settled into a pattern. Some of the over-elaborate furniture remained in storage, awaiting a decision,

144

but it was amazing how the long room could accommodate an armoire or, upstairs, a chiffonier. Dark pieces were complemented by white walls. The palette of colours was small: only in her wardrobe did Madeleine have a free hand. Now she was far from Paris she could see she was a project and would probably remain one. First Madame Récamier had taken her under her wing—the kindest, most anodyne interpretation—and now Freddy. Through a few diplomatic contacts and some in the wine importing business, a small circle was being formed. Madeleine marvelled that she had been blind to this strategy earlier. Her thoughts had all been on ordinary things: a successful lunch, the meaning of a look, the frequency of a phone call. She wondered if he had been bored or impatient. 'Thank you,' she would say after each meeting, and now she realised she was thanking him for something that was moving away and could never be confined to its beginning in the doorway of a restaurant and its ending when they parted on the street.

In Acland Street Madeleine selected a slice of chocolate kugelhopf from the window of the Monarch cake shop. She stood in line while palmiers and continental custard vanillas were put in boxes and slices cut from a Polish baked cheesecake. She ordered a coffee and took it outside to a table on the pavement, close to the road and the passing trams. Freddy would refuse to sit there, at a wobbling table with coffee spills and an overflowing ashtray. Sometimes dogs were tethered to the table legs, winding their leads around until they were pinioned. Madeleine could see her tastes, so long suppressed, were re-emerging. So much of her life had been spent in pleasing others it was a novelty to discover a taste for creaking old trams, exhausted shop assistants, a beggar lurching his way along the street and rattling a tin with a few coins inside. She fished in her purse and brought out a note which she folded to go into the slot. 'Thanks, beauty,' he said before he stumbled off, taking his strange dried smell with him. A tram, which she could see in the distance, began to move, but no one—dogs, pedestrians—seemed concerned and kept crossing the street in front of it. Freddy hadn't exactly forbidden her to waste time in Acland Street or made a comment about her thickening waist.

Now she got to her feet and set off towards the shop that sold candles and incense, soapstone carvings and cushions with twinkling fragments of mirror. She bought hyacinth soap and a hand towel for the bathroom. At the last moment she picked up a small black elephant. Some people had motifs, lucky charms. She had never thought of any for herself but if she had it might be an elephant.

At home she placed it on the bookshelf, on one of the highest shelves where it would be unnoticed.

Freddy phoned to say he would not be home for dinner. She read for an hour—she had a list of Australian authors—and then ran a bath. She used the hyacinth soap, holding it up to her nose from time to time. Then she lay stretched out, suds in her hair, arms by her sides, imagining she was dead. She pictured Freddy standing in the doorway, calling her name as he always did as he came through the house. There would be the tiny sound as his key was set down in the antique dish on the credenza and then his feet on the carpeted stairs. She tried to imagine the expression on his face, the first expression, whether it would be alarm, a rushing grief, or something more like exasperation. Perhaps his eyes would go first to her waist, thickened further by lying down, thanks to today's kugelhopf. And next her breasts, flat as two rum babas.

Kit came with Sylvie to her appointment at the Hong Kong and Shanghai Bank. It was clear the bank manager was nonplussed by the sight of them together, side by side in chairs a little lower than his own. The Grand Poobah, Kit thought, secretly pleased at Sylvie's appearance. Her hair was swept back on one side, and in that space dangled an earring shaped like a leaf. Kit's presence meant that any comment about the foolishness of Mr Arlington had to be censored. Doting older men were not unknown to the bank. Money might be impartial but there were usually human agencies involved, valencies that attracted or repelled. Sylvie, as if aware of these thoughts, had lightly touched her grandfather's arm when they were seated. Now they were both looking straight ahead, Sylvie at a painting on the dark-panelled wall.

No relatives had come forward to claim the property or dispute the will but the search would continue. Nor had the house been bequeathed. The owner had simply thought of the difficulties of young couples in securing accommodation. Sylvie tried to remember if she had mentioned the fruit shop. She might have done on one of the few occasions she had stayed for half an hour after returning Lovejoy. But the conversations had mainly been about dogs. Mr Arlington was amazed at the resilience of animals when they had been mistreated, how completely they seemed to forget.

'Forgive and forget,' Sylvie had said. How miraculously fur

grew back, eyes brightened and tails thumped.

'How old is the dog?' the manager asked, perhaps hoping it was one of the large breeds with a shorter life span.

'Not old,' Sylvie replied.

'Sometimes a random kindness can bring about a late change to a will,' the bank manager was saying. 'Not that kindness should be disallowed. It seems the changes were made in the last month.'

'Do you want us to see a vet? Get a certificate of health? Or a fortune teller, for a prediction?' Sylvie was becoming irritable. It was not her fault she had walked Lovejoy, answering an advertisement in the 'Personal' column. Something about the wording suggested it had been carefully worked out.

'And if we decide not to move in?' Sylvie asked. 'A dog only needs a bowl and a bed.'

'That was clear,' said the manager. 'Lovejoy is not to be denied his home. For the term of his natural life.'

'Have you read the book?' Sylvie asked.

Now the manager rose, placing his hands flat on the desk. Sylvie and Kit also stood. There were handshakes, some remarks about animals in rest homes, about decisions being made in the future. Kit left the name of his and Isobel's lawyer. Then they were walking along a passage to an outer door.

'Everything hangs on that little dog,' Kit said as they joined the stream on the pavement.

'I feel like taking Lovejoy somewhere wild,' Sylvie said, slipping her arm through his. 'Somewhere with brambles and farm dogs. A bull in a field. Somewhere he can have a real adventure.'

'Good for you,' Kit said.

At first Sylvie and Ben settled edgily into the house. Only Lovejoy seemed delighted as he rushed from room to room, all discipline abandoned. He was house-trained now and accustomed to Sylvie tugging on his leash and commanding him to sit when they were on the street in case she needed to stop and pick up an offering from the grass. This Lovejoy found puzzling: he was virtuously adding to the rich scents that were everywhere. Sylvie watched other dog owners do it: a certain sangfroid was required, as if her thoughts were elsewhere and this quick bending and scooping and sealing of the bag was something that might have been done by a night nurse before she came off duty. The problem now was that Lovejoy must be guarded, as their tenure in the house depended on him.

'Is there an escape clause?' Ben asked. He was tired of the stuffy furniture and carpets which the trust had had cleaned. Their own pieces, the very few, were stored in Kit's garage. And Sylvie too, though she didn't say it, longed for the simplicity of their rooms above Ma's Best Fruit & Veg where the sills were peeling and the windows jammed. Their parting from Cheung had meant a final enormous fruit salad to which Sylvie had added the last of a bottle of Limoncello. They had eaten it sitting by the window, looking out. When the fruit was gone they poured the liquid into wine glasses and polished it off.

Sometimes strangers came to the door of Mr Arlington's house, claiming they had the wrong address. Sylvie thought they were spies. Lovejoy rushed to the door, barking furiously. She hardly dared not answer in case the barking suggested Lovejoy was on his own.

'Let's give it away,' Ben suggested one evening when Lovejoy had made a mess on the parquet floor. He had eaten something on their walk and had to be bathed to remove the smell. Now the bath would have to be repeated. That night Lovejoy's face, restored to innocence, was intensely annoying to Ben.

They quarrelled in a desultory way and slept on the edges of the bed in the guest room. Mr Arlington's bedroom door remained closed; Ben had drawn the line at using it. At the foot of their bed Lovejoy snuffled in his basket. Sylvie was dreaming; she turned suddenly and groaned. Ben rubbed his feet on the sheet to warm them, then he moved across into her space. The bridging of night, he thought, though it was nearly dawn.

It was to this house that Madeleine came after her meeting with Isobel. Freddy did not accompany her. A room at the Hilton and taxis to and from the airport and to take her around; money for shopping, for gifts would be required. Madeleine knew he did not like families or family conferences. At Tullamarine, where he left her with time to spare, Madeleine had wandered from shop to shop and bought nothing. What gift could she bring to a daughter so long ago abandoned? She thought of many small things, as if gifts could broach the subject: a phial of expensive perfume, an exquisite scarf, a silver necklace like a collar. Instead it was liqueur chocolates she held in her hand as she came to the door with the barking dog. Isobel had told her about the strange bequest which was causing concern. Madeleine wondered if the dog could be left while they went out for a meal or if there were restaurants, as there were in

Paris, where dogs could be seated and served by waiters with impassive faces.

The barking increased, the door was opened and a young woman appeared in front of her. Tousled hair, flushed cheeks and a hand holding a leash on which a small dog was jumping. For an unsteady moment Madeleine thought she was back in Le Livre Bleu, summing up a customer as she had been taught. Her foot moved a little on the porch, then she was steady again. A young woman like Marilyn Monroe in *Blonde* who could lose herself in something large and tragic. But at the moment a young woman whose eyes were raised interrogatively and whose demeanour was impatient. Madeleine's fingers clutched the chocolates and resisted pushing them forward.

'Let me hold the dog,' Madeleine said.

Later she would be glad she said that first, before she identified herself. When she was back in her room at the Hilton, lying on her bed, she could console herself that she had offered to help. The lead had been passed to her, because at that moment the phone had rung and Sylvie had turned on her heel. Madeleine had stood in the doorway and the dog waited beside her. She bent to pat it and the box of chocolates slipped. In a second the dog had seized the corner and torn the cellophane. So Sylvie, coming back along the passage, had found her mother kneeling and blowing on Lovejoy's nostrils so she could get the chocolates back.

Getting to her feet, holding the leash in one hand, Madeleine felt she was not only rising from water but that her position had brought her to a new beginning. Sylvie had taken her for a land agent and the chocolates and solicitousness were simply a ploy. At least in dishevelment and discomposure they matched.

'Could I have a glass of water?' Madeleine asked.

Sylvie disappeared again and now Madeleine stepped inside. She closed the door and the little dog ran.

'Who are you?' Sylvie asked, turning from the sink with a glass in her hand. 'What do you want?'

'I'm your mother,' Madeleine said. 'You don't recognise me?'

'How could I?' Sylvie said. She held the glass out, and Madeleine took it. 'The last I heard from you was a parcel.'

'Postcards,' Madeleine said. 'There have been postcards.' Chosen carefully, she wanted to add. Views of the Grands Boulevards. Never tourist traps from the wire stand in the rue de Rennes, turned creakily on its axis until the shopkeeper looked up and asked if she wanted to buy the lot.

'Did you like the linen?' Madeleine continued.

Never would Sylvie be able to imagine the hours of searching, the thought that had gone into it. Madeleine had had the sheets put aside for twenty-four hours while she investigated one more shop in the Marais. 'Bargain,' Hugo had told her, but she had been too overwhelmed by the provenance and thickness of the linen, the way it felt to her hand when she slipped a finger under the ribbon or stroked a hem. The thought of lying in handstitched and monogrammed sheets made her feel weak. Something from Colette came back: that women and girls sewing had wicked thoughts.

'You'd better come in,' Sylvie said. She meant further in. She led the way to the kitchen and put the glass down again on the bench. Then she went into the bathroom and ran water on her hands and brushed her hair. It was a gesture her mother would have understood: that any scene that was to be played out demanded attention to one's appearance. Never did she fight with Ben without first sneaking a glance in a mirror, a knife blade—anything would do. Loss might come but appearance was a bottom line. Now she touched up her lips, outlining them as if there were boundaries beyond which her mother could not go, filling them in. She must sit her mother down and examine her face. She suspected her lips had fine lines. There was a perfume in the air, something hopeful. To hell with that.

Still she looked boldly enough when she was back in the room. Her mother was sitting at the small table used for breakfast. Her skin seemed to have been preserved as if someone had applied layer upon layer of creams and lotions. The skin of a slapper, Sylvie thought, for she was still discomposed and the question about the sheets had offended her. They made much— her grandparents and others—of her having tried to haunt her mother's house and scare off buyers, but her mother could walk dreamily along a street as if sorrow was the arrangement of a window or the fineness of old linen someone had probably given at least part of their sight for.

Then she looked more closely and she could see that no creams, even French ones, could hold back a creeping frailty, no night cream stroked in with the fingers could prevent a neck becoming like crepe. At least the sheets, as heavy and pure as a hard windfall apple or the scent of bread wafting over cobblestones, were true in the way centuries were true.

'We should begin again,' Madeleine said. 'I could go to the door and come in again.'

At this moment the knocker was struck and Isobel was standing on the porch, flustered a little, hiding the anxiety in her eyes, her hand reaching down for Lovejoy as if an animal was a talisman and whoever held the leash was protected.

They moved to sit at a long island with stools which brought their faces close. Twenty years earlier the kitchen had been modified and the island put in. Someone could work at it, chopping and dicing, running water into a saucepan, while those on the other side leaned on their elbows and talked or nibbled nuts or slices of cheese. Sylvie stayed on the side with the taps and Lovejoy sat at her feet. She fought to stay silent. 'He looks as if he has done great harm to someone,' Kit had said in the portrait gallery when they were standing in front of a cruel-eyed man in a wig. She had lifted her eyes and stared back. At ten she had small stores of venom. The eyes in the portrait, narrowed and bitter, suggested the stores would increase. Dimly, with a child's perception, she noticed the rich robe cascading from his shoulders, the chain of office, the gloves. She missed her grandfather suddenly. She would have preferred him to what was assembling: three generations of women, each with a stake in the lives of the others, each with a role they had elected to play. She turned the tap on—it overhung the sink like a lily—and the sound of water calmed her.

'Is there somewhere more comfortable we could sit?' Isobel asked. 'Since you are imprisoned in this house. Surely there are chairs?'

'I feel like a drink,' Madeleine said suddenly. 'Is there a drinks cabinet?'

'There's a bottle of brandy,' Sylvie said. 'Mr Arlington was drinking his way through it.'

'Let's have the balloons,' Isobel said. She could see them through the glass doors of a cabinet. She could think of nothing better than to stick her nose into one and sniff the rising fumes.

They leaned back on an old two-seater sofa, Sylvie in a wing chair. Everything had seen better days. And what were the better days of those who sat in them? Sylvie would have said it was her wedding, rowing with Kit across the lake, dipping her hand in the grey-green water. Isobel had too much to choose from: it might be the period she felt herself to be a spy, her felt hat pulled low, her ineptitude which oddly made her feel warm. For Madeleine, who had drunk half her brandy in a gulp, it was a memory of Madame Récamier on late opening nights when they closed the shutters and she handed over two thimblefuls of Calvados in two dusty glasses. Madame had believed in chaos: that her clients should be introduced to the creeping passage of dust as well as the smell of newly cut pages.

Kit, at home, was unaware of the conference taking place. Otherwise he would have offered to take the little dog. The dog was the problem. If Sylvie had not answered the notice in the 'Personal' column on a morning when she was sitting in the fruit-shop window, eating a new variety of peach squashed like a pug dog. And if the old man had not given in to caprice. But perhaps it was the living breathing creature, the animal snuggling into his side when he slept or, more likely, woke during the night. The young woman who took him out and returned him, each in a state of excitement, must be retained.

In the room that he and Isobel had no name for—study, library, den, its name had changed during the years—Kit ran his hand over the large globe that stood beside a club chair in the position of a lamp. He stroked the coast of Morocco and ran his fingers over Gabon and Botswana until his hand fell away into the Atlantic Ocean. He always thought of this globe as a face and most often as Sylvie's face. She had become his world, and the pits into which she fell resembled the great oceans. Not as oceans were when they lapped the shores of small islands or vast continents but as the Ancient Mariner experienced them, in their unknowable deeps. As a boy Kit had wondered—now he set the globe spinning and it rocked as if it was emitting a groan, which meant the stand needed lubricating—whether seas and oceans had some presentiment of a shore. Did the great volume of water sense a braking ahead or did it come as a trauma? He was ignoring the moon, of course, as humans always ignored something. The globe slowed and he patted it with his palm to make it settle. He thought he could talk to his own lawyer to see if Sylvie and Ben could leave the house and provision still be made for the dog.

At the house in question, Kit, if he could have seen through one of the long windows, would have changed his mind about the dog. Sylvie had gone upstairs to change. She had flung her jeans on the floor, pulled her T-shirt over her head and even put on new underwear. Then she put on a skirt, black with small flowers, and a black scoop-necked top. She ran a brush through her hair and applied concealer to her cheeks which were hot. She outlined her lips in the darkest lipstick she had, and sprayed perfume on her throat. Now her mother, who still looked oddly calm, should not daunt her. It seemed her mother was composed of layers, frail enough in themselves, that over the years had produced a surface that held her together. Her attraction for men, Sylvie thought, marvelling that what remained was composed of layers of adapting and pleasing.

Madeleine would have been very surprised at this diagnosis. She found a little downstairs toilet tucked under the stairs, and in its confined space she too was attempting repairs.

If there was a long sofa we could sit in a row like the three monkeys, Isobel thought, but there was only the wing chair which should be Sylvie's as guardian of the house. She rose and tried a slipper chair that had seen better days. How she longed to slip her shoes off and curl her feet under her. But other people's furniture brought a certain restraint. Looking around the room she could see it followed a reduced aristocratic style that might have been taken from *Country Life*. The furniture was arranged in nests: nothing touched the walls; there were no chairs like wallflowers. She thought of maids trailing vacuum cleaners with long cords.

'The house is a problem,' Isobel said to Sylvie when she returned and, avoiding the wing chair, sat beside her. Isobel eased a cushion behind her back. 'Kit is going to consult his lawyer.'

Sylvie said nothing: the subject had been exhausted. She suspected her mother, resuming her seat, was going to talk about the dogs of Paris. And on cue Madeleine started describing a woman kicking a pile of leaves over a yellow turd with the toe of her shoe in such a disdainful manner she obviously regarded herself as invisible.

'That's not the problem,' Sylvie said.

'How long do dogs live?' Madeleine asked.

'How long do any of us live?' Isobel said. Now they really were the three monkeys. Under conversation, under the most superficial enquiry from which all meaning had been bleached, like a drop of blood diluted and rediluted until it was little more than a stain, lay inchoate meaning. Words there were thin; looks, a gesture, took up the slack. If she offered to make a cup of tea, would it be seen as some kind of foreclosure? But she was too tired to get to her feet. It was easier to talk about dogs in Paris while Lovejoy circled the room, unaware that by giving Sylvie and Ben a lodging he was bringing grief.

'We should dine together,' Isobel said. 'Not tonight.' She was too weary for anything but toast.

'What about Lovejoy?' Madeleine asked.

'Baby comes too,' Sylvie said.

'I saw a dog coat in the rue du Four,' Madeleine remarked. 'It was like the suit of an astronaut.'

In two days Madeleine had flown. The morning after the dinner, Sylvie rubbed blusher into her cheeks and stayed in bed. 'You look ridiculous,' Ben said from the doorway. To Isobel she sent a message that she was unwell, possibly infectious. She cancelled her tutorials and imagined what a great ape might do. A fall in status was especially threatening for a female, though males, too, could slope away, defeated. At midday a bunch of flowers arrived from Madeleine but she did not appear. Had she done so, Sylvie might have added lipstick spots. She had tried the spots on Isobel when she was six and been sent to school with a scrubbed face.

When Ben got home Sylvie was out of bed, making macaroni cheese. The bench had pools of milk and flakes of cheese. She poured him a glass of merlot and held it out.

'How's your temperature?' he asked.

'Non-existent, as you well know.'

'Don't you think you're being cruel?'

'Sickness is always cruel.'

But he had no patience for banter.

'No crueller than my unthinking mother. She is more interested in Parisian poodles than me.'

'Lovejoy, the ice-breaker.'

Hearing his name, Lovejoy jumped up and Ben bent to fondle his ears. Conveniently, it hid his face on which he was afraid his thoughts might show. *How much more of this, how much longer can I bear it?*

But Sylvie was racing ahead: '. . . so smug when she was leaving, as if it had been a triumph. I almost think I prefer your mother, the pit-digging troll.'

'A good buss when you get home,' Russell had advised him. It was how he dealt with his frazzled wife and squalling twins. All afternoon Ben had been anticipating a harridan with carmine cheeks. He moved towards Sylvie and she raised a wooden spoon. An ambrosial gust of melted cheese issued from the oven.

He ground his face into hers so that her head felt hollowed out like a piece of fruit. He pulled her spine so hard he could finger the bones.

'It works,' he would tell Russell in the morning. But there was something Russell didn't know. It left Ben unaccountably sad.

Autumn came again, and with it the shape of Mr Arlington's garden was revealed. Some days, after she had toiled through Albert Park, braced against the wind and hurrying around the fountain which flung water in wind-directed swathes, Sylvie resented walking Lovejoy at all. A strange fear of authority had seized her and caused Ben to quarrel with her.

'I feel as if I am spied on all the time,' she complained when she was wearily winding a scarf around her neck and attaching the plastic bag to Lovejoy's leash.

Ben had been looking forward to eating, which was clearly not imminent. The front door slammed behind Sylvie—he thought it was the wind—and Lovejoy yelped as they went up the path. Never again, Ben decided, would he allow himself to be seduced by riches. They should simply have declined the offer—he could have said he was allergic to dander and the matter would have ended there. There were some at the office who were envious of his good fortune. He was advised to hang on and stake a claim. One wag suggested a team of vets or a dog whisperer if the dog looked bored.

He went into the kitchen—how he longed to be back in the poky flat with its gas rings with baked-on stains and the offerings of fruit on the windowsill. He always went to stand there when he got home, his hand feeling blindly and trying to identify the piece of fruit his fingers touched. And afterwards he would touch Sylvie's face in the dark, feeling her cheekbones and then the sharper bone of her chin. He loved the way one touch led to another, or he was unconsciously led.

He took down a can of pumpkin soup from the cupboard and heated it in a saucepan. Then he made a plunger of coffee. He lifted the soup off the heat and, carrying his coffee, walked through the rooms. For the first time in his life he felt insubstantial. Even Sylvie's boldness seemed to have gone. On the path a mound of leaves had piled up, almost like an artificial step.

He was not hungry: the warmed-over soup would do. Memories of the evening at Isobel and Kit's came back. Everyone had overindulged; he thought it had been deliberate. Something for the hands to do: raising glasses, lifting the lids of serving dishes and letting the steam escape—butter melted on beans and sprouts. There was a casserole that in his dazed state had looked like a tapestry. Sylvie's absurd mother had prattled on. She had talked about Paris and bookshops and restaurants. Kit had winked at him. Late in the evening they had tried to remember the words of the 'Marseillaise'. One line each, they had gone around the table. *Ils viennent jusque dans nos bras* had been one of his. He had acquitted himself well. Sylvie's mother had come to his aid when his turn came around again. Of course the deeper meanings were never translated. But the wine glowed red and then the brandy came, and he stuck his nose in the balloon and rocked it from side to side as if he was at sea.

PART THREE:

LOVEJOY'S LEGACY

A bitter wind was blowing through the garden and over the grave of the little dog which, like some human ones in old cemeteries, was covered with a tiny concrete slab and a headstone. Human graves of this kind felt a need to press themselves to the earth, to secure, in death, all that might have evaded them in life. The funeral had been conducted following the terms of the will: that the garden, though Lovejoy had used it only as a means to get out to the street, be the resting place, and that the body be buried three feet deep. Sylvie had been questioned extensively by the lawyer and had signed an affidavit that the death had been unavoidable.

A black Labrador carrying a bone in its mouth from the butcher—the butcher had been questioned and admitted that occasionally a mutton flap or a knuckle bone was given to the dog that seemed homeless. Such was the young lawyer's tone that the next time the Labrador visited the butcher took the precaution of taking him home for safekeeping. Lovejoy had been walking on the opposite side of the road with Sylvie, the leash in her hand as it always was when they left the park. Neither firmer nor less firm, she told Ethan Simpson, who regarded her aggressively as if he was longing for a charge to stick. Lovejoy had simply been overcome by life: the bone, the big black dog, all the suppressed instincts of living with Mr Arlington had been overthrown in a rapturous tug on the leash, which had torn it from Sylvie's hand and propelled him under the wheels of a car.

'You couldn't hold a small dog?' the lawyer asked, looking coldly into her eyes.

With an effort Sylvie returned his stare.

'Do you know anything about instincts, Mr Simpson?' she asked. Do you have any? she meant. Then she reflected he probably did. Cold ones, clinical in their execution. The Labrador, not relinquishing his bone, had darted onto the road as well, so perhaps there had been a meeting of spirits. The woman in the car, with the traffic banking up and honking behind, had stayed at the wheel, head in her hands, until a policeman arrived.

Mr Arlington's vet had prepared Lovejoy for burial and the funeral director had supplied a casket. There was no shortage of funds: thousands remained in the account for veterinary bills and food, the yearly registration. If Sylvie had wanted to employ a professional walker or groomer that would have been allowed. A professional walker, one who would have held the leash or plunged into the traffic herself. A professional walker with a pack of dogs of various sizes that would have become entangled had they attempted to cross the road.

'Now you are no longer needed,' Simpson was saying, and obviously it gave him pleasure, 'I presume you are not about to make an offer on the house?'

Future owners would be bound to ensure that the grave, level with the grass so the mower could pass over it, and its marker, were not disturbed. The old man had thought of everything, Sylvie told herself as she plunged down the stairs, carelessly as if she was imitating Lovejoy.

23 Gramercy Street had a slightly neglected air, though its paint gleamed and the gardener had done his work. Only a few leaves marred the path between the pruned roses. She would need to start collecting boxes for their possessions. She might find another Chinese fruiterer and ask for banana boxes with holes in their sides for ventilation. Ben had been cheerful that morning, seizing her in a rough hug in the hallway and turning her around, nearly knocking over the umbrella stand. He knew his mother was displeased, as if Sylvie's carelessness with the dog had robbed them of an inheritance. But now it seemed as if his reserve, new to him and puzzling to her, was being removed and things would be fine again between them.

Sylvie took her mug of tea to which she had added two heaped teaspoons of sugar into the garden and stood under the weeping cherry where the plaque was. The inscription was simplicity itself. *Lovejoy* and the date of the accident. Spooling back behind it were the years of companionship, romping and sleeping on beds, and all the imaginings that must have possessed Mr Arlington. The warmth as Lovejoy's body, sealed in its warm coarse fur, pressed against his crumbling bones. That warmth and the painful pressure as Lovejoy wriggled and settled had been worth having.

I knew neither of you, Sylvie thought, when the tea was drunk and a layer of sugar crystals remained at the bottom of the mug. She inserted two fingers and scooped the sticky sweetness out. Then she changed her mind and flicked the sugary drops over the grave. No one could fully understand the life of an animal, certainly not a self-centred human like Mr Arlington, but each had given something. She thought the black Labrador dog had whined when the car struck Lovejoy's body and, with horns sounding in her ears, she had bent over to see the light depart from his eyes.

·◦⋟ ⋞◦·

Madeleine's foray into motherliness, while not a success, still filled her with satisfaction. Satisfaction did not have to be shared, she realised, as the Boeing 777 had climbed into the sky and she settled into her business class seat. In a very short time the hostess, the veil of her scarlet hat unloosed, came by bearing a bottle of Veuve Cliquot. Madeleine raised the flute to her lips and looked through the glass at the sky. There was a society that watched clouds and identified them. Surely, she thought, it could not be as onerous as bird watching? Then she reflected that cloud superseded cloud and some were composite. She tried to think of a cloud name and eventually came up with cumulonimbus. Then she must have fallen into a doze, because when she woke a lap table had been pulled out and a white cloth spread. More champagne was poured and she drank it like water. It didn't matter if she was tipsy because the car would be waiting.

Madeleine slept again and, as if making a conscious effort in her dream, she tried to summon up the cobblestones in the rue du Dragon. Sometimes they glistened as shower after shower passed overhead. In summer, despite the efforts of the *balayeur*, they were dusty. In autumn dog turds were covered in leaves, something some elderly ladies took advantage of. Madeleine would dart from the bookshop to chastise a white-haired woman leaning on a cane while her grubby miniature poodle crouched in the gutter. 'Disgusting animal, as disgusting as its owner,' Madame Récamier shouted, but she had no weapon, only the latest Gore Vidal she had been in the process of arranging in the window. *Brûle en enfer*, the woman shouted back, and after the turd had fallen she kicked a few leaves over it with the toe of her shoe. Madeleine could see it clearly, more clearly than if she were awake. Two formidable women, young in spirit, holding their ground. They admired one another, she realised, and this was the message of the dream. The woman with the dog was thrilled when her *bébé* took longer than usual over his toilette simply to infuriate Madame.

The plane landed and Madeleine wished she had a cane to lean on as she queued and then went to collect her luggage.

'All well?' Freddy said, taking her arm. She knew no answer beyond a nod of her head was required.

They drove along the palm-bordered streets and she noticed the difference in the air, the demeanour of the people. Even the clouds had changed; the sky seemed wider. The great bowl of Port Phillip Bay stretched out with lake-like placidity. Once inside, and after a hasty kiss—another woman would have noticed a slight lessening of ardour, for Freddy was already embarking on an affair, making arrangements—Madeleine went to the bedroom window to gaze at the familiar layers of the view she was dependent on. The two roads on which traffic travelled in opposite directions, a favourite restaurant with a tiled roof, the strip of beach with its golden sand. The promenade, dawn, midday, evening, as regular as meal times, had not yet begun, but its rudiments were there. A quiet passage in music, she thought, not knowing how prophetic her words would be. Notes or human bodies that anticipated the movement of crowds or the crashing chords of a finale.

She would write to Sylvie, she decided. That would be the best way to begin again. Short letters at first and then more expansive ones. Longer sentences, like Henry James, full of parentheses which would probably make Sylvie impatient. She would not talk of France, for surely there was something condescending about rapturous descriptions of a place the listener had not visited. With a rare insight she realised her little 'tales' extracted a good deal of detail, most of it unpleasant or boring. Days when Madame Récamier hardly spoke a civil word or she discovered a hole in her shoe so she could feel the cobblestones. Why must everything be lived first? she wanted to ask, but then Sylvie's problems, over which she had no rights, came to her: a slight sadness in the eyes, the disastrous acceptance of the old man's will involving the dog; the strain of turning her life in another direction. Now there is less love at her disposal, Madeleine thought, though she had met Ben only once, when they dined together. At Isobel's she had gazed at the sepia-coloured photograph and wondered why she felt spooked.

She had walked with Isobel down suburban streets with overhanging trees and humps to slow traffic and, side by side, which was the best position for confidences, a few tentative things had been said. Nothing as profound as an apology or an explanation, for both would have been useless, but words that brought about a sort of ease. Both, as they trod in the leaves and watched others fall, were absorbed in the present. The present is what she would write about to Sylvie, nothing more.

There would be visits which might become regular. Perhaps four times a year, coinciding with the seasons. Winter for sorrow and introspection, spring for wilder words because the wildness would be recompensed by blossom. Then the thought ran out. By summer a healing might have been accomplished.

'What will you do today?' Freddy asked.

'Nothing much. Unpack,' Madeleine replied.

'I have a few appointments. I'll be here for dinner.'

'The Turkish restaurant?'

But he thought he would rather stay in, gauge the comfort he was expanding, evaluate how he could consolidate and preserve it. For a time he was watching every word.

Suddenly Madeleine remembered there was a glass ornament in her luggage, wrapped in layers of bubble wrap and rolled in her silk nightdress. It was in the shape of a fern, the curled frond. She needed to find somewhere where the light could shine through it.

Isobel lay in bed, disinclined to rise. Kit brought her a cup of tea and she noticed he was slightly stooped, accentuating the care with which he placed it on the bedside table. Automatically her hand reached out for it; automatically she turned her face so his lips fell on her forehead. Once, when she was in hospital sharing a ward with five other women, she had bent over one of the beds—the occupant had called out in a mild insistent voice and Isobel was nearest—and a horrid stench had issued from the woman's mouth. It had filled her with fear and a resolve to brush her teeth as soon as she woke. Now she ran her tongue over her teeth and noted they felt smooth and slippery. The body's wakening she had taken for granted when she was young; now it seemed like a factory in which someone switched on the lights over a cold concrete floor, or a nightclub seen in the unforgiving light of day, all tawdry drained colours that needed human breath and anticipation to animate them. A tiny quantity of matter had settled in the corner of her eye, and she touched her finger to it and then ran it under the lid and under the lashes that had never been luxuriant and were now thinning. During that stay in hospital she had resolved to regard her body in a different light. So many procedures, so many tubes and catheters, the nightly turning when she was aware of white figures on either side of her bed. She no longer cared what words she spoke or in what tone, though consciously she tried to thank everyone for the smallest service. Over the long days and nights her body had resumed its activities; its systems which were connected and yet separate entities, started up again.

Kit came back and took the cup. It was a hint. His hair was damp from his shower. Isobel felt a stab of envy at the neatness of his appearance, though she knew he too made an effort. Why should it not cost him as much as hers? Yet hers felt greater. There was something about the male body, she thought, as she got up and put on her dressing gown. She did not allow that procedures for the male body might be equally feared, equally intrusive. Feared more, she conceded, as the hot water streamed down her back and she turned her shoulders into the torrent, one at a time, to ease out the aches. How many absurd conversations had she had with her gynaecologist, another neat man, buffed to his fingernails. They had conversed for years over an unmentionable expanse of her body which he handled discreetly, telling her when the speculum was to be introduced or warming his fingers under the tap.

By the time she was dry and dressed Isobel was ready to do her face. But this morning, sober or tired of her thoughts, she looked back firmly at the face in the glass and gave it only cursory attention. It was easier that way. Besides she wanted to carry—and *apply*, for that was always Isobel's wish, even if it lasted for only five minutes—the lesson of those weeks in the ward. She wanted, as she went about her privileged tasks and her possibly privileged worries, to remember a woman she had become fond of and kept in touch with after they were both discharged. Honora's body had been hacked about by operations that were bound to fail, but her family had not been able to let her go. Great wounds crisscrossed her body as if she had been in a fight with Cossacks—Honora's words—to no avail. 'I never appreciated my body until now,' she said to Isobel the day before she died.

Now it was time for Isobel to get her body downstairs and do something useful with it.

Today she would start the annual cleaning of the bookshelves, one set of shelves at a time. It was essential to begin 'while her courage was high'. The words of Elizabeth Bennet propelled her into the study and lasted as long as it took to draw the curtains and raise the blinds. She fetched dusters and a bowl of tepid water to which she added a few drops of disinfectant, and began to take down the books and lay them out in long lines.

'Why now? Why today?' Kit asked, appearing in the doorway.

'Why not today? Have you forgotten your Primo Levi? *If not now, when?*'

Levi was several shelves down; it would be an hour before she reached him. Maybe she should attempt a new order: her most-loved books on a single shelf. But if she stopped to think of this, half the morning would be wasted while she read paragraphs or peered at inscriptions. Then there was the dilemma of what to do about books that belonged to others, some with *Ex Libris* stickers neatly inscribed and dated. She told herself she was simply here to clean, to shift the dust where it lay on the top edges and the spaces between. So many of the pages were yellowing where the sunlight had reached.

'Better you than me,' Kit said, retreating.

After two hours Isobel felt demoralised enough to sink to the floor and stretch herself out beside a line of books whose authors began with G. She lay alongside Jane Gardam and Helen Garner, Amitav Ghosh and Adam Gopnik. She had imagined the task would refresh her but the opposite was true because each author had brought back memories of herself. The naïve enthusiasm with which her sixteen-year-old-self had read André Gide, feeling if she saw him in a coffee shop she would be propelled to his side. She saw now that she had recognised her innocence and wanted to despoil it, not in the real world but through the safety of a book.

When her thoughts turned to Sylvie she recognised she had tried to influence her through books. Many had been unopened and politely returned. The Colettes had really been for herself; she had wanted to understand the sensualist whom Gide had called 'a great bee'.

Isobel sat up and rubbed a smudged finger across her forehead. She thought of Colette digging in the soil with her bare hands, with her dog and cat in attendance. Gloves and dusters were not for her, only the sturdy fingers, digging and probing. She doubted Colette ever undertook spring cleaning.

By evening one bookcase was complete: the books, dusted, were replaced. No decision had been taken about reforming their order: it was enough they sat on cleaned and wiped shelves that had been allowed to dry in the air from the open window. Isobel's back ached from lifting armful after armful of novels, biographies and autobiographies. She knew it would be at least a week or longer before she would tackle a second bookcase which contained history and travel, diaries of voyages and plant-hunting expeditions.

When Kit rubbed her shoulders and suggested an unpretentious Italian restaurant and something simple, like spaghetti carbonara, she could have wept.

Over the gingham tablecloth she tried to explain the despair that had come over her. She moved the miniature vase with its single carnation—scentless but long-lasting—closer to the window so it was reflected in the glass. It was the labour of the writers that had overcome her, which was odd for it should have been the contents of the books themselves. She had read a good many of them though she could not remember a single sentence—a few ripostes from Oscar Wilde, a pert remark or two of Elizabeth Bennet as she perambulated with Lady Catherine de Bourgh in the little copse.

'They wrote just to fill in time,' Isobel said when the steaming plates and two glasses of pinot bianco were in front of them.

Kit looked into her tired eyes, the lines radiating from them, the weariness that she could not conceal. She looked as though she had been herding the authors themselves, in their wigs and pantaloons, smoking jackets festooned with ash, hair standing on end as if in fright. He thought, as he lightly touched the back of her hand, that she took things too seriously.

'And now they are back in their places,' he said gently. 'Just as well . . .'

··❧ ❧··

Sylvie and Ben had moved into a flat. It was half a house: their half had the bay window, the other the French door, recently added and incongruous-looking. It was hardly soundproof: sometimes softly quarrelling voices rose from the other side. They were saving for a deposit, or Ben was, since Sylvie's earnings covered essentials. The will of Mr Arlington was still being settled: there might be a lump sum and there might not. Twice a week Sylvie supervised a tutorial. A new intake of students seemed to need her more. At least they looked up expectantly as she came into the room. A few had prepared work; a few made comments that were almost perceptive. The seminar room was usually required straight after: in the last five minutes footsteps were heard in the corridor and bags piled up against the wall. But if she had the room to herself Sylvie sometimes sat on for a few minutes, enjoying the sun on her face—the room was always warm—and thought about apes and her mother-in-law.

If the beautiful house that had been Lovejoy's home had been a mistake, so too was the latest move. Now they were closer, Ben's visits to his mother became regular again. Sometimes, to make matters worse, he came home with leftovers, which Sylvie refused to eat though she might only have opened a can of beans. Ben felt her resistance and took the treats for his next day's lunch. He felt his mother's warmth enveloping him as it had when he was a child and his father had died and she had become both overprotective and severe. He could never tell when one regime would change into another, for the warm protecting moods involved stories and hugs, hair stroking, especially after his bath, and goodnight kisses behind which he sensed, though only one kiss was given, an unrationed love.

Now, it seemed, he was linked to this again: the present and a residue from the past. When he was older and at school his mother had cut items from the newspaper and left them on his bedside table for him to read. Items about kidnapped children, boys lured by sweets or money, cars mounting the kerb as innocent children walked home from school. 'Did you read them?' she would ask, because there were normally two or three saved up. He would nod and say nothing and there would be no further comment. An extra fond kiss would be given that night, or a story whose hopeful outcome seemed to countermand the pieces of newspaper whose ink came off on his fingers.

Even as a grown man, a successful architect, he found it impossible to tell his mother what the effect of these missives had been. As a young boy he had read them carefully, sometimes puzzling over a word or something said by a policeman. He didn't dare use the dictionary but at the same time he was terrified his mother would question him. When his confidence grew he began to skim. There were familiar themes. The problem was the warnings were issued in the midst of comfort, ordered meals, attention to his childish complaints. If there was a difficulty with a teacher or a misunderstanding with a friend his mother would listen with an attention that had something spellbinding about it. Sometimes he forgot what he was going to say, sure that her attention would solve everything. The child who was snatched from the street or enticed into a house with the promise of seeing something—the real 'something' was not mentioned—was likewise surrounded by parental love and could not sum up the situation in time.

But his mother could not see the effect her efforts had on him. When he had deposited his schoolbag on the floor and flung off his cap he would go to his room and pause at the door. His eyes, however hard he tried to look elsewhere, would go to his bedside table where his present reading was piled, and under the lowest book there would be a piece of newsprint poking out. The only thing to do was read it straight away so it could be screwed into a ball. Then he would face his mother and lower his eyes.

Over the years—at thirteen he had cried Halt and flung a pile of screwed-up cuttings back at her—the effect had been both suffuse and incalculable. Only one story stuck: a small girl rescued by a dog and carried out from under a house where she'd been chained to a post, her body grey with dust and her hair as grey as an old woman's. The dog, in a later cutting— his mother had relented for once—was presented with a certificate, but Ben had nightmares about the little girl lying on a bed in the hospital and being carefully washed so her childish features were restored. For six months he entertained the idea of becoming a doctor. Then his best friend caught his leg in the spokes of his bike and a great flap of skin was torn off and it was all he could do to stay and support him.

Now, sitting opposite his mother, allowing her to bring his coffee and some small cake that must have taken hours to produce, Ben felt the unease that she had laid the foundation for resurface. She was talking of Sylvie, of his choice, but talking so obliquely, with such discreet pauses, as she rose for a napkin or passed a teaspoon, that he was almost fooled. Was the point of this unease that it could be reused? Was it a 'ground', a term he liked in music? *Greensleeves to a Ground.* He looked towards the window and watched a light shower stroke the glass. When his mother's back was turned for an instant, he pushed back his cuff and read his watch. He estimated he could bear another quarter hour.

At the door he allowed his cheek to be kissed and resisted rubbing his hand against it. He walked quickly along the street, ignoring the waving figure, and heard the door close. Sylvie's mother had insisted on kissing both cheeks. 'Faire la bise,' she would murmur. The powdery smell of her skin and the cloying perfume made him cough. Still she was an innocent . . .

Now, walking home through the dark streets—a visit to his mother always demanded a walk afterwards—he contemplated not just the breakup, which he knew was her hope and which she would put to him as a stumble, soon erased, but a move to another country. He could not be bothered with the fact that Sylvie's impossible mother was now closer. The idea that we are some part of another's design—like people embarking on farewell visits when a fatal illness is announced—was anathema to him. One of his colleagues had been diagnosed with a cancer that gave him a few months to live. Immediately he had plunged into activity: wills, uncompleted projects, dinners at which he appeared with tubes and morphine pump and, on the final occasion, a nurse. Ben thought he would go on a voyage and spend the remaining time staring at the sea. He would pack a suitcase of wine, the very best he could afford. He would sit in a deckchair in the moonlight and drink until he passed out. He would look for the freak wave and for dolphins. He could be wrapped in canvas and buried at sea. He envisioned the short service as he walked, the neat entry of his body into the water.

He was now at the entrance to the dismal converted house with the joined letterboxes. As an architect he should have known better than to tolerate its partitioned rooms and lowered ceilings. He didn't even have the energy to remove the plywood from the fireplaces and restore them.

In bed he pressed himself close to Sylvie like the wall that divided the house. Gradually the warmth of his body and a few drops of warm water from his shower flowed into hers and she turned towards him. She dreaded the days he visited his mother but didn't know how to stop them. There was something in the mother-bond she felt should not be interfered with. Her own mothering had been so little. Just before she fell asleep with her husband's back pressed into hers, as if by facing outwards they could face anything together, an insight came to her. It was that when she had dressed in a sheet and pretended to be a ghost to scare away buyers from the one house she had liked, it had been the warmth of the sheet she had wanted, some old comfort like being swaddled.

In Melbourne Madeleine was unaware of any change in her life. Freddy was a little distracted but she attributed that to the arrangements he was making to keep himself occupied, the business contacts and the appearance of work that was so essential to a man's self-esteem. He was being put up for a club, not the most prestigious but a good start. He knew just how to create a sense of mystery around himself. Cards had been printed and were casually passed around. His character had always been expansive and this spread ripples far wider than his expenditure. He also gave the impression, despite his sophistication, of being ready to learn. Several histories of Melbourne and the goldfields made their appearance; he was particularly interested in the substantial buildings that had been provided by the civic sense of the wealthiest philanthropists and would not have disgraced far longer-established cities in America or Europe. One by one he made a tour: the Royal Exhibition Building, the Mint, Parliament House, where he rested on the steps under the guise of admiring the view. Then he crossed Spring Street to take tea at another imposing edifice: The Windsor. It could not be called a fake but he had the impression it had descended from the sky, supported by giant hot-air balloons. Inside, at a table with a lamp and a fine damask cloth, tea was served with quiet ceremony. A napkin was flicked into his lap; he exchanged a few comments with the waiter and enquired about dinner bookings. A fresh pot of tea was brought and he slid a tip under his plate. Out in the street again he walked until he was tired, then boarded a tram. A cross-section of Melburnians talked or lounged: he must remember to avoid the rush hours when bodies were crammed against doors and the centre aisle swayed with strap-hangers.

Today, gliding through Middle Park and stopping to let off a handful of passengers, Freddy caught sight of a familiar figure on the station platform which had been transformed into a café. At a rickety table, with a tablecloth and flowers in a jam jar, was seated his wife, raising a cup to her lips and smiling to herself. In a second the tram had moved off again. He just had time to see her lift the lid of the teapot and peer inside. A tall young man in a long green apron appeared in the café doorway. Freddy smiled as the tram plunged into a cutting. He had no idea Madeleine could navigate, for it would have required skill to get to the station. She must have travelled towards the city and then changed back. Perhaps she had consulted a timetable, though he doubted that. Most likely she had sighted the tall waiter or someone on the platform and decided to copy the experience. Still it showed a pleasing initiative. On the way home he stopped at a superette and bought a bunch of flowers, cheap but colourful. He thought Madeline blushed a little when he produced them.

Despite Freddy's complacency Madeleine was forming a friendship with a waiter at the Middle Park station café. It was hardly a friendship on his side and nor did she suppose it had any real existence. He saw her, she imagined, after her third visit when they had exchanged a few pleasantries, as a middle-aged woman and himself free of the need to flirt. In France men were differently trained; there was the complicity of one generation learning from an older one, the passing on of tricks. But in this new country, as Freddy was fond of saying, opportunities were squandered. A man flirting with an older woman simply to keep his hand in might be imagining his girlfriend at the same age. The woman herself, by her grooming, her sophisticated conversation, might indicate the riches still in store.

Now Xavier, the young waiter, was carrying a rug over one arm, concerned that, despite the station's gingerbread overhang, she would be getting wet. The rain was so light and hair-like, as fine as babies' hair, that Madeleine wanted to laugh. She was holding her face up to it, raising her chin and exposing her neck. But she accepted the rug and allowed it to be spread over her knees. 'I'll be fine,' she assured him. But she would like another pot of tea. Two trams were passing and faces scanned the café but she felt as calm as an actress on a film set, refilling her cup and stirring in a spoonful of sugar. The trams disappeared and, as if the scene had ended, her hand reached out and touched the vase with its geranium. She stayed until the rain began to fall in earnest. Then she took her tray to the serving hatch and walked down the ramp as another tram came in sight.

She leaned against the window and thought of Sylvie. It wasn't her love she longed for—that was past and could not be undone—but her admiration. A flicker of admiration for the tiny initiative of a bored woman, still carefully groomed, still grateful for the ease life had given her, who had worked out a tram journey that brought her to a small oasis. Nothing could be less oasis-like: the screeching bird over her head as she got out at her stop, all the waving energy of the bay which today had a red-hulled ship on the horizon.

Nine months after the death of Lovejoy, and when Sylvie had given Ben an ultimatum about finding somewhere else to live or living in the flat on his own, a letter arrived from Simpson, Simpson & Vale. The house at Gramercy Street was sold and the grave of Lovejoy was secure. The slab and headstone could not be moved—it was part of the bill of sale—but who could tell if it would last beyond one owner? There was a codicil that had required investigation. If the care of the dog had been exemplary, a lump sum could be paid from the estate. But since Lovejoy had come to his death under the wheel of a car this, at first, did not apply. Yet the care, until that fateful afternoon, had been exemplary, and if Mr Arlington had been alive, awaiting Sylvie and Lovejoy's return, no fault would have been found. 'You both look as if you have wet noses,' he had remarked once when they burst through the door together. Lovejoy had found a hedgehog, sick and stumbling in the daylight, and undoubtedly hastened its end. It was the following day that the codicil was added, for Mr Arlington loved enthusiasm applied to a task. He considered Sylvie would not waste her life, and a gift of money, not so substantial as to deflect her from whatever purpose she had and not too small to wound, would show his regard. He might write a note to go with it.

In the event, that week had been his best, 'the best of the rest' as it was described, and ten days later he was sinking. Now the money was finally to be released. Lovejoy's death was not judged to be Sylvie's fault; the sale of the property and a share portfolio had released considerable sums to the charities nominated; this last sum would tie everything up.

Sylvie, sitting in the office of Simpson, Simpson & Vale for the last time—there was no way she would use such a firm herself— endured again the condescending stare of Ethan Simpson. She looked at his cold pale-blue eyes and anaemic fingers fumbling with a pen. She wrote her bank account number on a square of yellow paper. 'A few days, possibly a week,' he pronounced, and she thought he would hold anything back for the feeble pleasure it might give. They would use it for a house deposit;

with a little added it should be enough. And towering over it would be a loan which they would whittle at like climbers on a mountain attacking an ice wall with ice picks. None of this was apparent in her face, only the desire that he should not triumph or she seem overgrateful.

That night she took Ben to dinner. They drank a whole bottle of Villa Maria pinot noir and she was the one who went to the counter to pay.

'We owe something,' she said. 'Let's walk.'

A weight had been lifted from his heart, so he agreed. He guessed where she was going.

It was a fine night of magnificent stars. In the garden of 23 Gramercy Street starlight was falling on the tops of tall trees and the lawn was assembling its dew. The blinds were drawn and no light showed. They slipped through the gate and made their way to the rear of the garden where the little grave was set in the lawn. Sylvie had forgotten to bring a flower, so she pulled a white gardenia from a bush and laid it under Lovejoy's name. Passion to passion, she said to herself. And on the way home, holding Ben's hand, she questioned him about what he thought was the most important thing. But she didn't wait for his answer; she gave her own. It was passion.

Isobel, in the doctor's surgery, was pulling on her clothes: ubiquitous black trousers, crease-proof, elegantly cut but in the last few months loose at the waist. She could almost climb out of them without undoing the zip. Over her head she pulled a fine merino jersey, the kind she wore when flying. The temperature outside—minus 55 degrees—always horrified her and the thought of a few seconds in it was appalling. She could never convince herself there would not be a microsecond in which something would be felt. That it would be violent was undoubted: a rush of air, a wall of flame, a plunge into a sea whose surface was like iron.

Seated in front of Dr Margot Franklin, Isobel looked into the face that, too, was growing older. A companion face, she thought. Not exactly a friend, but a paid observer, a watcher of the skies. Dr Franklin's eyes had permanent violet shadows and the fine lines on her forehead were more deeply etched.

'You feel well?' she asked Isobel, who nodded. More tests were mentioned. How many phials, Isobel wondered. Last time there were three into which the blackish-looking blood had run. Yet the results had come back normal. But she would submit again and, since she had had no breakfast, she could even do it on the way home.

She could hardly confide in Dr Franklin that she was becoming tired of life—not a terrible tiredness, just something on the fringes—and that the tiredness was to do with her own powerlessness. She could bear a lack of power in her limbs, taking care where she put her feet, though that was humiliating enough, but the lack of ability to influence events, to forestall things, galled in a way that affected her spirit.

The time she had almost been caught by the married man Sylvie was involved with, and had had to pretend she was admiring the flying lady mascot on the car bonnet. Her hand had gone out to stroke it and then quickly slunk back to wipe itself on the side of her winter coat. She had been thinking of sugar combined with petrol. The car jerking to a halt and

Sylvie, suddenly seeing sense, fleeing. Absurd scenarios had kept her going. The man had given her an ironic stare—Sylvie was not yet in sight—and she had walked on, her hand in her pocket hot as if it had been scorched.

What she really longed for, before her strength deserted her and days would really have to be devoted to books and sorting her papers, was an adventure. Or an intervention, because that, she knew now, was her temperament. If a fly was drowning in a bowl of water she must fish it out, or if a plant was strangling another. If a child was being hurt she could not rest. Sylvie was not being hurt at present, not that she could tell, but there were the hurts of the past that could never be removed since nothing can ever be totally removed from a life, except in sleep or unconsciousness. And where should the intervening stop? And what if it did more harm, if it added to things better left sinking into oblivion, which might be a natural process. She had read an essay written by a chemist about the cleansing properties of soil, how fluids were absorbed into it, entrails and organs, and lastly bones, purified of muscles and sinews and nerves, until at the last they were reduced to powder and vanished. The essay was carefully written, frank but not intended to alarm, and that had been its effect on Isobel. A period of distaste, like the distaste she had felt on putting her hand on a dead rat, would soon be replaced by something far superior. The earth, as the chemist described it, was both clean and cleansing, taking each thing that was added to it and lovingly fingering it until it was broken down and absorbed.

Dr Margot noticed Isobel's distraction but the consultation was almost at an end—fifteen minutes in the case of older patients or where psychological counselling seemed required.

It had never been necessary before with Isobel, and she felt certain it was an aberration or possibly a mood.

'Do you get depressed in autumn?' she asked when a repeat prescription had been printed and Isobel was straightening her shoulders and preparing to depart.

'Not particularly,' Isobel replied.

Outside she took the scarf from her pocket and wound it around her neck. If she had been born in a different country and worn different clothes. A hijab perhaps or a burqa. If her movements had been curtailed from birth. Then she thought of Kit forbidding her to drive or accompanying her to the library to change her books, and her mouth curved in a smile. Smiling could warm not just the recipient, she decided; she felt a tiny warmth herself.

A woman coming towards her looked at her oddly and the smile widened as Isobel turned the corner. If she was to be so cleanly broken down, she might as well have an adventure. She might as well intervene to her heart's content.

Sooner than she thought, Isobel's intervention was required. A trust fund she was keeping for Sylvie would need to be broken into, to add to the gift from Mr Arlington, if they were to have enough for a deposit on a house. The day the money was banked, Ben took Sylvie, in an excess of happiness, to supper with his mother.

It had begun promisingly. Dessert and coffee in a hotel he knew his mother liked. She could not bear a heavy meal late in the evening. Sylvie wore a new Zambesi skirt she had been paying off. Her hair was freshly washed and she had sprayed herself liberally with Isobel's *Poême*. They could see Cora, already seated, as they came up the stairs that led from the foyer to the dining room. She, too, was coiffed and perfumed, resplendent in a jacket of gold brocade.

Sylvie, following the waiter, wished she had a Venetian mask with scrollwork and crimped lace. Cora did not fully stand; she set a manicured hand on either side of her place setting, as though prepared, then subsided. The waiter was offering drinks and dessert menus, asking if they would like to see the trolley.

'The trolley sounds good,' Sylvie said. 'I would like to see it.'

'The menu, I think,' Cora said.

Under the table Ben kicked Sylvie's foot and she kept her eyes lowered.

The trolley came, was examined and exclaimed over, and two dishes selected. Then it glided away, and Sylvie wished there was some other ritual that could be summoned: a flambéed steak, crêpes Suzette, a menu based entirely around fire. *Hover*, she said to the waiter under her breath. *Hover*.

'It's good news,' Ben was saying. 'Sylvie's dog-walking. The old guy had a heart. Must have taken a fancy to her.'

'Perhaps he didn't know what he was doing,' Cora said. She was prepared to say something about senility or a lawyer's cheap sense of closure. But both Sylvie and her son were silent.

The flaming steak might not have been in evidence but there were things to fiddle with on the table, forks to lift and set down. Ben wondered for a wild moment if the sweetness of the desserts would be counterbalanced, like a tart filling, by bitter words. For he sensed his mother longed to hold nothing back.

He could feel the heat emanating from her body, the tenseness of her spine. Perhaps her hand itched to overturn the sugar bowl, the jug of milk, the single yellow rose which seemed to be backing away.

'It was a wasted enterprise. Walking the dog,' Cora continued. She seemed determined to provoke.

'The dog who brought a deposit,' Ben said, lifting the teapot. 'Enough for a place at last.'

'You'll have to come and see it.'

'A good area,' Ben said. 'Not quite the worst house in the street.'

'The third worst,' Sylvie said. 'I checked. Third or fourth.'

The complicity was enraging and Cora's hand shook. She raised a spoonful of raspberry soufflé to her mouth.

'As if anything could make me approve,' she said, and the bitterness in her voice was unmistakable. Better to lay the gauntlet down, abandon her researches. Research got you nowhere.

'We hope . . .' Sylvie began.

'Why should you hope? Why not abandon it? Some of the best philosophers have.'

'What have you been reading?' Ben asked. 'It sounds like something very indigestible.'

The waiter hovered then and fresh tea was ordered. He did not ask if they were enjoying the experience.

Perhaps she is ill, Sylvie was thinking. In which case she would feel no grief. But she would need to control her tongue. She could see it was a supreme advantage. Yet almost instantly she plunged.

'From the beginning you were determined to dislike me,'

she began, looking into her rival's face.

'And why shouldn't I? My son makes a disastrous mistake and I'm expected to be all sweetness and light . . .'

'You don't know what you are saying, Mother,' Ben interrupted, and his voice was low. He observed his own hand as he refilled cups. It was commendably steady. Suddenly he longed for the autumn air outside, for leaves in the gutters and others on the pavement to kick his way through. And perhaps tomorrow a call to his mother's doctor. Or the offer of a holiday.

The bill was paid, his mother was handed into a taxi. He slipped his arm through Sylvie's and they walked. It was miles, block after block, before the residential street began, but by then they were in stride. A stamina built on opera cake and chocolate marquise. He thought he could walk with her forever, that darkness would never come. Something would happen to the world and twilight would be the default position. A shift in the heavens. Like the year he worked in London, stunned by the first afternoon when it was dark at 3 p.m. And Sylvie, concentrating on matching him stride for stride, only strove, as she rationed her breath, to remain silent; anything else was too dangerous to contemplate.

Madeleine too was surrounded by danger but it was a danger she could not see and this lack of visibility protected her. Freddy was unaware, since he had been successful in the past, that an arrangement might not always work; there might come a faltering or demands or, what he most dreaded, a breakthrough in which all control was gone.

He was interested to learn about bushfires; he questioned people at the club and read eyewitness accounts. He thought he might drive out and visit one of the stricken towns, view the flapping corrugated iron, the concrete foundation slabs and the blackened trees. A photo of a fireman holding a water bottle for a wombat with a scorched face to drink from was on the front page of the *Age*. Madeleine looked at it for a long time, moved by the fireman's gesture, for the wombat seemed to be accepting the gift and holding the bottle with its paws.

One evening when they were dining with another couple the conversation turned to philanthropy and how it could crown a life spent in business. 'A late satisfaction,' the man said, and Freddy agreed. So they mean to give a bottle of water, Madeleine thought to herself. Only it must be Perrier water and it must be seen, though a photograph was not necessary to the action. The woman opposite, in a dress suitable for the opera, smiled discreetly as the forms of philanthropy were discussed, and Madeleine smiled back. Both knew they were the necessary accompaniments; they could hardly have been acceptable in curlers and slippers.

All the way home Madeleine was silent. She was thinking of the shape of the wombat's nose, its no-nonsense curve as if it could never act dishonourably, as if every gesture would be unclouded. So unlike humans, for even at the pleasant and innocuous dinner, which they all agreed was a success and must be repeated, there had been undercurrents. The director of the gallery had approached and spoken a few words, and Freddy had instantly become more animated.

'I have a headache,' she said when the front door was closed.

In bed she lay on her side—the wombat's face was burnt

on one side—and tried to imagine its life after the fireman and the photographer were gone. Did it survive the night in the blackened forest? There were no living trees for it to climb into. Then she remembered there were animal hospitals and it might have been taken to one of those.

Freddy sat on in the lounge, nursing a drink. He was amazed, not for the first time, at what could undo a woman. A burnt armadillo—though there were none in Australia—would not have elicited the same sympathy, or any creature with scales or a protective shell. He foresaw his new life—he meant his new complication—would need careful handling, perhaps even a pause. Women's imaginations, even the most prosaic of them, leapt so blindingly far ahead. The woman he was seeing wanted companionship, but the price for living separately would be enacted in a regular routine. This, a compromise on his part, could be useful when he wanted a retreat. Still a disturbed routine sent a signal without any words being spoken.

Madeleine was sleeping when he came into the room. Her body felt hot, though she wore a fine cotton nightdress edged with lace. It was twisted under her. He pulled the sheet taut on his side and eased himself in. Sleep took a long time to come; he lay on his back thinking of the need both sexes had for a partner. His arrangement with the new woman was promising, but that was only the beginning. Neither sex presented the real self at the first encounters. Appearance counted but speech, he thought, hardly at all. Underneath what was being gauged were the accommodations that would be required and whether these were acceptable. Just before he slept he thought—and the thought brought a frisson of surprise—that this was the part he enjoyed most. It was like embarking on a voyage, stowing trunks below deck and then coming up on deck to look at a disappearing land.

··❧ ❧··

In the study, the shelves dusted, washed and dried, the books replaced, Isobel spread her fingers on the old brown globe and gave it a spin. Instantly it rolled away and the proportions of ocean and land changed. How absurd to think there was a missing continent to match the vastness of Europe or Asia. Or that huge serpents or whirlpools could furnish a boundless ocean. Anything to remove the idea of emptiness, whether it was a dresser decorated with plates or the rising shelves of books from which she had removed at least thirty to give to the hospice shop.

If the globe had been smaller Isobel might have lifted it from its stand and held it in her arms, pressed close to her heart. She would have uttered old-fashioned words over it, words that were half spells, half invocations. She would have held Sylvie's life close to her, and Madeleine's. Lives that were composed of plains and mountains and surrounded by sea. She closed her eyes for a moment, her hand still on the globe, and imagined sea monsters, giant squid that seized wooden ships and dragged them beneath the waves. And most perilous, like Niagara Falls which she and Kit had visited, a great falling away of water that signalled the end of the world. When the globe was still again, stopped at South America and the Pacific, Isobel drew the curtains and lit two lamps, one on a stand, the other on a low table. Sylvie had arrived, fuming about the disastrous supper.

'Should I refuse to see her again?' she asked Isobel. 'Make it a condition of staying with Ben?'

'Draw up a treaty?' Isobel asked. A few famous names flitted through her head: Versailles, Dumbarton Oaks, Maastricht, Vienna.

She had embraced Sylvie on the doorstep and now, in the study, she embraced her again, pulling the slender body close to her larger one, not caring about etiquette or the peculiar way men and women now embraced, their hips leaning well out with a triangle of light between them. She felt Sylvie's breasts pressing and flattening against hers and guessed Sylvie felt a similar pressing. If there was some way of convincing her that the world did not end in a great plughole and the ship sailed on, taking on fresh fruit and vegetables, and the sailors recovered from scurvy.

Sylvie flung herself back into the old reading chair with its velvet cover and matching footstool. She kicked the footstool viciously and it fell over. But when Isobel came back into the room with the tea things on a tray it was righted again and Sylvie was looking at the bookcase. In front of the books were spaced small ornaments, nothing of value. A cheap Madonna with hinged wooden wings, some tiny tea cups and saucers, too small for dolls, a row of black elephants lined up in order of height. The largest elephant had tusks, the rest were mothers and babies.

'What's the best thing to do with an enemy?' Sylvie asked when her hands were wrapped around a mug. She thought it was Isobel's thoughtfulness; she had brought a cup for herself.

'Perhaps there's some information in the bookcase,' Isobel said, sipping from her cup. She thought of Eliza Bennet and

Lady Catherine de Bourgh exchanging fire as if they were armed with muskets. There was far more fighting in that little scene than in the barracks at Meryton. Then there were the great battlefields in *War and Peace* across which Pierre wandered among fallen cannonry and torn bodies. The battlefield resembled a sea, too vast in its sweep and horror to comprehend. But she saw that Sylvie needed comfort, not literature. Something practical like a spell. A voodoo doll into which pins could be inserted. Sylvie could engineer another meeting and see if Cora clutched her side or rushed to the bathroom. Isobel's own mother had had a saying which had puzzled her as a child. 'Treat with ignore.' It usually meant one of the ladies who sat around the afternoon tea table had offended her and would be denied an invitation. But sometimes it was used differently. It was a withdrawal containing a rebuke, practically a weapon: one of those fearsome weapons that were multi-purpose, like a can opener that could take off bottle tops. A rifle with a bayonet.

'I wish you would pay attention,' Sylvie was saying, and Isobel apologised. She was so frequently giving advice in her head—usually long soliloquies which were raptly listened to—but when it was solicited she was at a loss.

'You could negotiate with Ben,' Isobel said, putting her cup back on the tray and deciding against a refill. 'His feelings need considering.'

'I know that,' Sylvie said. She could barely keep her voice under control. 'I know it is hard for him.'

'Will he continue the weekly dinners?' Isobel asked.

'He hasn't said he won't. Perhaps he is talking to her. He can't make a clean break.'

'But you can. You can make a decision. Retreat can be a good thing. Kit could give you a few pointers.' Isobel took the mug from her hands, refilled it and gave it back. She wished they were sitting side by side; she could have touched her arm or shoulder. Soon Sylvie would have to get up and use the bathroom.

'Excuse me,' Sylvie said, rising and going out of the room.

I must say something more, Isobel thought while she was gone. It's useless talking in abstracts. I should say an enemy is a good thing, a salutary thing. And if one ever becomes a friend it is the securest friendship there is. But all this was irrelevant.

Sylvie came back and Isobel had moved to the sofa. She patted the seat to indicate Sylvie should sit beside her. She touched a hand to the fair hair that fell forward, indicator of an interior state. Then she curled an arm around her farthest shoulder and pulled her granddaughter towards her.

'You are strong, Sylvie,' she said. 'This will pass and you will come through it.' She felt the resistance in the tense body return. Being told you are strong is not helpful. 'Come to me whenever Ben goes to his mother. At the same hour, for the same length of time. You can coordinate your watches. You can come to the tent of the enemy general.' Those tents were usually on a hill, she thought, when they had both risen from the sofa and stood in the middle of the old Turkey carpet. Now they embraced warmly and there was a feeling of love. Isobel felt her bones soften as she tried to transfer her warmth to the smaller, more compact body of her granddaughter.

··❧ ❧··

Kit had taken to asking Isobel what she was feeling. Usually it was at night, when they were in bed together. Like two figures on a tomb. But sometimes it was when he brought her a cup of tea or poured a glass of wine. Gradually they had both come to feel that they could not get through the day without an early evening drink. It allowed Kit to admit he preferred a small—two fingers—whisky and water while she drank red wine in the winter and white in the summer. The fire in the grate consumed its ingredients in order: old papers that Isobel was burning, fresh-faced kindling and cones, and then small logs which Kit sawed meticulously into the correct length. Isobel could remember fires where logs were pushed in by brute force and sometimes, glowing like crocodiles, fell out onto the hearth. How she had wanted Kit to enquire about her feelings when they were courting. Now she realised her own attention at that time had been on him: her dress, her look, the trouble she took with her hair, even her perfume had been designed for his feelings, his confidences. He had a man's natural diffidence; that she listened with wide eyes—she had practised opening them in an expression of surprise and delight in front of the mirror—was enough. And if her attention strayed he could bring it back by a caress.

'I hardly know what I feel,' she said one evening when she had helped herself to a second glass of pinot noir. A shepherd's pie was heating in the oven and an apple crumble alongside: twin dishes. For a moment, as she had set them together on the rack, she had thought of twin martyrs, perhaps exchanging quips, as they were turned in the fire.

The best days were those in which she hardly thought at all. Days when she drove or walked and her mind simply observed or her thoughts were simple, one dimensional. Thoughts that could not have offended an Inquisitor; thoughts a child might have, that Sylvie might have had when she was young, leaping from her bed and running the moment her feet touched the floor. Then she recollected that this part of Sylvie's life was closed to her; Sylvie had been with Madeleine and possibly already feeling unhappy. Then Madeleine had gone to France, with Isobel and Kit's help, and Isobel had attempted to mend the fractures.

'I've been thinking of the time Sylvie broke her arm,' Isobel said. She was not thinking that at all but she needed to say something and her eye had caught the old apple tree outside the window.

'The deliberate break,' Kit said. 'How she worked at it.'

'What do you mean?'

'She was determined to break a leg or arm. When I tried to stop her leaping from the tree she tried the roof of the garage. Usually she just winded herself and rolled.'

'Poor child,' Isobel said. 'Something else I didn't know.'

She had accompanied Sylvie to the hospital, sat beside her as the plaster was applied. She remembered a white face and had taken it for bravery. Sylvie had not counted on the pain to be undergone before the plaster was covered with signatures and drawings. Horses and fairies: decorum, since the teachers could see, had prevailed.

A desire to injure yourself. How common it must be, Isobel decided. Followed by the desire to have something firmly applied—plaster or chastisement, a punishment self-willed. None of it seemed to exist in Madeleine, who drifted through her life, oblivious of trouble, content to present a surface the way the two elderly harpies in *Gigi* had trained their protégée in arcane rituals, like eating ortolons.

'Ortolons,' Isobel said suddenly. 'Do you know what they are?'

'Some kind of bird?'

'Served whole. The important thing was to use a certain number of strokes to cut them through.'

'Ghastly,' Kit agreed.

'Still, if you wanted to move in certain circles,' Isobel said, trying to think what the modern equivalent might be. Knowing your single malts or cigars? Perhaps that was the problem with Cora: Sylvie did not match her idea of propriety, though Isobel and Kit had trained her in manners, courtesy to others, being kind to animals. Animals had been no problem. Kit had taken her to the art gallery or museum on Sundays to give Isobel time alone and they had peered at glass cases or free-standing displays while Kit tried, vainly, to connect an Edwardian dress or a piece of porcelain to a bygone age. He never told Isobel how deflated each visit left him. Still sometimes when they were walking down the broad steps, under the lamps which emphasised the building's grandeur, a faint hope resurfaced of some future effect. The wide lawn stretched almost as far as the eye could see. 'They must have driven up here in carriages,' he said to Sylvie, wondering if she would remember the Edwardian dress.

'Poor horses,' was all Sylvie said.

Isobel's imagining that Madeleine's life was easier because she was protected from introspection, or self-awareness, was wrong. Her passivity did not always protect her from shocks or shocking discoveries. Nor could Freddy always control events. His own comfort had always come first and this was now revealed to be a blind spot, for at the moment when his senses should have been most alert there was a failure of signals. The woman at Myer who had served him and brought tie after tie for him to inspect—he bought none but, charmed by her ease in a men's department, he had lingered. Zsazsa Szabó was the only woman on the floor, chosen for her personality which ranged from flirtatious to motherly. For Freddy she adopted, automatically, the air of a slightly world-weary, sophisticated woman whose interest could be revived by a bit of sparkling conversation. Freddy too rose to the occasion, forgetting the pain in one knee. He took his hand from the counter and stood straighter. She took his name, after he had looked through several catalogues, and promised to notify him the moment the new Boston Brothers ties arrived. Paris was mentioned. It was her dream to live abroad. She could easily have said Berlin or New York, because a few images came instantly to each one. Eventually someone else came to the counter and the conversation, regretfully, was at an end. Though he didn't intend to, Freddy turned back before he reached the lift, and a manicured hand—he could see the polished nails from a distance—wiggled in a little wave.

When the message came and he paid a second visit, she was not there. He concealed his disappointment and left a message expressing his thanks. He wondered what else he could buy. He had always admired the neckwear affected by Byron which protected and warmed the throat, concealing the Adam's apple which in older men became more prominent. Remembering a portrait of Byron working at his desk, his shirt rumpled and full-sleeved, he wished something other than the tailored shirt would come back into fashion. Perhaps he could weave that into a conversation.

A few weeks later he was having coffee with Zsazsa in an alcove on the third floor. Zsazsa had led the way, briskly, past displays of curtaining and beds, each made up, each in a little room like a stage set. The beds were smothered in cushions of all shapes and sizes; some seemed to have rolled from an eminence. Whose responsibility would it be to remove them, Freddy wondered. What was the etiquette? Or did each attend to the cushions on their side of the bed? Zsazsa, now she was not behind her counter, wearing a tape measure over her shoulder, retained her air of unassailable confidence. Freddy found this oddly restful. With Madeleine he played the role of overseer; it might be pleasant to hand over the reins. As he rose to hold her chair at the end of her short lunch break, he knew he could leave whatever arrangement there was to be in her hands. Even his role would be explained to him: it would make a change.

After she had gone, striding along the path between the beds, he resumed his seat and ordered another pot of tea. The waitress, he noticed, had been particularly attentive while Zsazsa was present. He walked more slowly towards the lift, pondering the pillows. At the last moment he retraced his footsteps and stood at the base of a huge sleigh bed. He chose the smallest pillow, black with a dusky pink rose, for Madeleine.

⋯⟩ ⟨⋯

Half an hour later—he had taken a taxi outside the store—Madeleine was unwrapping the cushion and holding it over her heart. The rose looked so much like a heart and was practically the same size. The stem which disappeared into the seam had three large thorns; some photographic method had been used, it looked so realistic. 'Not the bed,' she said firmly to Freddy. 'I want to see it more often.' She thought she might move it from place to place. After she had decided on the centre of a slipper chair she went to the mantelpiece and turned the page of the book that was on display there: a book of Southern plantation houses. It was one of her mother's habits to display a large pictorial book on a stand, to contemplate a pair of plates, or a single divided one, for a day or a week, like an exercise in meditation. Today's house had a slave cottage, diminutive, dull and weathered almost to an earthen colour in one corner, but it was so out of scale it could be ignored, as it would have been by those in the mansion. Giant pillars, chipped and mouldering, towered above steps that billowed like a crinoline at their base. Some of the shutters hung lopsided, but the mores of the period still hung in the air. It made Madeleine shudder.

Freddy's attention and the gift, she knew, were associated with guilt. He was such a planner, so attentive to detail and progress, that the smallest breach of the trust it was her role to maintain produced signs she had recognised from the earliest days. That night when she turned on her side to sleep she remembered Gigi. She had read the whole of *Gigi* because it was short, and then *The Cat* which was her favourite. Freddy had made love to her gently before he slept. He had laid his lips against her hair and run his hand down her side. Quite often she felt herself turning into an object with him: this time, as she lay on her side, her hip jutting and his hand stroking and measuring, she thought of a large amphora she had seen in an interior design shop where furniture and garden statuary mingled. Despite the rose cushion that was at this moment glowing downstairs in the green chair, her heart felt heavy. It was lucky that her natural lassitude gave her scope to merely seem to be enjoying something.

Gigi had been read twice and *The Cat* three times. She could never be a Gigi, though there had been times when her clothes were too tight or a shoe pinched. Still there were different kinds of resistance, and Gigi was not the only one who could leap into the unknown with her bold conversion of Gaston, the sugar heir.

Only once in her life had Isobel set out deliberately to defeat another human being. It was the third year of her marriage; they were part of a loose group of friends. They had all married around the same time, like lemmings, except instead of plunging over the cliff at the last moment they had joined hands with another lemming and put on a wedding ring. But there was nothing meek and lemming-like in their behaviour to one another.

Already the signs were that she and Kit would be among the lucky ones and last. They were settling into a calm which they tried—Isobel especially tried—not to show. In the first years of love Isobel had let her impressions blur, her instincts slip. But there was a woman in the group, Livia, already aware that her own marriage would not last, who was beginning to have her claws into Kit. It took a while to see it, for a kind of group philosophy prevailed: they were a certain kind of people, liberal and free but honourable at the same time, morals carried lightly. Slowly and then more quickly Isobel caught the signs. She made the mistake of speaking, showing that she knew what was going on. 'The Sleeping Prince will wake up one day,' Livia had replied. 'We'll see about retraction then.' She had developed a habit of resting a hand on Kit's sleeve or bare arm. In front of the bedroom mirror Isobel practised a bland face, an open countenance. But she couldn't bear a false laugh.

She decided against enlightening Kit. She was determined there would be a time when Livia was defeated. Kit need not know he had been fought over; she could do without flattering him in that way. Some engagements could not be avoided, but dinner invitations could be limited. 'We hardly see you,' Livia said in front of Isobel, and the hand came out and settled on Kit's wrist. Isobel noticed a slight flinch and smiled to herself. She felt her whole life was under scrutiny, as if she was being shadowed.

A pile of coats and wraps lay at the base of the hostess's bed at a party. Livia lay in them, calling feebly that she felt unwell. Kit who happened to be passing pushed the half-open door and leaned over the bed. (There was a convention of closed doors, and the coats made a delightful nest.) Isobel came into the room and offered to fetch a glass of water. She chose the largest tumbler she could find and filled it to the brim. Some of it slopped on the carpet. Just before she reached the bed she stumbled on a coat sleeve and the water poured over her enemy's neck and cleavage.

'I forgot the ice,' she said after someone else had gone for a towel.

'What was that about?' Kit asked when they were walking home.

'Heaven knows,' Isobel replied. Hell knows, was what she wanted to say, but boldness and restraint went hand in hand.

In the darkness between streetlights Kit smiled to himself. A woman could not know how delightful it was to a man to be fought over.

'Shall we stop going to these things?' he offered. He was thinking they had served their purpose. They had courted and coupled, the hunt was over. Unless someone was dissatisfied, wanted another round.

'Slowly,' Isobel said. 'Perhaps we could do it slowly.'

She took his arm and matched her stride to his as if they were conquerors.

The hooks, the hand on the wrist, the sleeve, were not so easily removed. When Isobel and Kit's absence was noticed there were phone calls. The phone was put down when Isobel answered. It was unavoidable that Kit should sometimes pick up. Once Isobel heard him say he was no handyman, and guessed a task had been set. She backed softly out of the room. Sometimes there was a car parked opposite. That was when Isobel read up about sugar in the tank and how to slash a tyre. The climax came one winter's night. The phone rang, startling them awake. Both turned on their bed lamps. Was it Sylvie? A sobbing voice poured from the phone and Isobel knew it was Livia. 'No,' Kit was saying. 'Phone an ambulance.' The sobs continued, broken by incoherent words.

'We should go,' Kit said, when the phone suddenly went silent.

Isobel was already pulling on clothes. In the car she brushed her hair with the miniature brush she always carried in her handbag. She rubbed her cheeks.

Livia was lying on a sofa, her feet on a footstool. A negligée and robe showed her figure to advantage; her tear-stained face was lightly made up. Isobel sniffed for onions, wondering if she had poked herself in the eye. Finally she pushed Livia into a sitting position. The emergency was a demand for a divorce. In the bedroom Kit, searching for a thicker robe, noticed rows of empty hangers.

Isobel had taken command like a general. Kit was ordered to make coffee. He never knew what words were exchanged but he did not doubt they were cold and sharp. No false affection lingered, just cold facts as imperceptibly the night gave way to dawn.

Isobel's desire to act was so much a part of her character, she could no more eradicate it than she could stop brushing her hair the moment she rose in the morning, or cleaning her teeth five times a day. The times in her life when she had not taken action were the times of greatest suffering. What intervention she could have taken on behalf of Madeleine she was never sure, for their natures were so different. Sylvie and her problems with her mother-in-law was a different matter.

Sylvie's account of her meeting with Cora had convinced Isobel that Cora was intractable. Yet she must be treated as Ben's mother. She tried to imagine Ben as a small boy, drawn into a web of motherly love. A stifling web that no child could see. Cora's excuse for not attending the wedding might have been a fantasy, Isobel thought. She had presumed, in time, they might have visited one another's houses. Then she noticed the dust that had already descended on the shelves she had washed the month before. The old globe was shedding paper flakes on the carpet. Still she did not care if her own sporadic housework was the source of another's sense of superiority. She touched the globe with her hand and it flew over palaces and mud huts, houses where children were crooned to sleep and others where they wailed themselves into unconsciousness, wracked by hunger pains. In between were the oceans, full of fish, into which wastes were poured. The globe was a great worry bead which she should turn each evening, letting the worries of the day go.

It occurred she might look for a friend or an acquaintance who knew Cora too. Someone who could ensure that she and Isobel were at the same gathering. An event at the art gallery where it was easy to avoid another person simply by staring intently at a painting while sipping a glass of wine. It was not always easy to avoid someone even so; they might be standing alongside when the speeches began, wishing they had secured one of the few seats. Nonetheless, she knew she was going to pursue Cora Taverner. It would be an active kind of enmity. The thought of spying again brought a return of energy. More walks at night, peering at lighted windows. More socialising when she had become rather lax.

Isobel climbed on the first rung of the library ladder and brought down a life of Lucrezia Borgia. Somewhere there was a history of the Medici family but Lucrezia would do to begin with. Isobel gave the globe one last shove before she left the room, wondering how many of the billions of people on it were at this moment using their wits.

Two days later Isobel was seated at a French café drinking a flat white. The café opened early and the aromas of coffee and pastries drifted out into the street which was still wet from cleaning. She planned to devote half a day to sleuthing. She was wearing walking shoes, and in her bag was a fold-up umbrella and a light waterproof jacket. Her first stop would be the library, to read the habitation index which listed streets under numbers and occupants. Though she could not see any immediate use, it might be helpful to know the names of the neighbours on either side. She might be forced to take shelter or even sanctuary. The café was filling up with its regular clientele, jovial after their first coffees were served. Soon Isobel was joined by a dark-suited businessman who held his briefcase between his knees and a young woman wearing a cap with tassels.

'Do either of you know a family by the name of Taverner?' Isobel asked.

They both looked at her blankly. The businessman thought he had heard the name. Isobel finished her coffee, thanked them, and left. She felt, if they met again, she could continue her enquiry or report progress. The businessman had murmured 'Good luck' as a fragrant *omelette aux fines herbes* was set in front of him and he placed his briefcase on Isobel's vacated seat.

Isobel wrote down the neighbours on both sides and opposite and, for good measure, added the householders next to the neighbours. In a nearby street there were a number of gentrified houses serving as small businesses: a manicurist, which could be useful, a shop that made cushions and bedcovers, and a tea shop. A few streets away was a doctor's surgery, a laboratory and a cooking school. She could be walking to any of these places to order a cake or have her nails attended to, or, more ominously, to sit in a cubicle while blood was drawn from a vein. Armed with her knowledge of the neighbours she could approach one with confidence.

Nonetheless she was pleased a light shower gave her the excuse to pull up the hood on her rain jacket as she passed Cora's gate. The windows were rather close to the street but they were dressed in such a way that various drapes and blinds made an almost impenetrable privacy. The owner could be overseas, Isobel thought, and it would be impossible to tell whether the house was occupied. There were two guest rooms furnished as exquisitely as a boutique hotel, Sylvie had told her.

Though she was no further ahead with her investigations than when she started, Isobel was pleased with her walk. She showered and made a cup of coffee. In a few weeks she and Kit would travel to Melbourne. They would visit Madeleine and resume the relationship, as much as could be salvaged. But first they would fly to Sydney so Kit could drive the coast road. It would be Isobel's seventieth birthday while they were away. For three nights before they decamped to a modest apartment they would stay at The Windsor.

Sylvie stopped outside Prospero's Emporium and peered in the window. The glass was grimy as usual and most of the exhibits seemed to be made of metal. Old canisters that had once held biscuits, ancient egg beaters and fish slices, a blackened kettle.

A tin bath was filled with preserving jars. It was oddly restful, she decided. In the halcyon years—a word she had used in her seminar, unpicking its sounds, orotund sounds as if someone had a toffee parked in one cheek—when she and Ben had lived above Ma's Best Fruit & Veg, Prospero's had offered an alternative vision. It was all dust; all things are reduced to dust. Nothing could be less like fruit with its gleaming glowing skins. Reluctantly she moved away from the door as someone came out carrying a lawnmower with golden wheels. She took a few steps to the left and peered inside the old fruit shop. A row of sewing machines with heads bent over them and a dressmaker's dummy in a cheongsam. Ben was at a conference in Adelaide. It was a day when her own seminar had not gone well: the projector had broken down while she was showing slides of the Toda people, and one of the secretaries had had to come and fix it. As she ambled through the park Sylvie thought of the work that, for once, she had put into it. Of course if the missing students turned up she could repeat some of it, fix someone with her beady eye like the Ancient Mariner on the church steps. He must have had charisma, Sylvie thought, as she began to descend one of the steep paths which were covered with chestnut burrs.

Ben had left a note on the kitchen table. It was a quote from Dante:

> *Do not be afraid; our fate*
> *Cannot be taken from us; it is a gift*
>
> Dante Alighieri x

Her hand shook a little as she held it; in her heart she had been expecting something worse, a more stringent quote, even a farewell letter. When she felt calm, or this is how she came to it, she smiled at the careful spacing and the punctuation that he had been at pains to copy. He was not an architect for nothing. In the early days of their marriage they had taken pleasure in concealing notes from one another; it had become a treasure hunt. There might be one in the tea caddy or under her pillow. Once, trying to unpeel one stuck to the underside of a cake of soap, Ben had slipped in the shower and bumped his head.

The night before they had argued in a desultory fashion about his trip. Why must it be compulsory? Sylvie had demanded. Only the PA would be left in the office; the rest would be cloistered in a lodge. Some kind of superior deal had been negotiated. Buffet meals, platters of fruit, drinks in the evening. Perhaps that was the cause of the bitterness: that Ben should be in luxury, drinking and socialising into the night, while she heated something from a tin. But Dante made her feel cheerful again. She took a Pacific Rose apple from the fruit bowl and cut it into thin slices; then she arranged a circle of nuts and dried fruit and two squares of dark chocolate on a square white plate. What would Dante Alighieri have eaten? Wine, naturally. She opened a bottle of merlot and filled a glass to the brim. The quote, on second thoughts, seemed less comforting, but the unspoken text was they would face it together. When Ben returned she would ask neutral questions but not superficial ones. Something along the lines of 'What was it like in the dark wood?'

··֍ ֎··

Isobel had asked not to be met and she was relieved when she and Kit came out onto the concourse at Tullamarine, pushing their trolleys, knowing that no one in the crowd lining the barriers would cheer or wave. A basketball team was ahead of them and a great shout went up and banners were unfurled. Then she thought of Madeleine, possibly alone in her house, possibly lonely, and wondered if she had deprived her of a pleasure.

Outside they took a taxi and Kit instructed, 'The Windsor.'

Her birthday treat was beginning. 'A taxi or a horse and carriage?' he murmured, taking her hand. 'Bread and water for the last week.'

'There might be a soup kitchen,' she said.

She thought she could volunteer. At the end of the evening she might be rewarded with a bowl of soup.

The taxi door was opened by a doorman in a top hat. He had a kindly face; it might have been part of the job description, Isobel thought, lifting her face towards him and smiling. The great doors, brass shining where the sun caught it, were flung open and they were in a world where gesture counted. A huge floral arrangement on a circular table with ornate legs rose towards a chandelier.

Instantly Isobel felt warmed. She told herself it was all pretence: the bread and water that would come later—not literally, but she would curb her spending until the money was recouped—were equally fine. Somehow, though, her heart wasn't in it. She could feel herself sinking into the luxury of it all, as if she was the owner of one of the designer suitcases on the luggage cart a bellboy was pushing over the thick soft carpet.

The room, when they were alone in it, was over-chintzy, over-heavy and yet strangely restful. They lay on the high bed together and Kit held her hand. There was a writing desk against one wall and a telephone to summon . . . Isobel wondered what she could ask for: the water in the vases to be changed, another half dozen towels? At dinner a little gift was slipped beside her plate. Inside was a wombat brooch. Its eyes, glowing against the tablecloth, were garnets: night eyes for hunting and feeding. The body, silver, was scratched to resemble fur. Tears came to Isobel's eyes at the continuity the gift expressed, for Kit had given her *The Secret Life of Wombats* many years ago. She had avoided reading it, knowing nothing of wombats and thinking she would not be interested. As a teenager the author had crawled into a burrow and almost become jammed. The great pressure of the earth above him, which might at any moment collapse, the great dome of the starry sky above. No one at the boarding school knew where he was, and he knew this too. And there was something else: the wombat's enviably strong back like a plank which could be used against an enemy as effectively as a studded shield. A wombat could run on its four paws and then suddenly stand upright, catching its pursuer a knockout blow.

'Let's not invite Madeleine and Freddy here,' Isobel said impulsively. 'Let this just be for ourselves.'

Later they lay in one another's arms in the overstuffed bed. The twin bed lamps glowed; the wombat brooch was propped against a water glass from which Isobel sipped during the night. The eyes then were truly hunting eyes, though she couldn't recall what wombats ate. Perhaps they spent most of the night digging. Kit was sleeping, breathing softly, though that would change as the night wore on. Sometimes he talked in his sleep. Isobel turned on her side and slid towards him so her back was pressed against his. A friend who was widowed had told her that this was what she missed most, more even than sex. But we have both, Isobel thought. Before she slept she stretched out her hand towards the brooch which she could not quite reach.

Madeleine had thought her parents might join her for lunch at the railway station at Middle Park. They might be pleased with her initiative, that she was becoming familiar with the city. They could cross the tracks as she had seen Xavier doing, carrying a takeaway coffee to a woman waiting on the opposite platform. The tram was just coming and Xavier skipped across the overbridge and waved as she stepped aboard.

Isobel, Kit and Madeleine had spent the morning in the city, where Isobel realised once again how she hated large stores and shopping. Kit had disappeared into a bookshop with a small art gallery attached. But the mood lifted once they were on the tram, Kit with a parcel of books under his arm, Isobel with a new scarf in her handbag and Madeleine, indecisive as usual, with nothing at all. The tram rushed through cuttings of brambles and graffiti-covered walls, and then they were at the station and climbing up a slight ramp. Isobel could tell Madeleine wanted to sit on the platform and look down on the passing trams, though a slight breeze was rising. They ordered and sat at a rickety table. A tram came into view and Isobel noticed with amusement how Madeleine raised her chin and looked straight ahead as if she were in a play. Kit pulled his jacket collar up and some of his salad sandwich fell on the platform. Isobel couldn't tell what she was feeling. Was it a farewell, or all the farewells they had shared, brought together on this shadowy artificial stage? As if he had read her thought or seen her shudder slightly, the waiter was beside her chair with an armful of blankets. Old assorted worn blankets, some with striped borders, the sort of blanket her mother had sometimes wrapped her loosely in, inside the bedclothes, and which she had clung to like the skin of an animal. Even Kit was pressed to take one, folded, on his knee. Finally the wobbling table was noticed and the menu was folded in half and pushed under it. Warmth and stability reigned. Isobel moved her hand across the table, clearing a path between the teapot, the milk jug and the jug with hot water, and took Madeleine's hand in hers. As if on signal, two trams appeared, facing one another. One was old, the other very new.

It marked something, Isobel thought later. As a treat it had little going for it: they endured the light shower against the scalloped roof until the drops thickened and fell with heavy plops on the plates. What a sight they must have made, stumbling in their blankets, shepherded by the waiter who had come running to rescue them. A genuine smile spread across Isobel's face and she looked at Madeleine as if she was seeing her afresh. She caught the glimpse of failure, the remnants never to be vanquished, of passivity offered as an excuse, and felt them brushed away. Inside they divested themselves of the blankets and handed them back. Then they were at a low table, ordering more tea, and Kit suggested a brandy each. Afterwards, when they were back at The Windsor, Isobel thought it was their damp hair that had washed away something old and stale, something fixed in their expectations of one another. She stood in the shower until she was warmed through. She thought she could smell the damp wool of the blanket, so scratchy and worn. It answered to a comfort she thought had gone forever.

·⋗ ⋖·

The passivity of her mother was not entirely lacking in Sylvie's character, and now she had the weekend to herself she gave in to it. There were essays on gender roles to mark but she put them aside. She thought she might go to a hotel on her own and have dinner with a book propped in front of her. Isobel and Kit would be full of tales about The Windsor: she would demand a full accounting, from the moment their suitcases were put down to the late-morning checkout. But when Sylvie thought of a hotel, she thought of a woman alone, as her mother had been in Paris. A woman who would be shown a small discreet table, perhaps near the kitchen so she had something to watch, though the swing doors would cause the edge of the tablecloth to lift as the air gusted forth and the waiters emerged, plates balanced on their palms and lower arms. A supercilious expression would be necessary, the hint of being a woman snatching an hour or less of repose from some mysterious activity. And the book would be as carefully chosen as an Isobel selection, researched and read about, the reviews compared for a consensus.

And afterwards? Now she had two whole days at her disposal, this 'afterwards' presented itself to her as something mysterious. The moment when the curtain came down in the theatre or the last note faded away and the orchestra laid down their bows, wiped the spittle from the mouths of horns and trumpets. That night as she commandeered the centre of their queen-sized bed Sylvie watched the last act of an opera from the Met. She found herself admiring the lungs of the soprano who lay dying on a bed that resembled a bier; when the end came Sylvie scrutinised her chest to see if it still rose and fell. The best came at the end, after the last bow and cheer, the last clap and foot-stamp had died away. Then the stage was raised, revealing underneath, in their black stage clothes, the great cast of stagehands and technicians who made the sets, arranged the lighting and the special effects, made the scenes segue into one another. Sylvie lay for a long time imagining them, the heroes, far worthier than the cast who had risen over their heads as if they were gods.

The trip, Isobel decided, was a success. Apart from the stilted meal with Freddy present, during which she realised she disliked him and that Madeleine had probably made a mistake. Still everything in the St Kilda Road house seemed solid, as if that offered a guarantee. Drapes, carpets, furnishings were all carefully chosen and the paintwork was fresh. The bay window had drawn Isobel to gaze out at Port Phillip Bay, stretched out so wide it didn't seem a bay at all. Far out, so their shapes looked like toys, were two ships at anchor. Madeleine's behaviour was different in her own home, more subdued and deferential, as if everyone must be considered, not merely in a superficial way, like filling a water glass or passing a dish, but in their desires, their interior comfort. Isobel saw at once that this was impossible and not worth the effort. No one could know the secret desires of another.

She, for instance, had no idea what Kit was thinking. His head was turned slightly sideways as he talked to Freddy. His expression was veiled, neutral, the words innocuous, but she guessed he was judging, trying to penetrate the defences which almost all men possessed. Not for the first time Isobel thought how different men and women were. In Madeleine she could read a great deal of surface unease, as if she struggled for the composure from which Freddy began. It had been a stiffish kind of evening, saved by the changing light—at one stage it was an almost violent blue—that came through the bay window. A palm tree outside it turned black. Madeleine got up and brought a pair of antique candlesticks to the table. A delicate vanilla scent drifted over the tablecloth, and Isobel moved her plate with a rind of cheese and a spidery stem of grape over a reddish stain in front of her. Kit and Freddy began to discuss cigars, and Isobel stifled a yawn. Any word would do, she thought, like a stone thrown into a pool. Cigar—great cigars I have known, evenings when they were smoked. Or it could go in another direction: the fall in tobacco prices, the ruthless advertising of big companies, did the directors of these companies smoke? And underneath, nothing, so the eye rested on something and gave it significance.

Eventually Isobel got up and began to help Madeleine clear the table. She could see this offended Freddy but she was suddenly too tired to play games. The disorder of the table was one thing but later Madeleine would have to move back and forth to the kitchen. Freddy, she decided, was a man who liked to create an impression; his wife was included, and now she was carrying glasses, two in each hand, Isobel intercepted a look that was slightly unfriendly. Would there be a reckoning later, when she and Kit were travelling in a taxi back to their last night at The Windsor? She hoped not, but she couldn't be sure.

At the door she grasped Freddy's rather soft plump hand in both of hers and pressed it firmly. 'I think Madeleine is looking a little tired.' She kept her eyes on his face as she spoke, so he knew he was being delivered a warning. She hugged Madeleine, pressing the flat of her hand into her back, drawing her as close as she dared. Such damage existed between them, but this action seemed to be narrowing something.

Then she and Kit were being bowed back into The Windsor. Isobel elevated her chin slightly and behind her Kit grinned at the bellboy. 'Another week and I feel I could have mastered the look.' On their way to their room, by the stairs, they stopped to peer into one of the prime ministerial suites. What bliss to live there, Isobel thought, as their two noses pressed against the glass. Especially blissful for a wife. A quarrel and she could storm off, not into the streets as a lesser woman might, but into the bowels of the hotel. There were so many places where a woman could hide. And so many staff to protect her.

The following morning they moved to a serviced apartment in Flinders Street. At first Isobel thought she could not bear it. The ceilings were low and the furniture, perfectly clean and neat, seemed to have shrunk. She complained to Kit that they should have arranged for luxury last. Then they could have flown home, admittedly only in economy class, still feeling superior. The effect of The Windsor, she decided, could last a week. But Kit was happier. They were on the third floor, and outside their windows was growing a London plane tree. Below in the street ordinary people, in ordinary clothes, were passing. Ordinary worries, Kit told himself. Worries could be dear and familiar. He and Isobel had those to look forward to. He had to admit he was worried about Madeleine.

Sylvie was walking along the street towards her mother-in-law's house. She had not directed her footsteps, she thought later, when she replayed the scene: she had simply felt compelled to walk in the rain. Instead of a raincoat she wore an old cardigan with missing buttons that came to the top of her boots. When she found herself outside the gate, her hand on the latch, it seemed natural to go in, because by then her feet were in a rhythm. A glass of water, she thought, as she pressed the illuminated bell beside the ornate knocker. I can at least ask for that. But her mind was streets ahead, in a reconciliation scene. She could not imagine them in an embrace but she knew it would give Ben pleasure if, on his return, she could report that she and his mother had reconciled. 'Things will be fine now between us,' she might say and quickly change the subject. Then she would hold out her hand and say, 'Come.'

Cora's obvious surprise and the way she exclaimed 'Sylvie' soon convinced her that the scene would need careful management. Cora was not a woman who liked to be surprised: surprises were what she gave other people and usually in a setting she could control.

'A glass of water?' Sylvie said, hopefully. 'I've been walking.'

'Ben is not here, if you are looking for him.'

'He's at a conference. In Adelaide.'

For a wild moment Sylvie wondered if the conference was like this. Open to suggestions on the surface but underneath raw power play.

'Surely you could afford bottled water,' Cora was saying. 'Aren't walkers supposed to carry it?'

'Serious walkers,' Sylvie said. 'I'm not serious.'

'You're not serious and you should never have married my son.'

'I'm serious about your son. As serious as it gets,' Sylvie said. She pitched her voice low.

'You know nothing about seriousness. A dropout, a stray, something the cat brought in . . . Something beyond salvage that he had to pick up.'

A lovely rush of energy filled the kitchen. Both women felt it. The woodwork was a pale green. It was like being undersea.

The next thing Sylvie knew was a stream of water running down her face. It had come from the drinking faucet. It felt like a cold swathe of hair. Instinctively she reached for the nearly-empty glass. For a second she held it like a chalice, then she allowed her fingers to open and it to crash on the parquet. Cora sprang back, shrieking. Then she rebounded and grasped Sylvie by the hair. Pulled closer, Sylvie spoke the word she had been longing to say since their first meeting, 'Bitch,' and Cora repeated it. 'Bitch, bitch, bitch.'

At least we are singing in unison, Sylvie thought, when a quarter of an hour had passed and she was in the bathroom, drying her face and brushing her hair. Her neck glowed red but the face above was pale.

In the kitchen Cora was making tea with a good deal of noise. The glass tumbler had been swept up, the pieces wrapped in newspaper and taped with parcel tape to preserve the hands of the rubbish collector. Care had replaced rage and flowed just as freely.

'Don't expect me to like you,' Cora said when they were sitting in easy chairs with their tea. The idea of sitting across from one another at a table was far too intimate.

But now that she had an acknowledged enemy—the acknowledgement was the important thing—Sylvie offered a small olive branch in intermittently lowered eyes.

'I'd much rather you didn't,' she said. It was Isobel who had impressed on her the desirability of enemies. At least here would be no flattery forthcoming.

'I disliked you the second I set eyes on you,' Cora said. 'Everything about you.'

'Right down to my shoes,' Sylvie said. She was trying to remember what she wore that day. Something new, she thought. She imagined she had made an effort.

'Shoes,' Cora said. 'There was no need to travel that far.'

'So I wasn't wrong,' Sylvie said. 'It's a relief.'

She felt a sneaking admiration that her rival had not wasted her time. Appeasement was simply more time to manoeuvre. She imagined them on opposing hills with a plain between. Tents in the setting sun and generals and scouts coming and going. Tents with flaps that swung like culottes. Some film . . .

'You can't concentrate,' Cora said, setting down her cup. 'That's just one of your troubles.'

Suddenly Sylvie was filled with glee. There must have been a last glimpse from the tent of the opposing army bringing up supplies while the light lasted. A last fix before the great rivals slept. Would Cora allow her to sleep?

Cora was getting to her feet, gathering up Sylvie's cup. Sylvie got up as well. She didn't ask which it was to be: war or truce. No strategist would do that. She could imagine the scorn that would follow. She simply said, as the door, the tent flap, was held open for her, 'Thanks for the tea.' The reply was indecipherable because Sylvie was walking. Nothing on earth would have made her turn her head. It might have been 'It changes nothing,' but she could never be sure.

Two hours before Ben returned, Sylvie was at the art gallery with Kit. Art, she knew, was his solution to everything. Opera for the direst, most dreadful predicaments, an orchestra for major but lesser ills, a string quartet for malaises. But his favourite was the art gallery. Select a painting that suited your mood and become absorbed in it until all else faded. On his first visit to London Kit had reeled out of the Tate blinded by an hour in the Turner Rooms. He had stared at *Steam Boat off a Harbour's Mouth* until he could feel the snow on his eyelashes. The ship disappeared and appeared again. On subsequent visits the same thing happened with the Thames and the Houses of Parliament.

He was early and watched Sylvie as she climbed the steps. Indescribably tired, he thought, casting about in his mind for a work that might serve. In the end he decided on Spencer Frederick Gore. There was a long leather settle they could sit on and gaze at *Tennis in Mornington Crescent Gardens* where several gardeners would have been required to find the ball. He was gambling on Sylvie finding greenery restful.

'I don't think I can understand marriage,' Sylvie said, lifting her eyes from the sickening greens and pinks, knowing her grandfather would expect her to gaze at it for at least two minutes. She thought he had chosen wrongly today. His choices were usually so apt: a portrait that could make her laugh with its presumption or, best of all, a tiny, almost forgotten miniature affixed near the juncture of a wall as if undeserving of attention. The tennis match said nothing to her; the figures were too small to engage.

'Neither can I,' her grandfather answered. 'I don't think anyone can.'

'Are there any paintings of people pulling hair?' Sylvie asked. Her head still felt sore, though no hair had come out. In the bathroom she had dipped her hands in water and smoothed her hair down. That was when Cora must have been making tea. Small wonder the tea clippers raced to England with fresh supplies when tea was so useful.

'Goya,' Kit said. 'You need a strong stomach for Goya.' There had been a travelling exhibition of drawings housed in one of the side galleries. The pity and horror of it was still fresh in his memory. The viewer pitied the victims, then themselves, and then felt responsible. Perhaps this accounted for the gallery being nearly empty.

'How did it end?' he asked, sliding his hand across the leather and placing it on top of Sylvie's. Isobel had told him about the fight.

'I can't tell,' Sylvie said. 'I can't tell anything with her. I'm glad it is out in the open. What am I going to say to Ben?'

'I'd say nothing,' Kit said. 'I'd strongly advise nothing.'

'And if it's like a venomous fang that refills with poison, what then?'

'Then we'll find a way of dealing with it. You and me together. Meanwhile I think you should come home with me and rest for a few hours.'

But first they went in search of a Goya. The travelling exhibition had long flown but there was still *Here Comes the Bogeyman*. They stood in front of it and some of the pain in Sylvie's heart melted away. She thought she saw enquiry in the look the young plump-cheeked woman was returning, and courage.

'I'm not at my best, Kitcat,' she said, slipping her arm through his and feeling the comforting soft tweed of his jacket with the leather patches. A supercilious portrait, she went on thinking, could only have reminded me of the perversity of human beings.

Isobel was out, and Kit propelled Sylvie towards the spare room where the bed was always made up. She took off her shoes and crawled into it like a creature that has lost its outer skin. Three hours later she was still asleep. She woke and heard voices. Isobel, Kit and Ben were gathered in the dining room. Her place was set and she slid into it.

The next week Isobel fished out an old wig from the attic. There were three: a redhead, a brunette and a blonde. The blonde was instantly useless; it wouldn't have been out of place in the court of Charles II. For a moment Isobel was distracted by thoughts of itching, the hot feel of mesh on the back of the neck. The brunette was moderately short and nondescript and had a fringe. She tried it on and dusted an old dressmaker's mirror to gauge her appearance. Kit looked up in surprise, hardly recognising her.

'What are you intending to do?' he asked. 'Sell insurance? Apply for the position of a maid?'

'Neither of those. I'm going to post a letter.'

'Addressed to whom?'

'Myself, naturally. A few words of self-praise, I think.'

On a card in the drawer in which she kept supplies Isobel wrote: *Boldness favours the brave* and signed it *An admirer.* She stuck it in an envelope and sealed the flap. She had no idea what she was to be bold about, what the wig, itching and unpleasant to touch, was meant to protect her from.

She parked her car by the nail clinic and walked, coat collar turned up. A soft rain landed on the brown hair and glazed the surface. She wore a preoccupied expression, as if deep in thought. A man coming out of his gate almost collided with her and murmured an apology. Here, on the other side of the road, was the house, carefully sealed as usual. She wondered what Cora did inside, which room she was in. Sylvie had told her there was home help and someone brought baking once a fortnight. Soon she was at the postbox, gleaming and fresh-painted, probably campaigned for by a little committee of women, since in most parts of the city they were disappearing. She slid the letter in and heard it strike the bottom of the box. Tomorrow or the day after it would appear in her letterbox. She might throw it straight into the trash. She turned at the pillar box and crossed the road, still preoccupied as if the letter she had posted had signalled the end of an affair, condolences for a death, a painful letter to a child.

To her horror she saw that Cora had come to her gate and was checking her letterbox. Isobel fished in her pocket and pulled out a handkerchief and covered her mouth and nose. But their eyes met and for a second, though neither gave a sign, she wondered if she was recognised. Instinctively she altered her posture, stood taller, walked more quickly. The eyes are the windows of the soul, she said to herself, feeling for the edge of the fringe which came almost to her eyebrows. At the corner the humour of the situation came to her and she stopped for a moment to catch her breath. 'I can report she is alive and well,' she could tell Sylvie. Then, as she reached the car, she tore the wig from her head and stuffed it in a rubbish bin.

'What was your mother doing walking along Cavendish Street in a wig?' Ben asked after his next dinner with his mother. Everything was going on as before.

'A wig? I don't think she owns one,' Sylvie said. She arched her eyebrows and opened her eyes wide, remembering a school play in which she had played a flapper.

Nothing more was said. Ben's mood had improved since the conference. He had presented her with a bouquet of snapdragons and, always a sign between them, an offering of fruit. She received it as solemnly as a great ape holding up a twig for inspection or examining a leaf.

Isobel was summoned to Dr Franklin's surgery late one winter afternoon.

'Come after 6 p.m.,' she said. 'That will give me time to clear the waiting room.'

Isobel thought nothing of it; there was no change in the voice, except a hint of tiredness. Often she suffered a low-level virus, a gift from her patients, all through the winter.

The familiar room was more bedraggled than ever. Dr Margot had never gone in for the minimalist look. Once there had been a full-size plastic skeleton until its metacarpals and phalanges were removed by children's hands. More appealing was a series of miniatures done by a medical student. Organs of the body made the formal acquaintance of other organs. The vermiform appendix bowed to a kidney and asked for a dance; the heart waltzed with the gall bladder. Isobel never tired of looking at the paintings with their soft colours, for apart from the organs and their strange behaviours the backgrounds were perfectly domestic. She was looking at a pancreas lying on a chaise longue when Dr Franklin came in.

Tired, thought Isobel. How tired she looks. She could do with a tonic.

Then she reflected that Dr Franklin had told her years ago that tonics and cough syrups were useless.

'Isobel,' she said, and instead of sitting behind her desk she came and sat beside her. They looked across the desk together. She had shrugged off her stethoscope and it was lying on the blotter.

'You look . . .' Isobel began.

'Isobel . . .'

They were talking over one another. A smile spread across Isobel's face but there was no answering smile.

'Tests,' she said. 'Do you remember having them? You didn't

ring the surgery to get the results.'

Isobel remembered how she had peered at the blood welling into the tube. Five tubes while she sat holding a piece of cotton wool over the punctured vein and the technician wrote her name and date of birth five times on the labels. The attention to the puncture point struck her as excessive. Once in the car she had torn the plaster and the wadding off.

'It's serious, Isobel,' Dr Franklin was saying. 'Very serious.'

Then the purpose of the later appointment was revealed: not fitted in at the end of a long day but deliberately chosen because it might take longer and be unpredictable. So many times they had walked to the door together, Dr Franklin's hand lightly touching Isobel's back or Isobel lightly touching Dr Franklin's arm. Part of the consultation included enquiries about family members; the doctor had twin boys.

Dr Franklin got up to fetch a file and when she was seated again Isobel felt the news might be about her sight. The desk, the wingback chair in which Dr Franklin usually sat—she saw that the wings of the chair offered refuge, the doctor could sink back against them and imagine she had disappeared—everything in the room was fuzzy.

'Am I losing my sight?' Isobel asked.

'What gives you that idea?' Dr Franklin replied. 'Your sight is fine.'

Then as the room reassembled and Isobel could see, in compensatory clarity, everything that had threatened to fade, the real news was imparted. Her overriding feeling was of sorrow for Dr Franklin who must be longing for the protection of her chair.

But Dr Franklin was drawing her back with details: tests,

new drugs, university research. Despite the five phials of blood, she was talking about the vagaries of medicine, how one philosophy succeeded another and none was certain.

'Will you call Kit?' she asked, looking at Isobel with concern. That too went with the late consultation: naked expressions. But Isobel could not let her naked expression show, because she did not yet know what it was.

At the time when Isobel thought her own walking might have to be curtailed, Madeleine had decided to walk a little every day. Her plumpness, never excessive, a couple of kilos at most, did not seem to displease Freddy who, himself, was growing plumper. Some of his suits had been taken out and new shirts had been bought. It was while she was delivering some shirts to a charity shop that Madeleine found she enjoyed walking the length of Fitzroy Street. The charity shop had moved and she had walked a further two blocks. On the way back she had stopped for coffee at a café with tables on the street. A group of students had joined her, sharing the bench she was sitting on. She felt pleased to be considered unthreatening—none of the students looked at her—and a little saddened too. After the students had rushed off like a flock of birds, she sat on, watching the activity of the street.

Shutters were rolling up; a woman swept the patch of pavement outside a dress shop; someone chalked a menu on a blackboard and lifted the chalk with a flourish. It had been Madeleine's task to sweep the pavement outside Le Livre Bleu, occasionally to clean the big front window, though clean windows were low on Madame Récamier's priorities. 'A smudged window,' she had informed Madeleine, 'adds mystery.' More important were fresh flowers which Madeleine bought at the market. Always the cheapest, except in early spring when extravagance was allowed. Few who stopped to admire the bright yellow daffodils near the cash register escaped without buying a book. Madeleine, resuming her walk, thought she admired people who were as cunning as Madame Récamier. Temperaments such as hers saw the connectedness of things, like raindrops driving people indoors—how often had she watched with amusement as Madame darted into the street with the huge umbrella she kept to snare a victim. New stock was a golden opportunity. 'Hold this,' Madame would say to someone browsing and hoping Madame's eyes did not alight on him. And then, once half a dozen copies of the latest Truman Capote were in his arms, would come the next move. 'Smell the pages.'

Isobel had told her that Sylvie had had a similar relationship with the owner of a fruit shop. So they had that in common, Madeleine thought, as she got up and walked back along the Esplanade. The palm trees were rustling and a tram was climbing the rise. Freddy had told her he would be out that evening. She began counting the steps between lampposts. Another tram rattled past and gave her an idea. The café on the station at Middle Park served dinner; she could eat there.

That evening Madeleine decided to travel the whole route to the terminus before turning back. Freddy would presume she was at home reading a book or watching television. She realised his imagining of her life stopped when he was not present. Sitting on the tram—one of the ones she thought of as middle aged: neither a dowager nor the newest bright yellow—Madeleine pressed her face against the window and marvelled at the dark squares of lawn, fountains and palms outside the towering offices in St Kilda Road. So many lights burning and only occasionally a figure passing behind the glass. The tram raced and sang on its tracks; cars with headlights on pulled up alongside, and passengers dropped down into the dark streets. Soon they were passing the museum where a crowd was gathered in front of the doors; further on a white dog lifted his leg against a spotlit tree. Now came the part that stirred Madeleine's heart: little shabby houses with screen doors and broken-down sofas under the windows so the owners could survey the street. Tidy gardens jostled untidy; skips and bins hinted at some futile activity. Yet Madeleine thought she might do something with one of these houses if she had a free hand and plentiful funds. The tram paused before it began its return journey; the conductor came through and looked at her curiously. 'It's my favourite route,' she said when he stopped beside her. 'Mine too,' he said. 'You see everything on this run.'

After that she felt slightly deflated. Soon she was back in Bourke Street and changing trams. Everything looked different in the dark and she must concentrate. Middle Park came quicker than she realised and she just pressed the bell in time. And here was the station, lit with fairy lights, and Xavier coming out onto the platform with a coffee in one hand and a folded blanket in the other. She got out—her legs felt shaky—and walked quickly up the ramp.

Afterwards Isobel wondered how long she had spent with Dr Franklin. Was it time that could be calculated, like the seven minutes for an ordinary consultation, taking in time for pleasantries and the writing of a new prescription? Was there an average? Dr Franklin had been insistent that Kit be called, but Isobel had resisted with equal force. She could feel the power of her resistance in the room which suddenly grew close. Then Dr Franklin relented, on the promise that Isobel would walk to the nearby taxi stand. She had no intention of obeying: that imperative had vanished along with the effort to please. A strange freedom was being offered her.

When the allotted time for such visits had passed, though she did not glance at her watch, Isobel and the doctor embraced. And the doctor walked her not just to the door of her surgery but along the passage and to the door of the clinic where the night air was pouring in, dampened by a light shower that must have been falling while they talked. It was one of Isobel's favourite scents, especially in autumn when the air carried base notes of domestic fires.

Isobel set off towards the taxi stand, aware that Dr Franklin was watching. She passed by one cab and then quickly turned the corner. No running feet came after her; the doctor would be inside now, tidying her desk for the morning. She had promised not to phone Kit.

Isobel had had to work hard to extract that promise, and a feeling of self-pity had almost undone her. She must concentrate only on the moment, bring all her force to bear on it, since there was nothing else. And Dr Franklin, recognising something of this, something in Isobel's eyes or her expression, had capitulated though her own face bore a grimace. Never before had Isobel seen so clearly how one person moves away from another, how separate lives are, despite propinquity. If someone had come out from the alley she was passing and struck her on the back of the neck, she thought she would have been grateful. For the knowledge to be taken out of her hands, for the roles that she and others must instantly assume. At this very moment Kit was probably drinking a dry sherry and worrying about putting the casserole in the oven.

Down one long straight avenue Isobel kept walking. Then when she realised she was lost she turned back and reached the taxi stand again. A single cab with a turbaned driver was waiting. He switched on the interior light as she opened the rear door, and she shivered a little as he turned to greet her. His appearance was neutral, friendly, his eyes kind but tired.

'I saw you go past,' he said, after she had given him the address.

'I needed to walk for a few minutes,' Isobel said, hoping silence would prevail.

The cab was decorated with a great many ornaments: the dashboard was practically a shrine. It was oddly warm and comforting, sharing the space with a little luminous god. Isobel sank back against the shabby seat cover, the ancient springs. Tears, unbidden, ran down her cheeks and she stroked them away with her fingertips. A tissue was passed from the front seat, the turbaned head looked straight ahead. Only once, just before the cab pulled into the kerb, did their eyes meet in the mirror.

'No charge,' he said when she was opening her purse.

'But I insist,' Isobel said.

'No, Madame. No.'

··◦··

'Surely it is too cold to sit outside?' Xavier asked Madeleine when she was seated at the small table at the end of the platform, the one likeliest to receive gusts of wind and rain. But Madeleine left the blanket guarding her seat and went inside to consult the menu. She chose corn fritters with bacon and a glass of merlot. She could tell the staff thought she was an oddity, despite the ring on her finger when she laid her hand flat by the till. She thought how her father disliked rings and what they symbolised. 'Married but unhappy,' he would say. That could mean another ring. Or one on each finger: I can't make up my mind. The day Freddy had dragged her into the mairie in the rue Bonaparte—no special dress, no bouquet, just a rose from a street seller—she had convinced herself it was romantic, forceful in the way men expressed emotion. Her hand was imprisoned in his; if she had tried to free it, it might have attracted attention. Somehow he had had the measurement of her finger. Later she remembered trying on a ring in a backstreet jeweller's, an antique ring with a carnelian. The witnesses had been two cleaning ladies who were grateful to put down their buckets and mops. 'Done,' he had said as they came down the steps and out into the sunlight again.

Now, as she waited for her meal to be brought, she moved the ring up and down on her finger. Already it was tight; one day the band might sink into her skin and need to be cut off. If she had an operation it would be covered by tape.

A tram was approaching, its interior lit up. She wondered, as she dug her knife into a fritter, if she appeared a mystery woman, eating alone, a blanket with red stitching slipping from her shoulders. Someone like Lara in *Dr Zhivago*, a novel Madame Récamier had a low opinion of even though she had placed a new translation in the window.

Months later she had wondered if economics had been behind Freddy's impulse, and even his pressure on her hand, the sudden drawing of her towards him, the kiss in front of the charladies when permission had been granted, had all been taken into account. A gesture not only cost nothing but the violence of it could be an entry on the right side of the ledger. She knew that profit and loss was pleasing to Freddy. He would frown at stinting where it showed: the table, her clothes. He would have calculated that impulsiveness made a good story. For months their circle had been regaled by it and women had looked at him admiringly.

Xavier had exaggerated the cold and the platform was filling up. Madeleine let the blanket slip from her shoulders and another waiter, noticing, collected it. The trams seemed to increase in number; the stars glowed overhead. A young man, solitary like Madeleine, asked if he could share her table. She smiled and her smile stretched the corners of her mouth wider than usual. He offered her a cigarette, and though it was years since her last Gauloise she accepted.

To prolong the pleasure of the young man's company Madeleine ordered a dessert, a slice of apple cake, but when it arrived she realised she could not manage it. Diffidently she moved the plate towards the young man. While he ate, Madeleine looked at a row of terrace houses in the street opposite the station, imagining herself a buyer, choosing the laciest balcony, the most colourful front door. Could she live without Freddy, his endless guidance? She saw now how all-pervasive it was. *His* wedding, she thought, and a little flare of anger rose: *his* spontaneity, for he had begun telling the tale that very evening when they had guests to dinner who could not be cancelled.

The young man pushed the plate back towards her. He stuck out a finger and caught the last of the crumbs.

'Would you like another?' Madeleine asked. 'I could shout you . . .'

Then she realised it sounded forward and she blushed.

'I wouldn't mind,' he said. 'I'm on the last week of my allowance.'

'Noodles,' Madeleine said. 'Sausages and mince.' What she had lived on. Crêpes and day-old croissants. With only a little persuasion he accepted a large slice of chocolate cake. For herself, another coffee.

Probably she wouldn't sleep. Or would fall asleep just before Freddy came home, padding lightly up the stairs and dropping his clothes on the carpet. The slight creak as the bed adjusted to his weight. How absurd if beds could write their autobiographies, the heavy and the light bodies . . . Another tram drew up, someone bounded out, followed by a sleeping child in a pushchair.

The young man stood up, pushing back his chair.

'Thanks for the cake,' he said.

'My pleasure,' Madeleine said, remembering to look slightly distracted as if at that very moment she had decided on the second terrace house from the end, the boldest one of all, with its black door and shiny yellow knocker which gleamed in the dark.

'Have a good week,' she called, thinking of his allowance which would be replenished.

'You too,' but already he was on the ramp, crossing above the tracks, his hair shining in a street light.

For one week, though the doctor phoned, the doctor's nurse—both calls when Kit was in another part of the house and Isobel answered in a voice that was disengaged, almost cheerful—Isobel said nothing. She had chosen this week for herself, foreseeing that, in what was to come and what was still unknown to her, she herself must be ahead because of the comfort she must supply. And in between this strengthening, which felt like the kind of exercise that the body objected to, squeezed into her daily life were the moments she took to mourn. Very short moments, because the pain was intense and raw. Just holding a cup of coffee in her hands as she gazed through the kitchen window, her hands warming and then stinging on the sides of the mug, was more than a comfort: it reminded her of the time when her hands would be cold and the last task done. They would not be holding a coffee mug, she told herself, because her grip might have gone. She might be sucking on a shaving of ice, handed to her by Sylvie, or having her lips moistened by a cotton bud. And these tasks, she foresaw, would be accompanied by an almost angelic solemnity, as if all the tasks in a life were like that, or could have been, if she had been self-aware.

She set the coffee mug down on the sink and crumpled some bread for the birds. Someone had told her the bread should be moist so a crumb did not lodge in a beak and cause choking. Still the birds had done without moistened bread for so long she thought they might have adapted or at least knew what to expect. A blackbird landed and its tail lifted. For a moment it seemed to look at her with yellow eyes. Some lines from Keats's *Letters* that she had been reading when she met Kit came to her, about the bright purposefulness of creatures as they went about their business, contrasted with the dull-eyed despondency of humans. She had taken the *Letters* with her to her favourite place in the university grounds, under the canopy of an oak so ancient it wore a plaque naming the date of its planting. If she closed her eyes she could imagine the ceremony: perhaps a woman, though more likely a man, with a bright ceremonial trowel, digging the sapling into its prepared hole. Someone, not the dignitary, would tamp down the earth, moving around the little tree in a circle, so despite wind and rain it felt anchored.

The blackbird was darting across the grass now, its head cocked when it stopped. It seemed to be listening to some underground music which only heightened attention could discern. And the bold steps, of remarkable unhesitating speed, were part of it too. Boldness and listening. One day she would examine these as they applied to her own life. Of course she would be found wanting, but that was a human concept and there were other measures. The blackbird had reached the edge of the lawn now, where the rose garden began. Suddenly it dived and speared at the earth.

PART FOUR:

LEAVING

Madeleine Rice's departure from Melbourne was as furtive as ever Madame Récamier could have wished. 'Cunning,' she had said to Madeleine one winter afternoon, when despite the rather economical lighting she favoured, the shop was dim. They were sitting at the rear, unpacking books, while an eye was kept on the door. The door had a bell attached which gave Madame a few seconds to dart forward, since there was no sale without movement. The boxes contained mainly American titles: the ubiquitous Joyce Carol Oates, some Bellow which had sold out thanks to an interview in *The Paris Review*, Barthelme, Roth, of course, for whom Madame had a *tendresse* that was probably unwarranted.

'Have you learnt nothing from literature, not to know that?' Madame Récamier's eyes gleamed in the gloom; she reminded Madeleine of a crocodile half-submerged in water. 'Even your Jane Austen, your Henry James is full of cunning.'

Madeleine had merely kept a neutral expression. She did not see where cunning fitted into her life. Madame had lived on her wits and now made it a philosophy that the books that surrounded her should validate. They were sipping Lady Grey tea, a blend Madame preferred; coffee was reserved for the mornings.

Still something of Madame's advice must have rubbed off on her, for Madeleine had observed, in the weeks before she left, Freddy's longer and longer absences and something in his manner that resembled the style favoured by some American male writers: cool, all-observing, with personal feelings held back.

She had confided in Kit. She had phoned him one evening when Isobel was out—Kit did not say where she was. It had always been easier to talk to him than to her mother and, besides, he offered a male perspective. It seemed he had instantly recognised a pattern, even if he did not say what that pattern was. The self-satisfied male who sets up his surroundings with a care few women can emulate, and which is unlikely to be noticed by the women it contains. Such women usually praise their spouse—it was usually a spouse—for possessing exquisite taste, taking an interest in female matters. Kit had not been impressed by Freddy on the occasion they dined together. Madeleine was flattered by her husband's proprietorial manners, Kit could tell, but he saw them simply as a shrewd economy, the expenditure of very little effort but making sure it counted. He had been tempted to tip his wine glass over the table to get a reaction; then he thought Madeleine would have to wash the napkins.

An airfare had been sent on the condition Madeleine followed his instructions. She had packed a small suitcase and left it at the florist's she patronised. Then the following day, a day when Freddy had told her he might be late returning, she had taken a taxi from Fionola Florist to the airport. Kit had promised to meet her when she landed. She requested a window seat and leaned her head against the cabin wall. The man beside her was silent and she was grateful. Only when they were standing in the aisle, readying to disembark, did they exchange a smile.

Her father, standing behind the barrier, had the advantage of height: she sighted him first and his changed face. Her worry that the florist would already have phoned Freddy, who paid the bills, evaporated. She just had time to recall the floor-to-ceiling fridges where peonies and carnations and roses were stored and how the glass door had a sheen of condensation when Kit was at her side.

The week when Isobel spoke to no one was long past; she could hardly remember it and the false freedom it had offered. It had taken at least a week of excruciating talk for Kit to be reconciled to what he thought was abandonment. He seemed to be going back through their life together, to the vows they had made—wholehearted and overspilling words as they stood with their arms around each other—or the long soul-searchings after Isobel's one regretted affair.

Isobel had thought of dressing up to greet Madeleine; then she had decided against it. She was wearing a light merino jersey and a pair of wool jersey slacks under the bedclothes that were neatly pulled up with a wide swathe of top sheet like a sash. The pillows that, on occasion, Kit had flung impatiently on the floor or against which her head rested while they made love on the quilt were neatly arranged in sizes and shapes. A line of books reached as far as her toes; with the bed roll at her back she could change the one she was reading. At present she was skipping through *Middlemarch*, reading the Dorothea sections—Casaubon had just been discovered dead at the stone table in the garden and Dorothea was free. Later she might reread the great swell of the ending which was like the middle of the ocean.

The door banged and Kit made sure she heard their approach. Isobel ran her hands through her hair and reached for her hand mirror. Her lip liner was in place, the little lines above her top lip held back. She need not think for how long. In the few seconds it took to climb the stairs Isobel made a signal of her own by knocking a book onto the floor.

The first thing Madeleine noticed were the circles under her mother's eyes as if someone had tried a colour there and failed to wipe it off.

Now Isobel pulled the cover back and invited Madeleine to join her. 'Take off your shoes,' she said.

'Your mother likes to imagine it's a sixteenth-century bed at an inn,' Kit explained.

'I couldn't bear the low ceilings,' Isobel said, when the pillows had been divided and Madeleine was propped up beside her.

Madeleine had a great longing to cry. She wanted to go back and prepare a dinner party, to act for the rest of her life as if nothing was happening.

Downstairs, in the kitchen, Kit filled the jug and waited for it to boil. It took less than a minute but he didn't know how to pass the time. His head drooped and he wondered if he would become one of those stringy old men with a head like a gooseneck lamp. Then he thought it was the shape of a human embryo, the bean-like head, as if even at the commencement of life thought, or something that resembled it, was important.

··⧽ ⧼··

'Just an hour,' Isobel said, 'and then I want you to be with your father. He needs your company.' More than mine was unspoken.

The bed was wide and warm; the warmth of her mother's body seemed to move towards her across the sheets. On the flight Madeleine had prepared her own story, her suspicions of Freddy whose desire was always to arrange life to suit himself. Now her story was being pushed away, she might never tell it. Then she thought her mother was indicating that her father would be the recipient and it would be a distraction for him. The traditional thing was to go for a walk; no matter how heavy hearts were, a walk was considered beneficial.

After an hour Isobel indicated she would sleep. Before Madeleine left the room she replaced *If On a Winter's Night a Traveller* which had fallen on the floor. Then she bent and lightly kissed Isobel's forehead. There was a sound like a groan and Isobel turned on her side.

'I'm going to leave Freddy,' Madeleine said to Kit when the walk began. They were in a park created in a gully. Paths followed its sides; there were trees dedicated to prominent citizens. At the bottom of the gully was a lake bordered by rushes; Madeleine thought it might once have been filled by rusted car bodies, stained mattresses. There was something threadbare about the park, despite the flourishing trees, some of which had grown canopies to block the sky.

After they had walked in a circle Madeleine and Kit sat on a wooden seat. It too had a plaque.

'How long?' Madeleine asked.

'No one can tell. There can be remissions.'

In front of them were two paths, one that led to the lake. It hardly mattered which one they took. Madeleine would suggest coffee somewhere before going back.

'If we could move from being born to a plaque,' Kit said, getting up. He looked at her suddenly, remembering her as a young child, a poor sleeper. She had sleepwalked as well. A little figure in a white nightgown with a frill around the neck and hem walking softly down the hall, the eyes open and glazed. His own sleeplessness had begun with her. A sense of danger had woken him so he was alert in seconds. He had known not to touch or make any startling movement. Nonetheless he had been unable to resist extending his hand, the way one approached an animal. He allowed her hand which was held in front of her like a blind man's stick to touch the tips of his fingers. When she didn't recoil he softly enfolded the hand in his. She had bequeathed him the sleeplessness, and over the years it had not been without advantages. And then there had been Sylvie.

'What is it to me?' Cora Taverner had said when Ben gave her the news.

The Tuesday dinner had been resumed, except now the date was frequently broken. In reality Ben dined with his mother about once a month. Sylvie made no comment; he simply wrote *Dinner with M* on the whiteboard near the fridge. 'How was the monster?' she asked. How was the Minotaur? She had other names up her sleeve. 'Let's not speak of it,' she said in the days when it divided them. 'I won't ask what you ate.' 'And I won't tell,' he replied with a grin. After that his appetite was better, and when he got home he poured himself a stiff whisky and lay back on the sofa. There was always enough food for four: dishes filled with vegetables, lamb chops of which he could manage four. What did she do with the leftovers? He suspected she threw them out on the lawn or they went in the garbage. He had given up trying to turn any of her attitudes, recognising it was futile.

The heartlessness of her remark stung him and he nearly choked on a piece of lamb. He held his napkin up to his face, feeling his face turn red.

'On your head,' he said, when he had swallowed some water. 'These antediluvian attitudes.'

'I admit they are very old,' his mother said, pushing the water jug towards him for a refill. 'At least I recognise them.'

'And their source in the swamp,' he said, holding the napkin in his hand and screwing it into a ball, out of sight, below the table edge.

'Your marriage has made you squeamish,' his mother went on when the plates had been removed and dessert laid.

'Why shouldn't you stay a primitive?' Ben continued. 'So we can remember you as a force of nature?'

'Whatever pleases you,' she replied, turning aside her head. 'Draw from me whatever you want.'

'And if we want nothing?' he persisted. He couldn't speak for his sister, of course. They might compare notes one day.

'I expect you imagine my funeral,' she said. 'You'll find it all prepared and paid for. You'll have nothing to do but attend. That's if you can be bothered.'

Her napkin was screwed up now too. He saw her hand, laden with its gross old-fashioned rings, tremble as she rose from the table. The chair with its padded cushion rocked and then righted itself.

Ben got up, throwing his napkin onto his plate, and followed her into the kitchen. She was standing against the wide door of the double refrigerator, once the pride of the house. Perhaps she had some idea of cooling her cheeks. Her illogic was illustrated even here, he thought, for the outside of the fridge was warm, the cold was inside.

He took a deep breath and placed his hand on her back, the way a man would hold a woman at a public dance. A tea dance, in his mother's case. The absurdity of it had always struck him, or had it been Sylvie who had brought it to his attention? 'Anyone would think a policeman was watching,' she had remarked. They were watching a costume drama on TV. Some sloe-eyed film star with his 'no touch' hands splayed like a starfish. *I mean this woman no harm, officer.* And afterwards the hands would be everywhere, pressing, fumbling, squeezing . . .

Remembering this he increased the pressure of his hand, so it was practically a caress. His mother turned and hurled herself at him, sobbing, and he was forced to hold her between himself and the fridge for a good two minutes.

An hour later, when he was driving home, Ben felt like a ghost. His mother had promised she would go straight to bed but in fact she was pouring herself another Drambuie. She had put down the liqueur glass and got a tumbler instead. Then, since there were only two fingers left in the bottom, she poured that as well. The warmth spread through her entire body and soon she would sleep. Ben on the other hand seemed to have lost all his blood; his movements as he drove were automatic; he would not have been surprised if a traffic cop pulled him over and told him his lights were not on. He had promised his mother he would phone the next morning, from the office. Already he was dreading it.

He sat in the car for a long time before getting out. He saw the light in the room they called the study go out. Sylvie would have been working on her seminar notes—she was teaching a new paper, reading copiously, 'like sinking through water', she described it. The door opened suddenly and she was there in her nightdress and dressing gown, her feet in a pair of his socks.

'What is it?' she asked. She was hoping, whatever it was, was final. A stroke had carried off his mother. Attempts to revive her had failed, despite heroic efforts by the ambulance officers. She saw he was practically slumped over the wheel.

'Come,' she said, extending her hand. She was still in her primitive society. No ambulance existed there, though there was a bandaging with leaves and bloodletting.

'Don't ask, don't ask,' he said when there was a plunger of strong coffee in front of him and they were both sipping. The unguarded creature he had seen had terrified him as much as a stream suddenly disgorging a crocodile. Something had struck at him, and even if he had managed to evade most of the blows—he had feinted and comforted until the rigid heaving back had become just a back again—he knew he could never go back. If she was dying he would brace himself for another assault. He imagined sheets pulled up to her chin and her eyes watching him, the cold power.

·◦﹥ ﹤◦·

Madeleine was back in her old room. Freddy had phoned and attempted to talk to her, but the call had been diverted by Kit. 'Let's not involve lawyers,' Madeleine overheard him say. His voice sounded sharp, impatient. Then the subject was changed to Isobel. Any visit must be postponed. The implication was that matters could just be allowed to drift.

At least the spare room was impersonal: early in her married life Isobel had been taken by the decorating style of one of her mother's friends. Rooms were plain, dressed with good simple fabric, heavy imported cotton quilts that made a scallop shape on the carpet, plain sumptuous things which somehow drew attention to themselves and were oddly comforting. The spare room, being little used, was the only room where the look had been maintained. Now, standing in the doorway, Madeleine thought she was bringing her own chaos into the room and the brown quilt was giving her the averted gaze of a monk.

'I won't stay,' she had promised her father, but he had waved his hand dismissively. 'Let me know when you want to answer the phone,' he said. She knew that Freddy was at a disadvantage. Probably the other woman was being ignored and he was playing the role of a man settling his private affairs. His complacency came to her, the layers of it, as she sat on the bed and felt the thick rich fabric with her fingers.

She borrowed the car and did errands and bought groceries;

she drove unthinkingly, looking for a beach. A lookout would do. Once she found herself on the motorway, aimlessly in the stream of traffic, alarmed and looking for an exit ramp. She escaped into a quiet suburb; overhead a great bridge bore the traffic away. She found a private house open to the public, with kindly women and a display of pamphlets in the front room. Tasselled ropes made a path through the furniture. It was impossible to imagine any activity around the vast dining table with its elaborate place settings, its arrangement of wax fruit under a glass dome. At the top were the nurseries and the servants' quarters. Gone were the flocked wallpapers, the cloaks and mirrors, and something rougher took its place. Pillows with striped ticking lay on the bed of a maid, and a trunk sat at its foot: the initials read *E.P.B.*

Half an hour was all Madeleine could bear. Luckily the grounds were spacious and laid out in a way that welcomed the elements. Rain or wind could sweep across the vast lawn before it descended into copses and a tennis court. There were seats under the giant elms. No human life seemed as spacious or as impervious to events. For the first time it came to her— ironic given Isobel's diagnosis—that her own life was closing too, that all the preparation that was to come would end; that the lessons, particularly Madame Récamier's sharp rebukes, would no longer apply. Freddy would settle or she would return to him after a suitable pause which she would attempt to see as a correction and which he would eventually ignore. As if in contradiction a pile of leaves, raked under a nearby tree, shifted in the breeze and a few topmost leaves fluttered down. It was like a detail at the corner of an eye, a slight blur. From somewhere out of sight came the hum of a mower, keeping the vast spaces immaculate, and then, as it came closer, she could see the head of the gardener against a little rise.

At the dairy Madeleine bought supplies, though none were necessary. She bought chocolate for her father and newspapers he would probably not read. And she bought two bunches of paper whites, too early and probably forced, though she liked to imagine they grew somewhere in a field and had been brought on by unexpected days of sunlight. Her mother had talked to her of spring when she was a child, trying to show her that winter was reversed in these blooms and colours that had something extra about them, an extra vitality that came after the earth had sealed itself away. They had made a poster together, or it may have been a project for school. There was a good deal of yellow crayon and cotton wool for newborn lambs.

Sylvie had timed her visits to avoid her, and Madeleine suspected she was in contact with Kit. She walked slowly back to the car. She could not challenge it: Sylvie had enough to contend with. Her mother-in-law had been admitted to a private clinic. Sylvie would not visit her either, but great tactfulness was required.

Madeleine arranged the paper whites in a thin tall vase. Its cobalt blue seemed to increase the green of the stems and made the flowers creamier. Isobel patted the bed beside her and Madeleine sat down. Then after a while she cast aside the pillows and lay flat. Isobel's hand was over hers but she couldn't speak. Tears ran from Madeleine's eyes and down her cheeks, and she stayed still, trying not to give a sign, though she knew her mother knew.

'I'd like you to find me the Arundel tomb poem,' Isobel said.

'Not yet. Sometime this afternoon.' She felt they could talk about it, about those who came to visit it, to lay a warm hand over a stone replica, those who privately mourned before the tourists came and grief was general and mainly for themselves.

Sylvie sat in front of the Albert Park fountain, on a bench at first, and then she went forward until she stood at the rim where the spray from gusts of wind could reach her. Her exhaustion was profound and yet the morning's tutorial had gone well. No one had contradicted her when she offered too strong an opinion on patriarchy. Sensing her mood was more important than understanding. There had even been some note-taking. And all the time she had felt like putting her head in her hands, asking for *their* comfort. Her students might have had stories they could offer: dying grandparents, siblings with shortened lives, someone nursed at the sacrifice of others. And what would her tutorials have become after that? Co-conspirators, a team of detectives? She might parcel things out between them. Still she knew that was not what they wanted. The spray fell across her body as if she was wearing a sash: one cheek, one breast and one side of her skirt. The wind dried her as she walked.

'Not today,' Kit had said, and then, before she could protest, he had hung up. There had been a sound in the background, like the click of a door.

'Not yet,' Ben had said when she suggested visiting his mother. Surely it would be safe with nurses in attendance?

'Aren't I the cause?' she had said. Her voice sounded sharp, defiant.

'Further back than you,' he said.

'In the primeval swamp,' she began.

'Please.'

And she had left it. There were words on her tongue that would have reduced his mother to a stain.

For a wild moment she thought of taking a bus, the way she would take one to the zoo. To the asylum, she would say. And in a changing room or whatever it was called she could borrow a white coat. She had a clipboard in her briefcase. She could survey her mother-in-law through the morning's seminar notes. *The importance of societal cohesion. The rewards of subservience.* She was passing a gym. Privacy was not desired. A line of machines faced the passers-by; legs pumped and flushed faces seemed lost in dreams. One young man with damp spiky hair winked at Sylvie. She grinned back and the elements of her world fell back to earth again.

In the afternoon Madeleine took the book of poems to her mother's room. Kit had helped her find it: the familiar slim volume in which the poem appeared was missing, or perhaps Isobel had moved it, but Kit found it again, in an anthology. Madeleine had no doubt her mother would explain it to her. Explaining was one of Isobel's strengths or perhaps it was an insatiable need. It never occurred to her that the other person might not need an explanation or that the other person did not start from the same place. Isobel's words had washed over Madeleine as a child. She had listened politely enough, but their temperaments were far apart. The Colette books with their beautiful covers had looked pretty on the shelves of her miniature bookcase but they had contributed little more than colour. Vaguely, she sensed that the contents were meant to be a warning, one that she would absorb through her skin. But since the dangers they illustrated did not exist in her world and her temperament was unlikely to seek them they were irrelevant.

'An Arundel Tomb', marked by a bookmark, and said over softly in her room in case she was asked to read it aloud, was obviously dense. It made Madeleine think of a boiled sweet. In her childhood two had been permitted at the end of each day: she had dipped her hand in the jar in search of a peppermint-flavoured one, with pink stripes. The ones she hated were black with white stripes. Then she had to brush her teeth.

'Did you find it?' Isobel asked, looking up, and raising herself. 'An inexhaustible poem,' she said when her reading glasses were balanced on her nose. 'You must have seen such tombs in France.' Isobel had run her hand over tombs in abbeys and in the open air, marvelling at the weathering of stone. Marvelling too that whatever remained—a little fine dust, a bone falling into powder—was so far far below. And the poem had the same feeling, despite the lovely details: one hand holding the gauntlet, the other receiving the caress of three fingers, the little dog at the countess's feet. And was there a pair of stone hearts to be imagined inside?

'Read it to me,' Isobel said. They were lying side by side, as all her favoured visitors did now: daughter, granddaughter, Kit. Others stood in the doorway or sat in chairs. Sometimes there was a furtive glance at a watch or an appointment in place. When she looked back on her gallery of friends Isobel realised there were few who could let a day float, so the marking of the hours became artificial and everything was governed by light.

Hesitantly Madeleine spoke the first lines. But even the little practice stood her in good stead.

> *Side by side, their faces blurred,*
> *The earl and countess lie in stone,*

Then Isobel took the book back and read the next verse. Madeleine the third, Isobel the fourth, until they reached the seventh. Then they began again with Isobel first. Over and over until the understanding came. It could never be pinned down, any more than a single skull in an ossuary can be separated from another, or finger bones, fanned out, remake a living hand. The thoughts were so vague and deep that only stone could hold them down. The dog and lion were fire irons or door stops.

When Madeleine got up there was a dent in the bed. She smoothed it with her hand.

'Leave it,' Isobel said.

On a bench at St Dymphna's clinic Cora Taverner sat with a nurse attendant. The ground sloped, deliberately, so those who were at liberty to roam, once they had descended to the rim of trees and shrubs that screened the road, had a steep climb back again. The cars passed in a gully; there was no hope of waving one down; all that would be seen was a hand waving from the bushes. Most of the residents soon took on an appearance that separated them from other human beings. Cora would not fall into that trap: her stay would be measured in weeks, and once the period of rest was over there would be counselling sessions, group therapy, long warm baths, reading and music. Solitude was considered empowering, though at first a nurse would be present.

St Dymphna's was exclusive and in the summer months there were garden parties, pony rides and open-air concerts. Cora was adamant she would not attend group therapy. She felt she might not have been admitted at all if her collapse in front of Ben had not led to endless bouts of weeping and sleeplessness. Her doctor had persuaded her, emphasising the healing properties of rest. 'Could I take an assumed name?' she asked, and he had agreed she could choose another name for the staff, though her real name would be on the files.

Now Nurse Barton addressed her as Phoebe and Cora felt she was changing into another person, one whose character was being built up day by day. Phoebe Vanderbilt was a business woman who sat on the board of a company and endeavoured to sort out its finances. The men on the board deferred to her opinion since she had inherited a large number of shares. In bed at night Cora added to what she was learning of Phoebe's life. She dressed her as she had once dressed her cut-out dolls, bending the tabs that held the paper afternoon dresses in place, adding a flared coat or a hat.

Ben had visited twice at the beginning; now he came once a week.

'Couldn't you go just once?' he said to Sylvie. 'She's a different person.'

'Only if I can become a different person too,' was the reply.

She had consented to come with him and sit in the car. He disappeared around the corner of the administration block and set off along a wide white path that glowed in the moonlight. In half an hour he emerged from the darkness. Sylvie slid across into the driver's seat and drove them home.

'Sorry,' he murmured.

'Sorry,' she murmured back.

Sylvie was almost too weary to brush her teeth. They stood side by side at the basin, she with her soft brush, he with his hard, sharing the cold tap. A longing to be a child again almost overcame her. And Ben? He who had had that world, how did he feel? But she couldn't ask. Now the guardian of it was herself being tucked into bed and the door left ajar so the passage light could provide security. Passing feet, instead of the feet of just one, would pass in the night. A torch . . . but Sylvie had just got to the thought of eyelids being prised up when she was felled by sleep. Beside her, flat on his back, Ben flung out an arm and his fingers curled over his palm.

Freddy was prepared to pay Madeleine an allowance while their separation was finalised. He regretted that his marriage of convenience had ended, that he had made his private arrangements too soon. It was beneath him to ask what Madeleine had found out, or been told. One of the dinner guests might have made mischief. Now her mother's illness gave a perfect vagueness when enquiries were made. However long the death took—his one encounter with Isobel had been the dinner in St Kilda—there would be a great many things to attend to afterwards. Gradually Madeleine's absence would not be remarked on. He might insinuate a collapse or grief delayed. The relations between a mother and a daughter . . . he could raise his arms in a helpless gesture. All that knowledge passed down, except in Madeleine's case it had not been. She had fled. Given her feebleness, he thought she had been bold, bolder than he gave her credit for.

He would sell the house, he thought, and take an apartment. The next stage. She might be induced to visit; they might come to some arrangement. She had loved the Vera Wang vegetable dishes he had given her, loved carrying them to the table and lifting the lids. In the steam and butter and scent of herbs her cheeks had glowed. 'Sweet,' one of the guests had said, when she was out of earshot. 'You have a sweet woman there.' A woman who could look so charming taking the lids off vegetable dishes would make a good nurse.

There were days when Isobel still went walking. Short walks with compulsory stops. She became good at selecting an object before the need to stop overcame her. A well-tended garden, after passing one that was an untended wilderness, was a relief. Even a lamppost around whose base someone had planted a few geraniums. She suspected she fooled no one, but it was natural for old women to catch their breath, to overestimate their stamina. Sometimes, after she had gone, angrily brushing off his concern, Kit got out the car and slowly followed her. He too had to stop to preserve the illusion of independence. In the glove pocket of the old Peugeot was a book, *The Meditations of*

Marcus Aurelius, which he sometimes read, unseeingly. Or he listened to the car radio. When Isobel stepped back inside she was greeted by an exuberant fanfare or Haydn symphony. She was grateful when this happened, for it covered her fumbling.

'Don't say anything,' she said. In about a minute her breath settled and she felt calm and even pleased with herself. She refused to go back to bed.

Sylvie, when she had a morning tutorial, came in the afternoon. Her quick step on the path, the ring of the doorbell, pushing the door open at the same time so she was in the hallway before the chime died away. Her briefcase fell on the floor as her satchel had when she was a child. Isobel had never been able to persuade her to unpack it straight away. She must rush forward like a homing bird to find her grandmother, to ensure that the life they had built together was undisturbed. Everything in the house was the subject of intense scrutiny to Sylvie: how long would a vase of sweet peas last? She peered into the water at the bottom of the vase, then inserted her nose among the petals to see if the scent had changed. Any rearrangement of the furniture was upsetting.

Isobel had not encouraged the wild embrace that Sylvie wanted to offer. In her case it could be returned unconditionally, even more powerfully than the offering of a ten-year-old child, but what of the world, more cruel and judgemental? A wild embrace was too naked; it put power in the hands of a viewer as well as the recipient. Isobel shuddered at the idea of reserve on one side, a cold calculation of what could be taken advantage of. And she had not been wrong. Except she need not have stepped back as Sylvie bounded into the room, murmuring something about her school bag and its half-full drink bottle. It was one of Isobel's regrets now: an equally fierce embrace, a naked showing of her love, might have obliterated the expulsions and the love affairs that were to come.

Now she squeezed Sylvie's hand as hard as she could, until her bones ached. She pressed her lips against the still-fresh cheek, feeling the soft invisible down. She directed the conversation—this was still her role—to the foxglove finger stalls Sylvie had worn to breakfast for three mornings until they split and had to be thrown out.

Sylvie claimed not to remember, or she was wanting Isobel to preserve her breath.

'You took the vase upstairs and had them by your bed,' Isobel said. 'In the morning you must have plucked them off and put them on each finger. You ate your breakfast with them on.'

What use is the past? Sylvie was thinking. Even this memory claimed something of Isobel's life. Instead of foxglove finger stalls there should be something else. She was weary of messages and memories, for there was almost always a message. *I loved you, I observed you. Even when you didn't observe yourself.* Isobel had stood in the doorway when Sylvie had fallen asleep with the night light on, her fingers spread out on the quilt, each finger inside a purple sheath.

Sylvie was longing to lie down beside her grandmother and talk, but Isobel was resisting. So she went into the kitchen instead and made tea. A row of herbal teas were clustered on the bench. Angrily Sylvie lifted the flaps and raised the packets to her nose. They were all useless; she could have stewed rose petals herself or steeped dandelions. She chose chamomile, vanilla and manuka honey and the largest teapot, for she might stay for hours. Anything to put off the moment when she was dismissed. It was done so gently the dismissal was hardly felt but still she felt it. Her grandfather would hug her and walk with her to the gate as if she were going to school. He would touch her shoulder or rest his hand against the nape of her neck.

Isobel did not touch her tea for a long time, until it was almost lukewarm. Sylvie took a gulp of hers and almost choked. Her cheeks flamed and tears ran down them. It was useless telling her to go slowly. But at least it achieved what she wanted. She lay beside Isobel on the bed and had her hair stroked.

'I don't want to be here when my mother is here,' she said and her voice, rasped by coughing, had the complaint of a small child.

'I might become too weak to make a timetable,' Isobel said. She was thinking of the Gare du Nord and how on her first visit she had practised what to say to the ticket clerk. She had chosen well; the rush hour had passed, and the clerk, a middle-aged woman, had relented and spoken in English. In return, Isobel had ventured a sentence or two in her halting French and been rewarded by a smile and a 'Bonne journée.'

Now Sylvie was attempting to press her body close to Isobel's, but Isobel was unresponsive. In her new state she was becoming painfully aware of the wills of others. Often they were concealed under good temper and helpful suggestions but they were forceful nonetheless.

Kit came in and sat in a chair at the foot of the bed. Isobel felt herself under observation, under guard. That afternoon there was another doctor's appointment. If she could have she would have postponed it, but she and Dr Franklin were engaged in a battle about her treatment, how much of it Isobel would permit. Isobel knew she must argue now, and convince her that her arguments were rational. That was the hardest, for no sooner was she in the familiar surgery, with the familiar paintings and the fresh flowers on the desk, than she felt herself overwhelmed. She might have been a child again— Sylvie perhaps, on the verge of a tantrum. The energy it took to control herself, the responsibility of returning the doctor's sympathy which was there behind the cultivated neutral look and likewise threatening to break through. It would have been better, Isobel thought, if they could both have rolled on the floor and howled. Instead the onus was on her to be cheerful and comforting. Statistics were produced while Dr Franklin fiddled with her pen, turning it over and over in her fingers, and Isobel, careful not to make it look like a tic, smoothed her skirt over her knees. At least they hadn't got as far as experimental drugs and university trials. She would not die a guinea pig. Isobel's mind wandered at this point and she wondered if those who were guinea pigs and failed automatically bequeathed their bodies to science.

Still, when the visit was over, and she had not weakened, Isobel had come to one conclusion. She knew she wanted to be by the sea. Kit could find a simple cottage for rent. Luckily it was winter and many of them would be closed up. Shutters would be fastened over the windows; sand would have drifted over the floors. Even a few days would be enough. To look at the sea and read, to drink wine in the evenings. To give herself up, in whatever feeble way a human being was capable of, to that great force! It would take some persuasion, because Isobel wanted to be there alone.

·∙◦∙·

Phoebe Vanderbilt woke in the pre-dawn greyness and wondered where she was. Then the room at the clinic assembled itself: the bed in a certain position, different from her own bed which had always faced south, the bedside table with its utilitarian lamp, the tall thin wardrobe. The walls, a light green, were still grey, but the greys in the room were changing, some darker, some fainter. She lay still, thinking of her new identity. Ben had not visited for ten days and she felt certain he would not come; a new excuse would be invented.

Outside in the passage Cora heard the soft plod of feet. She got out of bed, sipped from a glass of water on the bedside table and went to the window. A white mist was rising from the lawns; the window, pushed open a few inches, let in cold air. What would Phoebe Vanderbilt do? She would not waste time looking out at drenched lawns, nor would she put on a dressing gown and slippers. She would dress and put on sturdy shoes. To encourage herself she pushed the window open further; the cold air touched her bare shoulders as she removed her nightdress and put on her underclothes. Slacks and a warm jersey, a woollen hat that could be pulled low over her forehead. Hair colour might be a giveaway, she thought. She was into the pattern of Phoebe's thinking now. She should make her bed; it was something both identities would insist on. She left her dressing gown draped over a chair and her slippers underneath. Money, she thought, and could not tell which of her voices was prompting but she admired its practicality. On his first visit, the day after she was admitted, Ben had left a hundred dollars in notes and some loose change in her handbag.

Before she opened the door to the corridor—cunning would be required for this—she took out her compact and dabbed at her cheeks. She applied lipstick with an unsteady hand. A vigorous brushing of her hair and the hat clutched in her hand. More soft footfalls, so she sat on the bed, waiting. And all the time the calm voice, like her own real voice that had always sustained her, that had encouraged and guided her through widowhood and had erupted in rage only when Ben had married Sylvie and she had been abandoned.

She counted to fifty before she opened the door a crack. The bathroom door at the end of the passage was closing; in a few seconds she heard the hiss of the shower and then a quavery voice singing. I can't stand this madhouse any longer, she thought. Her soles were rubber, and she walked softly along the passage and through the door that led to the garden. There was a moment's panic when she saw it was locked, but she pressed the snib and it opened and she was in the cool damp air. She regretted not stopping at the dining room, set for the day's breakfast, and helping herself to several pieces of fruit and some of the untoasted bread. Still she had plenty of money. And she had her new identities: Cora Taverner and Phoebe Vanderbilt. How well they complemented each other. *Take care on the slope, the grass is slippery*, one said, while the other urged speed. As much speed as was possible. In her haste she had left her watch behind but that might be an advantage; it might be presumed she was in the shower. *Anyone can find out what time it is*, said one of the voices, and she thought it was Phoebe. The grass was green now instead of green-grey. The sun was rising and on the highway below the sounds of early morning traffic. *Long-distance truck drivers*, the voice said. *Coming to*

267

the end of their shifts or just starting. She remembered they ate hearty breakfasts, packed with carbohydrates. She realised she was ravenous.

··⌘··

While Phoebe Vanderbilt was walking gingerly at the side of the highway, aware of her need to keep her dignity, Isobel was thinking of beings swallowed up by the sea. Not that she would wade into the sea until she was out of her depth and allow a wave to carry her away. There were too many accounts of bodies being returned, barely recognisable, half-consumed by sea life and buffeting. The first dead body she had seen was a man at the beach. She was walking with her father in the shallows, his large bare feet and her smaller ones no more than ankle deep in the pale grey water. A little further along a small crowd had assembled, and when they came closer her father had taken her hand and they had waded out a little further until the shore was clear again. But Isobel had seen the blue feet under the canvas cover and the poor drowned head, the partly open mouth and the staring eyes. What stayed with her most though was the rough canvas cover that might have been brought from the yacht club nearby. 'It might not be the sea at all,' her father had said. 'It might have been a heart attack.' Isobel had pressed her fingers into his hand and moved her feet closer to his as they went on walking. He had a habit of showing her things but only in a way that could be controlled. True to form, though she felt queasy, he had stopped for ice creams.

Kit, she felt, would not allow her to be alone; there would

have to be a schedule of visits and hourly checks. What if she went walking and fell over? Or she might collapse while paddling and be pulled out slowly by the tide like a piece of driftwood. It was impossible to explain to him that she simply wanted to watch. And to listen. All the thoughts she had had, many of them repetitious and futile, unique perhaps to her character but advancing nothing, when it would have been better to have been still. All the things she had feared and planned to avert, most of which had never arrived, and those that had arrived and undone her. Her best solace had been music with its perpetual movement, its effort. She might make a note of the colours of the sea like the bald notes her father had made in his diary. 'Wind: southwesterly; clouds: cumulus'. *Sea, grey-green. Sea, navy blue. Sea, battleship grey.*

At night Kit slept in the guest room, and for him it was as if he was already in the middle of mourning. Not the beginning, which he thought was the moment he and Isobel met in the hallway outside the old lecture theatre in Princes Street. It was not yet summer and they must have shared the same lecture theatre for months. He did not regret it: he was no fan of instant attraction any more than he was fond of rushing for the bathroom with a clenching stomach. After such violence there were always repairs to be done. Isobel when she got to understand him realised he was economical in everything except money. With that he was indifferent and generous. But his movements took the shortest possible route, even if it was just crossing a room. In a room full of people it would annoy him that a trajectory could not be made between the doorway and the window seat on which he planned to sit.

Every year, as the first warm days were heralded, Professor

von Rieger delivered his lecture about the fetid odours—like Newgate Gaol or Smithfield Market or an East End slum—they could expect in the lower lecture theatres. He would produce his simile about the canary: if one were carried into this hellhole as a test for air quality it would fall dead without a cheep. The professor had shrewd eyes in his creased face. Everyone tried to look as if the comparison was as daring as the canary. Kit stretched his lips into what he thought was a wide smile. A few sycophants clapped, and one or two girls, used to screaming and shrieking and fending male students off with indignant cries, made bird-like noises. Kit was thinking of the cruelty of humankind to use what was powerless and discard it for a nobler purpose. The canary with its tiny fluttering heart—how many beats a second?—and the fist-sized heart of some hulking miner, annoyed that his bravado was being usurped by a bird.

They had filed out, sniffing the air and the faint overlay of heat it was beginning to wear, and in the corridor the heavy door which a student had let go swung against Isobel's heel. Kit pushed the door back—it was as heavy as a fire door—and turned to look at her. She was looking down ruefully at the heel of her shoe where the leather had been scraped off and hung down. Her heel ached too but shoes were a luxury on her allowance. The last thing she needed was sympathy, and the tall young man who had stopped to push back the door had the wisdom not to offer any. Despite his strictures on early attraction there was a tacit understanding in both their eyes.

'I love the way you go about things,' Isobel said to him later. She didn't say she thought it was his finest quality but she thought it was. In any problem—except the most extreme that might have required violence—he knew the order of steps to take and always began with the one that was the most gentle. He had taken her satchel from her so she could look at her shoe properly.

In the years of Sylvie's turbulence, years which felt to Isobel as though they would never end and sometimes made her wish for catharsis, Kit had adopted the same strategy he had applied to her shoe. At first she had thought it was cowardice but then she saw the wisdom in it. He would scoop up the schoolbag which had been flung against the wall and lain there for hours; he would give Sylvie a ride to whichever school she was in the process of being expelled from by the expedient of hovering near the door, selecting a scarf from the hat stand or lingering over the newspaper. At this time he began her love of art by taking her to exhibition openings and allowing her to dress in outlandish clothes. There was an orange scarf wound about red-dyed hair, an evening dress of Isobel's of faded wine velvet with seams through which strained stitches showed. It was worn back to front, its tiny covered buttons falling from a deep V. Glances and sneers were directed at Sylvie but Kit knew they were uncertain: similar colours were on the walls. 'Go up close,' he said to Sylvie, for most of the guests were assembled in the middle, sipping delicately from their glasses, though a few men were quaffing near the drinks table. Soon Sylvie had a little crowd of men around her. Her eyes caught Kit's over their heads and he winked. She was in perfect safety. The following morning Isobel, heart-heavy, would walk up the driveway that led to the headmistress's office and plead for a stay of execution.

Kit was right. After a dozen or so gallery openings in outlandish clothes Sylvie did quieten slightly. Her attendance at school improved to three days a week. Sometimes, in the lunch hour, she read a book. At night, when sleep didn't come, she still climbed out the window. Here too Kit found a solution. He didn't follow her as Isobel would—they had nights of being on duty—but he was determined to spare Isobel. He pretended to an equal restlessness, said it was hereditary—he invented a line of insomniacs—and took Sylvie night walking. He taught her to observe the shades of grey the night brought forth, the movements of cats—gangs of them seemed to gather, their night eyes flashing. The sounds that were suddenly accessible, especially the sound of water which was sudden and loud. She protested violently at first; she never discussed her plans and whether anyone was waiting for her. Even this was solvable, for Kit discovered an all-night greasy spoon and they sat in a booth drinking coffee and sharing a plate of greasy chips.

The cook, enormously fat, in a stained apron tied under his great paunch, glared at them from small piggy eyes, his cheeks flushed. The plate of chips was slammed down on the counter and the sauce bottle thrust forward. Kit's manner, as always, was calm and polite. He acted as if the chips were foie gras and the stained Formica a fine tablecloth. Secretly he was wondering how much a human stomach could stand; he was bound to suffer and must remember to take some dyspepsia tablets when he got home.

Sylvie moved a hot chip around on the plate and nibbled the end of it. The salty heat burned her throat and then warmed her as if she had suddenly put on an extra layer of clothes. The cook was now breaking eggs into fat of dubious provenance; the edges frilled up instantly in protest. Then Sylvie and her grandfather were out in the pre-dawn air. Kit murmured a polite 'Thank you' in the doorway and there was a sound like a grunt. On the way home Kit introduced the game of inventing a life. They had played it when Sylvie was at primary school and amenable. They had done the life (sad) of the class bully, the teacher who incessantly cleared his throat (a mystery illness), the class pet (longing for acceptance). As always Sylvie was reluctant to join in and Kit, feeling the beginning of gas in his stomach, had to check his impatience. But two streets later and the life of the cook was taking shape. He was divorced (naturally) and bitter that his wife (thin as a whippet) had run off with a waiter. Kit thought it should be a long-distance truck driver. He was remembering the cleavers on the wall, the cast-iron skillets. There was no one to wash the man's aprons, no one to bring to his attention the rancidness of the oil. He was pugnacious and had beaten someone in a fight.

'Children, do you think?' Kit asked as they turned into their street. Isobel's bed lamp was on but they saw it quickly extinguished. And when Kit came into the room she was lying flat on her back like an effigy on a tomb.

Sylvie was determined to avoid her mother. Why, having finally secured a husband, must she leave him? And why, having no contact with her own mother, must she suddenly be there to nurse her? Once they had almost met when Madeleine had delayed her leaving to look at a book with Kit. Sylvie was approaching and just in time Madeleine turned and walked away. She was used to tact; it had made her an inept saleswoman in Le Livre Bleu.

Now, walking swiftly away in the opposite direction, the one that would take her further from the nearest bus stop, Madeleine knew only that she must avoid confrontation. She did not think of herself but her mother to whom she owed an unpayable debt. The longer walk did not matter and indeed she passed a taxi rank, which was useful to know. Freddy was planning a visit; he did not intend to see her parents; they would meet privately. Madeleine had not mentioned this, even to her father. But she hoped the second bold action she had taken in her life—the first was going to France and not returning—might have left some trace in her manner.

Sylvie stormed through the front door, banging it, and was reprimanded by Kit.

'I thought you were going to keep her away,' she shouted. Then, as quickly, she lowered her voice and looked ashamed.

'Don't expect me to play God,' her grandfather said. 'Play him yourself.'

He knew Isobel had not slept well but he could hardly ban Sylvie from seeing her. That time would come and he told himself he would be firm.

'Wait a while,' he said to Sylvie. 'I'll go first.'

Isobel was awake, but she made a signal with her hand. She held up five fingers which meant a short visit he was to interrupt. Sylvie, of course, would always try to stretch it to ten or quarter of an hour. Her privileged status was at stake. That evening there was another appointment with Dr Franklin, and Isobel would need her strength to prepare herself.

··❧ ❧··

Freddy visited, and Madeleine met him not on neutral ground as she had expected but in a lawyer's office in a courtyard with restaurants and fashionable shops. Since she had left Melbourne Freddy had had time to evaluate things. His sense of betrayal had grown, and at one of the first enquiries about her absence he had stumbled and replied in a way that showed he had been left. It occurred only once, he saw to that, but the explanation—her mother's health, Madeleine's desire to be part of the nursing—was unconvincing even if it was true. Hence the lawyer's office and the desire for a speedy settlement. However, he had not counted on Kit. Madeleine would succumb to any will stronger than her own—there were millions of such people, it was not a personal flaw, simply the way the world operated with small acts of kindness and cowardice. Now, as Madeleine approached the office, Kit rose from the pavement seat he was sitting at, pushing his coffee cup aside. They climbed the stairs together and he held her elbow gently in his big palm.

Freddy was waiting and Kit caught the flash of annoyance on his face as he rose to his feet. Madeleine moved towards him, as if on a string, and Kit saw the expression reined in, but the reflex was not as it had been; there was a separation coming between an underpinning emotion and the charm that was meant to cover it.

Nothing was decided on that day, although this had been the intention. Kit saw the charm slide further on Freddy's face as another meeting was proposed and documents exchanged. He placed his hand in the small of Madeleine's back as they left the room. Then a mischievous idea came to him: they could watch Freddy exit from the large patio opposite, filled with tables and chairs, potted palms and busy waiters.

'Should we have a newspaper?' Madeleine asked, but there was the menu, black with white writing, that could be held up. A look of fun passed between them. Her humour had always been shy, delicate, to do with small things.

Freddy emerged just as their coffee was being brought; the waiter provided a screen. Over his shoulder, Madeleine saw a downcast look as Freddy turned and walked away towards High Street. In earlier times he might have stopped to look in a boutique window or to admire a display of lingerie, gifts that he found useful to have on hand. Now she wondered what they concealed, those gifts of silk and perfume that were intended to cover her skin and to soothe it with their scents and smoothness.

She drank two cups of coffee and realised she was shaking. The sight of someone she had slept beside, who had presented her, on the day of their marriage, with a black silk negligée in an elaborate box. Clearly he felt wronged, though it was she who had received the anonymous letter saying *Your husband is seeing another woman.* A woman's hand, she thought, sprawling and bold, perhaps impulsive. The envelope had been typed and the card—it was a card, not a letter—showed an overblown rose.

Her father showed no inclination to move and she sat on beside him, imagining they could stay there all day. They could order lunch when the surrounding offices emptied and all the tables were taken by young professionals in suits. Then they could have afternoon tea or coffee and retire to one of the nearby bars to sample the tapas spread out on the counter. They could walk home together through the theatre-going crowds, past the doors of the Aotea Centre or a little experimental theatre with programme sellers in costume in the foyer. Instead they walked to the parking building and wandered about looking for the correct floor.

'What shall I do?' Madeleine asked Kit.

'Why do anything?' he said, negotiating a roundabout.

She had never been able to put her life in order, for she had never seen herself as the centre of it. Even the years spent with the Lévêque family had been an attempt at assimilation. She had hoped they would never come to an end, that her faltering mastery of French conversation would mean the invitation to stay another year would be endlessly extended. The Lévêques had seen her as English, backward and innocent. Their own daughters were models of practicality: each year was planned in advance and if the outline was not quite realised the plan was simply modified.

Kit thought that provided Madeleine had enough to live on she might do some charity work, perhaps at a hospice, or take art classes. There were film festivals and music recitals, opera lovers who met at private houses and were entertained by one or two of the stars of the opera that was being performed. He had seen photographs of some of the opera lovers and didn't think they looked promising, but the setting, summer gardens or hot soup and toddies by an open fire in winter, could make up for it.

'What will you do this afternoon?' he asked when they were home. Obviously he wanted time alone.

'I will go to the library,' she said. She thought there was an author reading.

'Let me know the minute you hear anything,' Kit said. He knew his tone was faintly dismissive and tired. Still he wrapped his arms around her and stroked her hair. At least her taste in perfume was good. It wafted towards him: *Boucheron* with its underpinning sense of coping and cheer.

··𝕤 𝕖··

Phoebe Vanderbilt walked slowly along the footpath that bordered the highway. It was soon apparent that she was very unfit. In her home and at St Dymphna's she walked briskly, telling herself it was exercise. However, a long walk was beyond her. She needed to think and it was hard to think while her breath was ragged. At one point she stopped to consider an idea: if she left a sign her pursuers might go in the wrong direction. She fumbled in her handbag and took out a handkerchief. It was initialled in one corner. When her breathing was calm again, she retraced her steps, looking for a place to leave it. Not caught in tree branches, because someone might not look up; they would be hurrying, looking for clues on the ground. She blew her nose on the handkerchief and crumpled it in her fingers. Quickly she left it near the base of a pohutukawa tree, resting between the roots. Then she walked swiftly back in the direction she had come. Her breathing was exactly as it had been before.

A van was pulling in beside her and the head of a young man peered out.

'Are you all right, missus?' he asked. A tattooed arm—some kind of snake—came through the passenger window.

'I need a lift,' Phoebe said, moving towards the snake, her knees trembling. 'If you would be so kind . . .'

He came around the back of the van to open the door for her, held her arm as she climbed aboard.

Now, when she needed her handkerchief, it was gone. There was a box of tissues on the dashboard.

'May I?' she asked.

'Help yourself, doll.'

The next five kilometres were in silence.

Furtively Phoebe looked at herself in the little hand mirror in her purse. Wrinkled eyes and smudged cheeks looked back, but she was used to that. They did not seem worse than usual.

'Alice Bowerman,' she said at last, giving a third false name, her grandmother's maiden name.

'Jake Reynolds,' the young man replied, lifting the snake arm from the steering wheel and offering a left-handed handshake. A southpaw, Alice thought, pleased she could remember the word.

Then they hardly spoke. Alice watched the white line. Each stripe as it disappeared under the wheels gave her pleasure. She thought of her white handkerchief under the tree. It might already have been found. She imagined it being held to the muzzle of a sniffer dog, the lace brushing against its fur. It might be bewildered by her backtracking.

And then she was lost in a cloud of fumes. That was her one complaint about the van: it smoked rather a lot. She settled back against the vinyl seat and allowed herself to relax. And since it was her grandmother whose name she was resurrecting she imagined her too. She was reputed to have a sense of fun and played the violin.

Cora Taverner, Phoebe Vanderbilt, latterly Alice Bowerman was right in assuming she was missed. The superintendent was notified and the bathrooms and toilets checked; Phoebe had obviously dressed, because her nightgown was under her

279

pillow, but her clothes still hung in her wardrobe. The breakfast shift was beginning; there were trays to be carried and first medications. No one followed the path to the road, and the handkerchief lay under the pohutukawa tree where it was soon spotted with pollen.

Thousands of white centre markings passed under the tyres of the Volkswagen Kombi, and Alice Bowerman was feeling almost comfortable. Jake might be receptive to her advice. He was taking a load of paintings on velvet to a craft market. Dusky maidens, guitars, roses, cats and dogs, tigers, their lushness increased by the rich material that provided the background. Alice thought he must have an undeveloped taste, one that she could perhaps correct. This might take time, she realised, and their acquaintance was likely to be short.

'A tiger sounds almost too rich,' she said. She was careful to keep her tone encouraging as if the richness was her fault or a fault in the buyer.

'It's the best seller,' he said. It was also the easiest to do because no one questioned the patterning of the tiger's coat if he got it wrong.

'Could I come as far as the market with you?' Alice asked. She could examine the market stalls and then sit at a table and have a cup of coffee while she thought of her next move. She would not go back to the clinic. But first she needed somewhere to stay where she could attend to her appearance, for she was in no doubt appearance would play a large part. It would be almost as important as the tiger's stripes on velvet. She might use a fourth name—her father's grandmother's maiden name this time—to cover her tracks. In her purse her fingers touched the hard and consoling edges of her Visa. She always paid it on time and was rewarded by having a high limit. She thought it was ten thousand dollars.

··✤· ·✤··

Dr Franklin walked Isobel to the door in the customary fashion and the hand rested again on her shoulder. A shower had dampened the pavement and the doctor looked at her with concern. But Isobel longed for it to rain heavily, once the doctor had gone inside, so she could be drenched before she got to the car. The primitive pleasures she had missed or guarded herself from were returning to haunt her. She had been forbidden by her mother to lie in wet grass, damp clothes must be changed; now she wished she was sewn into her clothes and soaked to the skin.

The few steps to the car took longer than usual but her legs were still steady and Kit was standing by the passenger door. 'The next time it rains,' Isobel said, 'I'm going out in it. Don't try to stop me.'

'I'll bring an umbrella,' he said, starting the engine.

'Just you dare,' she said.

The flesh is weak, she said to herself as they drove along the familiar streets. But the spirit felt raging. She felt as if she could tear the car apart with her hands, walk through walls.

Kit was thinking he must bear all this; he might even have to hose Isobel while she stood in the back garden, out of sight of the neighbours. He turned so he could see her profile. The subtle changes in her face were most discernible when she turned her head. The look was stern, older than her years. The skin was tightening. Bred in the bone, he told himself. *What's bred in the bone will come out in the flesh*. But Isobel's flesh had been so sweet. No pendulous arms, no dewlaps, no turning into the Woman of Willendorf. Of course he had not known her as a child when her skin would have been smoother still and in the care of her mother. Her mother had guarded it until the day the heavy door of the lecture hall met her heel and he had taken possession, holding her shoe in his hand and then handing it back. What a beautiful word 'cobbler' was, he had thought as they walked to the little hole in the wall where a cheerful Italian face looked out and exclaimed *Nessun problema!* She had not, of course, allowed him to see this flesh except in stages. He knew it was not her inclination—the reason she now wanted to stand out in the rain, preferably a thunderstorm—but the custom of the times.

'Wet grass,' she said, turning to him. 'What possible harm could there have been? All those absurd stories about damaged kidneys and becoming infertile.'

Someone had bled through a mattress: the story had gone around her mother's afternoon-tea circle, that coven of silk-clad witches. Isobel, sometimes invited to pass cups and hand the cake stand to one of the witches in the interests of honing her table manners, tried to block her ears when someone's gynaecological symptoms or a banned book which one of the group was circulating in a plain cover were discussed. Still she did steel herself to look at the flesh on display and to marvel at the effort each put into keeping it up. Beneath the silk strong support was called for, an armour overlaid with softness. In her opinion it was a honey trap and it was no wonder their husbands seemed bewildered. On the day of the mattress story she longed to go and lie on a grassy bank soaked with rain and then dew. And on her third date with Kit, perhaps with this bank in mind, she had flung off her clothes in his room, surprising and delighting him at the same time.

There would come a time when Dr Franklin would visit. Later there might be the hospice. In the meantime there were Sylvie and Madeleine. Never before had the necessity of living day by day, hour by hour, been clearer. She was on a tightrope and each step was a separate entity. The steps before her stretched out along the nearly invisible wire; the steps behind her promised nothing except they need not be taken again. She thought she knew what funambulists faced. The roar of the crowd and the roar of the falls might cancel one another out. Both were far below, the water curving and falling, the crowd half-waiting on disaster so they could say they had been there, they had seen the body shudder, try to right itself and fall. Live in the moment, Isobel thought that evening as she pulled off her hat—the habit of hiding her face had solidified in mere weeks—and Kit helped her out of her coat. Then before she could protest he led her to the centre of the round rug on the library floor where they had often danced a slow waltz and hummed in each other's ears. He held her loosely against him and then, though he was careful to watch for signs of distress, he pressed her as tightly to him as he dared.

With a new scarf around her head, Cora-Phoebe-Alice was admiring a display of fruit and flowers at the Artisans' Fair. She could not purchase any, of course, because she had no transport but she stroked the skin of a dark-red apple with a forefinger and spoke admiringly of the quality of the produce to the stallholder. In return he cut her a small stem of pale-green grapes. She exclaimed at their sweetness and smiled back at him. A plan was taking place in her mind. She would phone her doctor first. She would talk seriously and firmly, suggest there had been some kind of catharsis, like a person waking from an induced coma. She knew the doctor would take a good deal of convincing. She might have to be examined by a panel. There would be paperwork. She would be sober, rational. But now she needed to go home.

'Do you know anyone who is driving back to Auckland?' she asked the man who had given her the grapes. 'Is there a bus?'

He looked at her shrewdly, as if summing her up. 'I can give you a lift at the end of the day,' he said. While he spoke his fingers inserted parsley in a gap between leeks and green capsicums.

'There is still a lot of the market to see,' Cora said. 'I could come back if you would be so kind . . .'

He could drop me at a taxi stand, she thought. She fumbled in her purse and pulled out some of the loose change.

'Let me at least buy this apple,' she said.

Ben's reaction to the news his mother was missing from St Dymphna's was to bury his face in his hands as he sat at his desk. This attracted no particular attention. The firm had a big contract on. It had been hard-won and only now were the fishhooks apparent. The marketing department, aggrieved that they were not continually praised, had retreated into sulks. There were endless meetings to discuss strategy. As Ben rubbed his brow he seemed to be rubbing away not just his worries about his mother but the triumphant night when they had gathered in the first-floor bar of the latest in-hotel and drunk champagne until the barman threw them out.

He called Sylvie from the safety of the washroom. While he waited with the tap running, he looked at his face in the mirror.

Sylvie answered and sounded abrupt. Quickly he turned off the tap.

'What do you expect me to do?' she asked. 'Surely they'll be searching for her by now?'

'Could you go out there and take a look around? Without saying who you are.' He knew it was her free afternoon.

She caught the weariness in his voice and held back the harsh words she wanted to say. She owed her mother-in-law nothing; she had long ago decided to have no more contact with her.

'You'll owe me,' she said, and now her voice sounded lighter. He would never know the effort it took. He would owe her for that too.

The 'better' in marriage is often in small things, Isobel had told her once. The holding back of a harsh word, the gesture of making a meal despite being exhausted. A tiny gesture that, beginning almost in despair, brought a renewed energy. Sylvie tried it a few times in the flat above Ma's Fruit & Veg. There was one memory—just one—which she held on to, like a sampler over a bedhead saying *Home Sweet Home*. She had roused herself at the end of a horrid day to cook Ben a special meal. She had run downstairs for the vegetables to eke out the meat. As she chopped and diced she felt energised again. It was almost like the feeling of being in love. And Ben, coming along the street, had been assailed by cooking smells and a white magnolia which was in bloom, and could hardly believe it was for him.

'Darling Sylvie,' Isobel had said once. It was years before the diagnosis. 'This is something I've found useful. Take a good memory of yourself and hold it to your heart. Pull it out when you need it, as a reminder.' She had these memories herself, though they were not so much memories as cameos, little film scenes. A few from childhood, a few from the early days of marriage. Herself at her best, or the best she could be at the time. They were not just comforting but useful. They were a shield. Sylvie remembered this as she drove. She did not expect the day to be part of anything she would wish to remember or in which she would play a starring role.

She drove to St Dymphna's and parked in the visitors' car park. Unsure which of the long buildings to enter, she walked about, looking for an office. She found it discreetly tucked away along a corridor. There was no one inside, so Sylvie pressed the bell and waited. Eventually a dumpy woman in a blue smock appeared.

'I'm looking for Cora Taverner. I'm a relative,' Sylvie said.

The computer was consulted and then the phone was picked up.

'Taverner,' Sylvie repeated. She could not imagine Cora being unknown. She had expected a grimace to appear, quickly masked.

'I'll get someone,' the woman said, and Sylvie could see she was pleased to get away.

'We have no one of that name,' the matron told her. 'How

did you get the impression she was in here?'

'Someone mentioned it,' Sylvie said. 'Perhaps they were mistaken.'

'Is there a problem with this Mrs Taverner?'

'Not that I am aware of. Unless people come in here because of problems?'

Dislike flared between them for a moment. She would give a good injection, Sylvie thought, though I wouldn't like to be on the receiving end. Still she didn't want to draw attention to herself in case there were developments.

'The information must have been wrong,' Sylvie said. 'I'm sorry for taking up your time.'

She could feel eyes on her back as she walked towards the entrance. She took care not to hurry, and raised her right hand to her hair to give the impression of someone puzzling over a piece of false information.

Then there was nothing to do but drive. It hardly mattered in which direction. Sylvie did not care if she never saw her mother-in-law again. She had never deserved Cora's implacable dislike or known precisely on what it was based. Her rackety past? Three school expulsions? A headmistress at the same bridge club? It hadn't concerned her to be branded. It had allowed her to see straight through the formidable matron who might at this moment be phoning security to check her car registration.

In the meantime it was pleasant to drive. She drove out into the country where gardens gave way to farmland. At the last house cows were grazing in a field; several had their noses under a fence. She drove through a small town with a market on its outskirts. Another half hour, she told herself, and then she would turn back. The market looked interesting. She might stop.

Freddy Rice had returned to Melbourne with nothing finalised. A letter from a legal firm informed Madeleine that a settlement would be drawn up. She suspected her desertion would be taken into account; her attempts to be a good wife would not. Oddly, she was not sad; she had simply failed to fit into a role that someone had arranged for her without her volition. She had been like a paper doll, changing from morning to afternoon clothes, evening dresses. Now she felt some pity for Freddy because he at least had been faithful to his vision. She thought she would ask for an allowance to be paid into a bank account. Instead of selling the house he could replace her with another doll.

It would have puzzled Madeleine to know that Freddy himself was sad. Angry that his arrangements were in disarray but sad because he had found her passivity and natural good humour restful. He began to think of delaying procedures. Zsazsa, whom Madeleine had seen him with outside Myer, shocked by the unaccustomed animation of his face and gestures, had never been intended as a replacement.

Madeleine had moved from her parents' home shortly after her arrival. She had taken a small furnished apartment whose owners were overseas. It was not suitable that she should occupy the room that had originally been hers and now seemed to be regarded as Sylvie's. Surprising enmity seemed to have sprung up between them, despite flowers and messages. She was learning that the efforts we make for others are not only unappreciated, they are not even considered and provide a romance only for ourselves.

After an afternoon visit, Madeleine sometimes walked with Kit. They walked without speaking, both feeling drained. And upstairs Isobel felt drained as well, longing for silence. Sometimes, in their absence, which was never more than half an hour, Sylvie arrived. Kit returned and found her lying on the bed. Neither could guess at Isobel's agony, though her hand reached to touch Sylvie's arm. Sometimes she feigned sleep, wondering if her eyes would fly open at the end and someone would run their hand lightly over the lids to close them. Sometimes too her body had intimations of coldness, stiffness. But there was always something for her to concentrate on: Madeleine and her marriage, Sylvie and hers, Kit and what would become of him. The only true amusement was what had happened to Cora Taverner. An enemy, Isobel thought, turning on her aching side. An enemy, with all the astringency that implied, was worth having.

That afternoon when she had been sent in pursuit, Sylvie had pulled into the market car park in search of a rest room and a coffee. The market was emptying, which made moving between the stalls easier. There were portaloos at the back and Sylvie feared for a moment she might be trapped inside, but she emerged safely and went in search of a coffee. While she drank it at a table that wobbled on the bare earth she thought of what she would say to Ben. That without a clear sighting or some definite information she was bound to fail. She would say she had searched the market and questioned a few people; she would purchase something—some fruit or preserves—to prove it. And she would be sure to be home in time to cook a favourite meal with a bottle of wine. She was hardly aware of a woman observing her from the corner of a stall that sold earrings on little cards, long ropes of beads and wooden toys. Sylvie stood up and walked towards the fruit and vegetable stall, planning the meal. One quick circuit and then she would leave.

Cora Phoebe Alice—she was no longer sure which name she was using—had moved in the opposite direction, convinced Sylvie was leaving. She had not counted on the lure of falafel balls and organic limes. The stallholder called to her as she came around the corner. 'Not long now. Another half hour if you still want to wait.'

A silent, vigorous nod of the head, but Sylvie had turned. The strange figure in front of her, the familiar face, the enveloping unflattering scarf. For a moment they looked at one another in distaste. Cora raised a finger to her lips to entreat silence. Then she turned back to the stallholder and explained, 'A friend has turned up. But thanks for your offer.'

All the stalls were dismantled by the time the patrol car drove past an hour later. The lace handkerchief still lay near the trunk of the pohutukawa tree. There was no police dog in the car.

'A friend has arrived,' Sylvie mimicked as she drove home, Cora, at her insistence, in the back seat. 'Perhaps we need a new definition of the word. And that colour doesn't suit you.'

A deep laugh came from the back seat. A bark subsiding into a chuckle. Then came hiccups. Let her suffer, Sylvie thought. Heaven knows I've suffered enough at her hands. Perhaps she will die of thirst or choke.

There was a stray barley sugar, its wrapper covered in dust, in the glove box. Sylvie passed it over.

'I suppose you'd like to poison me,' Cora said. Then, when Sylvie did not respond, she said, 'Straight home. I've things to sort out.'

Already, in the back seat, she was reassembling herself. Her true name had come back and all it implied: bridge club, afternoon tea, the reading group that met each Thursday at Rapunzel's Books where the towering shelves surrounded them like a cloak. She realised how much she had missed them and her own incisive judgements which the others listened to with respect. Leaning back in the seat, she stretched her legs out and wiggled her toes. First of all she would kick off her shoes. They could fly up in the air and land where they liked. A deep hot bath, a strong gin and tonic. And then she would make plans. There would be phone calls; her voice would be measured, authoritative, as if she were discussing a new novel.

They drew up at the gate and Sylvie got out. Her mother-in-law got out more slowly. Her feet were swollen: the plan to kick off her shoes would have to be abandoned.

'Come in for a moment,' she said to her daughter-in-law.

Perhaps there will be an axe murderer lying in wait, Sylvie thought. She would close the door softly and leave him to it.

But there was only the curious abated smell of a house that had been empty. The dust which had gone on falling—dust had no conscience—stirred as if taking a breath. A petal fell off a rose in a vase in the hall. The phone began to ring, and they both jumped.

'Leave it,' Cora said. 'I want to gather myself first.'

'As long as it's just yourself,' Sylvie said, but her mother-in-law did not hear. She was pushing open doors, opening windows.

In the kitchen there was a coffee cup and spoon on the draining board. Ben, they both thought together. He had come looking for them. Suddenly Sylvie's heart filled with pity, as if they had both tried to tear him apart.

'You should have come to the wedding,' Sylvie said. 'Then all of this wouldn't have started.'

'I suppose you would have liked me in a boat on the lake. You could have pushed me overboard.'

Now it was Sylvie's turn to laugh. She thought of the swan that had approached and attempted to rake the side of the boat with its beak. Kit had poked at it with the oar and it had sailed off, its hateful red eye still glaring. Tears ran down her face and she laughed until she choked.

And that was how they reconciled: over two glasses of water.

Instead of the legal papers she was expecting and which she would have taken to her father, Madeleine received a handwritten letter and a cheque. Perhaps cynicism was coming late to her, for she was more interested in the familiar handwriting than the carefully worded sentences. She saw Freddy signing the cheque with a flowing hand, the Montblanc pen sliding along the lines and ending with a flourish at the signature: a man accustomed, as he was in his heyday, to signing piles of correspondence brought by a secretary. She looked at the signature and it seemed nervous, less confident. He must have known that she would show anything to her father; boldness and caution had warred in the phrases. *I miss you. Any other arrangements in my life are now permanently over.*

Yes, you were selfish, Madeleine thought. You thought selfishness was a virtue. Tending to yourself and having others share some of the burden. No thought of the sight of yourself dining with another woman, bending over the table towards her, urging her to choose the most expensive dish on the menu.

She folded the letter in half and put it in the folder where she kept her passport and other documents. The letter meant that, until she replied or came to a decision, her clothes would not be sent on, she would still wear her father's old plaid dressing gown which he had insisted she take. She lifted it from the end of the bed now and drew the sleeves together, matching seam to seam. She hung it over the back of the chair where the plaid was incongruous against blue velvet. Then she picked it up again and buried her nose in it, trying to distinguish its scents. Her father, certainly: the scent of his skin, though he was fastidiously clean. As a child when she had come into the bedroom to wake him she often found the hair at the back of his neck damp from the shower. He liked to wake and shower very early. She slipped her small hand under his neck. 'Yes, Madeleine,' he would say. 'A massage would be very good.' She had no idea what a massage was, but she pressed her fingers into his neck until he sat up and ruffled her hair. 'Let's get breakfast for Isobel.'

Wisdom, Madeleine. This old dressing gown smells of wisdom. Of soap and an open window to let the steam out. Of a body eased back into bed. An arm drawing another body close or simply lying in the curve of a warm sleeping back.

Tonight she would examine the letter again.

'You know best,' her father had said. Provided you use all your senses, he meant. Gather all the evidence: the words, but the hesitation of a Montblanc pen as well. And between the words were concealments, the words not spoken. Words too had spokesmen, Madeleine thought. The best words, the best sentence came forward, and the rest stayed in the background. She closed her eyes for a moment and she was back in Le Livre Bleu. Madame Récamier was boiling water on a gas ring for their mid-morning coffee. It was a wonder the curtain that closed off the alcove did not catch fire, it was so close. Why did the scent of coffee suddenly attract a little rush of customers so both she and Madame always had to wait?

That afternoon Madeleine did not go to her mother. It was Isobel's greatest wish to have time alone, but Madeleine was the only one she told this to, as if there was an advantage in hesitancy, an extra sensitivity. Instead there would be Sylvie, hovering. Sylvie bursting with the news that once things had been sorted out with doctors and lawyers Cora was longing to visit. Madeleine went to the cinema, sitting in an aisle seat so she could creep away under cover of darkness. The movie, with subtitles and Gerard Depardieu, was sentimental and yet there was an underlying rigour, almost a brutality. A bitter quarrel between a mother and son took place among the bean rows in a garden. The ending, as so often happened, was a car drive through a vista of manicured fields.

She came out and walked slowly towards the bus stop. She looked in a few dress shops, playing the game she had played with Isobel when she was a child. 'What would you choose?' Isobel would ask, and Madeleine had pressed her nose against the glass and tried to decide which toy, which book was best.

Once she had pointed to a Venetian mask, a cheap touristy thing, with dangling ribbons attached to each earlobe. She had carried it triumphantly home and held it up to her face in front of the mirror. A sinister mocking face—the mask smiled— looked back at her. It was the dress mirror in Isobel's room, and her chubby legs in their white ankle socks looked incongruous.

Could she be independent again? Choose for herself? Live within constraints? Or go back to security that required efforts of her own? These efforts were largely passive but they were efforts nonetheless.

She was becoming bolder, though. Without hesitating, she went into one of the boutiques and bought a long cardigan. It was synthetic, and woven through the fabric was a glittering thread.

Sylvie and Ben sat in his mother's dining room. At a single place setting on the table that could seat ten were the remains of a meal. A quilted placemat, a crumpled napkin, and a wine glass with a lipstick stain. How many glasses, Ben wondered, for his mother was drinking again.

Over the ruthlessness he had known since childhood was a hectic gaiety.

'When?' she was asking Sylvie. 'When can I visit?'

But Sylvie was being evasive. She could not know how much her grandmother hated the idea of closure, had hated this woman, hated even more that weakness should overthrow the judgements she might have made in health. 'I'll enquire,' Sylvie said.

Cora was fetching another bottle of wine. She had been welcomed back into the bridge club. A dashing story had been made of her escape. She would send a cheque to St Dymphna's clinic. She might enquire about endowing a seat with a plaque for the grounds. Sylvie had rescued her; the young man in the van had become the hero of a romance. Much was made of the handkerchief thrown down as a decoy.

Sylvie recognised the energy; she had felt it herself. She was not yet old enough for it to leave exhaustion in its wake, though there were hints. She glanced at Ben and shrugged her shoulders slightly. He took the signal and got up.

'Bed,' he said to his mother. 'A good sleep. Take something if you need it.'

'I have, darling. I have,' she said, and he thought she meant the wine. 'I took a sleeping pill before you arrived.'

'Then you must hurry. Sylvie will clear the table.'

So Sylvie had washed the wine glass, the plate and cutlery, the bowl and whisk with which Cora had made scrambled eggs. Her pity was fading. She squashed the egg shells with the flat of her hand.

Ben came downstairs and they crept out of the house, closing the door softly. 'She used to creep out of my room like this,' he said. 'I used to watch her. I practised walking backwards like her. It's not as easy as you think.'

They tried it when they got home. Any ruse so he will sleep, Sylvie thought. She felt she loved him more than ever. She made him go first. For a while he kept to an imaginary line, then he collided with the wall. 'Imagine I'm Queen Victoria,' Sylvie instructed. But when her turn came she was worse. Five steps and she struck her hip against the hall table.

'Perhaps they practised,' Sylvie said, as they undressed on either side of the bed.

'Who?' he asked, his clothes dropping from his hands.

'Disraeli, probably. He was a favourite. Perhaps he could scoot backwards like a monkey.'

'Can monkeys go backwards?' he asked.

Then he was asleep, fallen into blissful oblivion.

The frames have always interested me as much as the paintings, Kit said to Madeleine the next time they were walking around the Auckland Art Gallery. Surely he would succeed with either his daughter or his granddaughter. He doubted that the love of art compensated for the tragedies of life: the elaborate gold frames seemed to suggest a good dose of money was required. When an anguished face or an event met their eyes the frame offered confinement, a consolation of sorts. It was like Dr Franklin's surgery: the walls closing around a tragic prognosis. He had noticed the white petunias in the narrow bed under the surgery window seemed to be struggling as if X-ray results, blood tests, pulses and temperatures reached that far.

They were standing in front of a painting of a young girl in her bed. Her face had a greenish tinge. There was no School of Illness that he knew of, though there would have been enough adherents. An attendant stood by a small window; a jug and ewer was on a table, along with medicine bottles.

'Let's find something else,' Madeleine said, pulling at his arm. 'Landscapes, abstracts.'

If Madeleine returned to Melbourne there would be the

magnificent National Gallery of Victoria. She might become a Friend of the Gallery, a serious supporter. There would be lectures and meetings. He thought of Willem de Kooning's *Standing Figure* in the sculpture garden where the grass was cut at different lengths and made a pattern. Nearby, Balzac had his nose in the air and his dressing gown wrapped around his body that Rodin had surely elongated.

Now they were walking past watercolours. The frames were lighter and the works had an airy accomplishment; perhaps Madeleine could take a class. Kit suspected they required a good deal of thought, an examination of layers and the order in which they should be applied. One of his favourite words came into his head: *water meadow*. He doubted he would recognise one if he saw it: he imagined a surface that was lush and deceptive, waving grasses and reeds and, underfoot, water that rose through the soil at each step.

He longed to ask Madeleine her thoughts. She was so quiet. But it was restful too, while he talked about frames which, privately, he thought most straitened artists would hock for food or wine. Of course the frames came later, centuries later in some cases; they were more a comment on patronage or the use of public funds than art itself.

They sat outside and Kit suggested a glass of white wine.

'Isn't it too early?' Madeleine asked.

'What does too early mean? I think if I could start life again from the first breath I'd never stop running. I'd go without sleep . . .'

'Don't,' she said, placing her hand over his. He looked down at it and then ran his thumb over the soft skin under her index finger. There were two little liver spots, nothing more.

The wine came, a light riesling from Alsace.

'You'll be able to drive?' Madeleine said.

'Of course. But I think we should have a cake as well.'

When two little friands were gone, and two coffees, they walked in the gardens for half an hour. I shall remember this always, Madeleine thought. Whatever happens. It was not just a fancy; she had selected this image as it was occurring: the tall figure beside her, the silence between them, the sound of small shifting stones their feet made in the gravel. 'The world is nothing without images,' one of the authors Madame Récamier had invited to the bookshop had said. A reverent crowd had stood in the aisles between the book tables. Apéritifs had been passed around, dishes of olives. Afterwards a passionate argument had taken place: the writer had been challenged to explain how those without images lived. Madame had been very pleased by the evening, though she had not repeated it for months.

Remember, remember, remember, Madeleine said to herself as they came to the gates. It had been the best day in ages.

Spring was arriving. For Isobel it had always been a game to detect the greening of the trees in the park, particularly the oaks. When the first signs appeared, though 'appeared' was too strong a word, 'intimation' came closer, she would walk each day to gaze at their swift yet almost imperceptible visibility, the unfurling of tiny wing-like leaves that would eventually become an imposing canopy. At first a hint of greenness hung about the tree like the lightest watercolour wash. A shower could obliterate it or sunlight bleach it out. Now it would have to be imagined. Strangely this did not make her sad. So many memories were surfacing and joining up: in the periods she was free from pain they came, insistently, clamouring to be re-examined. Isobel thought that, unknown to her, they had consolidated so all the weather in which she had watched the leaves, sun and storm, lashing or light winds, was combined in a triumphant flurry of green.

Kit would find some consolation in art, Isobel thought, when her attempt at consolidating the oaks was over and other thoughts intruded. He would take Sylvie and Madeleine to look at paintings; he might ask them to choose a favourite. And which would he stand in front of to remember her? Not a portrait. Perhaps it would be his favourite Hitchens with its bold sweeps that needed no human presence to sing. A wide painting suggesting a continuum and also, though the strokes were light and bold, a solidity underneath. The Hitchens had a plain oak frame, refreshing after all the gilt.

Kit came and stopped in the doorway. Isobel looked at him in annoyance. Even now she was expected to provide signals. Then, in an access of pity, she recognised his fear. His longings were as complicated as hers: he needed an overview, he needed to hold her in his mind. She thought he was seeking similar images for himself: Isobel from the doorway, Isobel closer up, Isobel when we first met. And how could any of them hold against the flow of time—perhaps his reason for liking the Hitchens with its sweeping strokes like the movement of a pendulum. She knew he had been making arrangements for a nurse who would stay overnight. She put out her hand and patted the space beside her, and he bent and took off his shoes.

'Dr Franklin has found someone,' he said, taking her hand and stroking each of the fingers. 'Someone quite old and experienced. I would have preferred someone young.'

'Young and bustling,' Isobel said. 'In a uniform that is slightly too tight.'

'How well you know me,' he said, turning aside his head as if he was examining the books on the bedside table.

'That's good,' she said. 'It's one of the best things.'

Then, because their speech was beginning to resemble a child's primer, they stopped talking. In her head Isobel's questions went on: What had been her allotment of words? Had she used them up? Would—more frightening—they be winnowed for meaning and import? She remembered a woman, a stranger, coming up to her in the street and repeating to her something she had said and thanking her for it.

'I'm sure it was nothing,' Isobel had said, but the woman refused to be deflected. 'It meant everything to me,' she insisted, before hurrying away.

Now, with Kit beside her, Isobel fell asleep. Her body ached but it ached more to move so she seemed to sink more deeply into the mattress. Sleep surrounded her, like Kit's stroking of her fingers; it drew an outline like the outline of a body in one of the hundreds of thrillers she had read. Absurd thrillers where the furnishings of the room were described before the feet were sighted sticking out behind a desk or the body slumped in a chair with a dagger protruding from its chest. Far away she felt the touch of Kit's hand—he was running his finger up and down her middle finger, which was glowing like the index finger of E.T.

Kit was thinking about the nurse, wondering if he could

ask for someone younger. He meant fresher. But the next morning when Rosemary Summers RN arrived for a visit he was reassured. She was thin and bony but her eyes were bright and, if it hadn't been inappropriate, he would have said merry. He guessed she was experienced in many fields.

After she was introduced to Isobel, he offered her coffee and they sat in the kitchen together. She did not discuss Isobel and he appreciated her tactfulness. Instead she asked questions about himself. His career, how he spent his retirement. It turned out they had been at university together; they might have passed on a path between lectures, though her subject had been biology. She had wanted to be a doctor but money was not available.

When she had gone Kit bounded up the stairs again. He felt lighter than he had for weeks. Thin bony Nurse Rosemary would be more than a match for what was to come.

Madeleine had not replied to Freddy's letter, nor to a follow-up letter from his lawyer, suggesting negotiations be postponed until further instruction. For the first time in her life she was becoming aware of the power of not acting. It was what she had always done: with the Lévêques; the return home, followed by the return to France; the bookshop. Now she had the leisure to examine her behaviour. She thought of love and the warnings her mother had perhaps intended the Colette novels to convey. Had Isobel wanted a Claudine who had the wit to surrender to an older man as if she was bestowing a favour? Or an Annie who carried a revolver? She thought the great disadvantage of being a woman was this need of love; in men, the ultimate disadvantage was to conceal it. For the first time, since Freddy had prevented the thought from arising, Madeleine clearly saw his dependency. Yet it had been his strategy to make her the grateful recipient, the one honoured by an attention measured out and punctuated by displays of reluctance on his part. He had concentrated on what he could offer: an apartment or a house, status, an occupation. Yet it was not an occupation as the bookshop had been. There it was necessary to dust the books, change the flowers when Madame had pruned the dead ones and rearranged the survivors. 'The cheapest' she always instructed Madeleine as she set off for the market behind Notre Dame.

It was on one of her return trips with a bunch of alstroemerias that Madeleine had gone inside the church. It was midday and a Mass was in progress in one of the side chapels. Around the edges tourists were passing, reading plaques, taking photos of the rose window. Madeleine was close to the little group of the faithful when a middle-aged woman knelt with outstretched arms and then placed her forehead against the stone floor. Behind her two women stepped forward, ready to raise her to her feet.

Madeleine walked through the nave and out through one of the great doors into the courtyard. It did not matter if she lingered because it was part of her lunch break. (Madame Récamier had suggested, since she was Anglo-Saxon, she might need only an hour while Madame took the customary two.) What was the woman praying for? she wondered as she navigated the cobblestones and tried to avoid a young gypsy girl with a handwritten sign. There had been such offering in the obeisance, such an emptying of something—was it the heart?—as if nothing could be received except in a vessel emptied and scoured. She was thinking of the old coffee pot behind the curtain, its base almost worn away by the heat from the gas ring. The face of the woman had been emptied as well, and as the hands of her supporters raised her up she seemed oblivious of the drama of her gesture.

Now Freddy had made a gesture, but it was of a different sort. Already he was sketching for her his way out, the changes he would require. And how long would the terms last? She rather thought there might be an element of revenge which would be released very slowly so she would hardly feel it, except in a prickling sense that she was failing.

Sylvie had found a bach by the sea. It sat on a little hill, a child's drawing of a hill. Behind it a gravel track ran through the grass; in front, beyond a small square of lawn, mowed a few times a year by its owner or a local schoolboy who sometimes forgot, diminishing ledges, increasingly invaded by sand, led to a narrow beach. An old sign, on which wind and salt had worked to obscure the lettering, warned against swimming. At high tide it was still possible to walk on the strip of sand; low tide meant five or six could walk side by side and only one had their feet in the water.

A track led down, steep in a few places, but posts had been placed at strategic spots; children ignored the track altogether and rolled down over the ridges. At the bottom a seat of hard burnished wood, iron legs and ornate scrollwork on the arms, surprisingly comfortable because its back sloped, had been bolted onto a railway sleeper. It was the one chore the owner insisted on every summer. No sooner had he arrived than a pot of varnish and a brush were produced, the seat was given a wipe-down and a new coat of shiny varnish.

Inside there was sand on the windowsills and the mantelpiece above the swept-out fireplace. The floor felt delicious under Sylvie's bare toes, as if she had opened a box of Turkish delight and blown on the icing sugar. Everything inside was second-hand: the beds from someone's childhood, one with a rabbit on the white headboard. The dresser had a frilled edge and part of a Willow Pattern set stacked in piles, for the wind would have set a display plate tumbling. Green-rimmed saucepans with worn enamel gouges rested upside down on newspaper under the sink. It was perfect. A cupboard held supplies of sheets, towels, pillows. Everything was comforting and soft as if the sea, without any visible touching, had produced a symbiotic wearing away. Blankets like clouds.

Kit had been doubtful about the project from the beginning but Sylvie, with all the fire and determination that Madeleine lacked, had convinced him of the holiness of last wishes. That Isobel asked for it less now was not a factor: it had been stated in advance as a request, at a time when requests could be made; it was nothing more than tact. Then there was Nurse Rosemary who was giving him confidence. A sort of Mary Poppins, despite appearances.

The owner was located and a flexible arrangement made. Two days, Kit thought, or a single night. A few hours' notification and instructions about the key. (In a tin buried under a hydrangea bush, marked by a stone.) A few feet away, as if someone had been interrupted at weeding, was a trowel.

A thief, Kit thought, when the trowel struck the stained lid of the tin, would have lifted only the stone. It was important to him that there be no frantic searches for keys, no need to phone the owner again. If Isobel was to come there must be ease and grace, as much as was humanly possible. Nurse Rosemary stood beside him, in the wind that rushed up the slope, her thin figure braced.

Inside they opened the windows and the front and back doors which made a funnel. The stale air dispersed and the scent of the sea flew in. Nurse Rosemary removed a bird's skeleton from behind the dresser. The idea, she thought, was foolish but must be humoured.

Madeleine, sitting beside her mother, wondered if she should talk to her. So often now Isobel seemed to be half-asleep. Should she introduce herself in case Isobel thought she was Sylvie or the nurse? Was a kind of confession required? A recital of regrets, sincere and brief, so any vanity was expunged. Then gratitude, then love. She thought of the concerts she had attended with Freddy, the sung Masses, the programme in her hands and glancing down at *Kyrie, Gloria, Agnus Dei*. Neither she nor Freddy was religious; she held his arm as they walked down the aisle of St Paul's Cathedral and Freddy nodded his head at acquaintances. Afterwards the programme went into a drawer with the programmes for musicals, cabarets, The Rolling Stones.

The one word Madeleine longed to say was 'Mother' but she could not think of the tone to say it in. Dying men said it on battlefields, young men who before they died and their bodies slipped underground reverted to childhood and the mother who would appear in answer to a call with a glass of water in her hand and a promise to leave the night light on.

The front door opened softly and there were voices. Nurse Rosemary appeared in the doorway, wearing her expression of calm. Despite the deep lines there was no overriding expression, no sourness or cynicism; the lines could have been a pattern like stripes on a tiger. Madeleine, getting to her feet, smiled, and Nurse Rosemary smiled back. An open face with distinguishing marks.

Before she left Madeleine bent over and kissed her mother's brow. Isobel's eyes fluttered open and for a second Madeleine thought she was not recognised, then a calm expression spread over Isobel's face and there was a word that sounded like 'Darling'.

All the way to the bus stop—she had turned down her father's offer of a ride—Madeleine said the word to herself. *Dar-ling. Dar-ling.* She felt she could have torn it to pieces, for it was a word her mother had never used until now. She rested her back against the bus seat and tears leaked down her cheeks. Every house the bus passed, every shop, every factory seemed to be saying *Darling*. And above them the clouds, the clear-washed blue of the sky. She half-expected a small aeroplane to appear, trailing a banner. Madeleine clenched her fists, but she had herself under control when the bus stopped.

The great irony was that when the visit was accomplished and Isobel was settled in her bed with its special mattress near the window, and the window open, the sea glinting in, the invigorating air filling the room and Sylvie walking about with bare toes, the irony was that Isobel was thinking of a lake. She was in a rowboat with Kit. She had swapped places with Sylvie, who stood patiently on the shore. She was wearing the wedding dress her mother's dressmaker had sewn for her, and the long veil that was tucked under her. The dress was a long sheath with leg-of-mutton sleeves and the material was ivory satin. There was a cushion under her, and the veil was trapped between the cushion and her buttocks. Beneath the satin was the pristine underwear bought from the shop that sold ready-made gowns. Her stomach was clenched, not just from fear of motion sickness—something she had not taken into account—but from a slight elastic pressure of the fabric. She expected, when she undressed, her stomach would be quite swollen. It was swollen now, when she reached a hand down to touch it.

'Derrière,' Isobel said, and Sylvie leaned over to catch the word. 'They used to always say "derrière".'

'Where?' Sylvie asked.

'The dying say strange things,' Nurse Rosemary had warned her. 'It's best not to take them as last words.'

But Sylvie's attention was acute.

'Where?' she asked again. Her mother should have been here to hear. But Madeleine thought she had a cold coming and had begged off.

'In the best shops,' Isobel said. She closed her eyes and was perched on a high stool, so high she would twist her ankle if she slipped.

'Derrière and bosom.'

Those were the two areas to be controlled. Before they were offered to a man. That evening it was Kit who had hung the dress on a hanger while she disappeared into the bathroom. She had looked down at her stomach, pink and striped where the panty girdle had left a mark. She took a towel from the railing and rubbed furiously at the stripe. Then she sat on the toilet seat for a while, running her hands through her hair which was flattened too and lacklustre.

All this was odd because Isobel and Kit had slept together on their third date. Isobel had acted like Claudine and given herself before she could be seduced. She had taken the initiative from which no lover could recoil. The little piles of clothes then had been undistinguished—cotton bra and knickers, a sweatshirt with the university crest and a straight denim skirt. She had thought of everything except getting back into them, turning her back and hoping Kit was still wrapped in the sheet. And Kit, as she had intended, had been amazed by the fierceness with which she had given herself. He still remembered it. Hiding her innocence, staking a claim on all the unexpressed passion that, through the years they were together, would be available as from an inexhaustible well.

He had seen the passion parcelled into many things: the attentive way she read and made lists of further reading from footnotes; the way she cooked with her recipe book balanced on a stand as though the assembly of eggs, flour, butter, spice was a kind of music. There had been an old book from a Benedictine monastery in Connecticut from which she had cooked casseroles and crumbles using cheap cuts of meat and windfall apples, and lectured him as long as her interest lasted. Things were perfected and then left, but not before the essence was extracted and stored. Only a week before her diagnosis the monks' cookbook had come out again and she had made oatcakes.

'As dry as accidie,' Kit had said, and she had looked at him with a flash of understanding.

'When have you ever experienced accidie?' she asked.

'At work, often,' he said. 'With you, never.'

'Liar.' But she was amused and the oatcakes had had to be served with berries and whipped cream. There was a limit, even to monks.

Her passion, apart from bed, turned out to be colour. It had evolved over the years and was always changing, adding touches and juxtapositions, finding new theories. It might be something as small as four books on a footstool. Kit could swear she arranged the colours there, though two were from a second-hand bookshop and two bore library markings. It was unconscious and yet something she checked on, adjusted. An awareness that a painting was in the wrong place or the bookcase looked better with some titles sloping like fainting guardsmen. She was a follower of 'the liquefaction of Julia's clothes', for curtains trailed over the edges of carpets, shawls embraced the backs of chairs, and petals at the base of flower vases were to be regarded in their falling.

Kit thought he had been guarded by instructions, now that Isobel lay pale and confined, her movements limited, her breathing light. The thought that he would have to continue to carry them out filled his heart with a pain that almost caused him to stagger. He thought he might tear down great swags of curtaining and bury his face in them, smearing them with tears and snot. Quickly he left the room and went outside. He sat on a garden seat with a distant view of the sea. Far out, on the horizon, a ship was passing. He tried to imagine the lives of the men on board, their longing, now the port was in sight, to be on land, passing the hours in time-honoured ways with cards and betting. In all the years Kit and John Cook had worked together at Beca Carter Hollings they had invented ways of being together. After days spent poring over plans and negotiating with clients, some of them almost certainly mad, he and John had been able to pass hours in near-silence. 'Drink?' Kit would say and John would nod. 'Another?' A glance at a watch and a shake of the head. It might have prepared him, Kit thought. But first would come a pain he felt he could hardly bear, a madness that he must take pains, with whatever energy he possessed, to conceal. He must let it out in very small measures so, if the relief was tiny, the edifice held. The body has wisdom, he told himself, as he turned his attention back to the sea as if observation on his part could decipher that endless, futile-seeming motion. Already he was embracing his daughter and granddaughter more. I'm in it for myself, he thought. I'm preparing a path.

Sylvie came up to him when he went inside again, stiff-limbed. He pulled her against him and stroked her hair.

Isobel was glad to be back in her room. Gladdest for the presence of Nurse Rosemary. So much seemed to have happened to Nurse Rosemary's body already. The thinning of flesh, the wrinkles that took up some of the slack, the deep lines where the skin might be expected to be smooth. A deep line across her forehead was like the cut of an axe. But Nurse Rosemary evidently did not see herself in this way. Isobel imagined a tease and a competitor with boys, her long legs carrying her over the playground or up into the branches of a tree. Now she moved soundlessly around the room, doing things not in a cringing tactful way that would have driven Isobel mad but with swift darts as if Isobel was being attacked by a thousand small irritants it was her responsibility to repel. Isobel was amused. The bed sheet was tightened by a swift tug of skinny fingers; a glass of water, half drunk, replaced. Expressions chased themselves over the worn face as Nurse Rosemary arranged the day's pills in a pattern. Isobel wondered who she would go to next.

'I never nurse children,' Nurse Rosemary said, as if reading her thought. 'Too many wrinkles. I come into my own at Halloween.'

'The kindest witch in the West,' Isobel said, smiling.

'Only the West? The North and South and East, I was hoping.'

'I'm very grateful to know you,' Isobel said.

'It doesn't take much,' the witch replied, striking her fist into a pillow that had dared deflate. 'Not for you or me.'

A harsh wind was shaking the garden. Petals were falling, and leaves and twigs. Kit wished Isobel, propped up on pillows, could be spared the sight, but she found it exhilarating. Wan-looking clouds as if at the back of the wind something like an old half-washed-out watercolour had been discovered. Isobel had always meant to paint watercolours when she was old. The pots of water, the cleanness of them, and the deliberation she imagined it took: all these appealed to her. Her subject would be flowers, giant carelessly observed flowers: a Christmas lily, hellebore, a dying rose. None would be observed in botanical detail or accuracy: as the water ran over the precious paper she would attempt to convey the emotions she felt when she looked into the petals of a camellia—like the dome of the Chrysler building—or the tenacity hidden in a frail viola. Kit would come in and she would set the brushes down or add a last swathe of water to take the flower back to its origins. Her grandmother had painted on panels of wood: English primrose, shasta daisy, bleeding heart. Isobel thought there was a Japanese influence in the way the flowers stretched from one side of the wood to the other. How, with her twelve children, had her grandmother found the time? There was a notebook of comments, written in a fine nib, showing a page could be arranged as well as a panel. Kit thought the panels might have come from an old wardrobe, the varnish too hardened to remove.

How many days, Isobel was thinking. What she meant was how many days before disintegration set in, before Nurse Rosemary's sparkling and mocking eyes hid a trace of strain, before Madeleine and Sylvie, still carefully avoiding one another as if one was holding a whip and the other doing a penance, found relief in a great quarrel. And after that would Kit have the strength to apply balm, to assure her that all would end well? No one would believe it, least of all herself, and she might be surrounded by one of those weeping Victorian scenes with everyone gathered and the bed in the centre, a wide nave filled with what in a few days would shrink to a casket. Her own control, too, was slipping.

'How much of me is left?' she said to Nurse Rosemary during the early morning's bed-straightening, before the tea was brought in a flowered cup.

'What do you mean?' Nurse Rosemary said, bending over, perhaps to conceal her face.

'My blood is awash with drugs, none of my organs is functioning naturally. I can still breathe and speak but that's all.'

On the sheet Isobel clenched her fist and then loosened it. It was the equivalent of preparing her face.

'I don't see how you can ask,' Nurse Rosemary said, pushing her fingers into the small of her back to show she was mortal. Isobel thought of uttering a small groan. 'Nothing is lost, don't you think? We don't own it but we don't lose it either.'

'You think there is still a child inside, a newborn baby still sleeping? The first and best sleep of all.'

But that was as far as Isobel got that morning, for it was time for an injection and then Kit came to check if she was up for visitors.

'Does anyone check with the Queen?' she asked rather tartly. 'Doesn't she have to stand for hours?' The injection was taking effect.

Over the next few days, as unconsciousness made itself felt, Isobel felt herself being colonised as surely as explorers in a new land raised flags and issued proclamations. No matter if the natives did not understand the language or a treaty was cobbled together by lamplight with a skinful of whisky. But she clung consciously to the idea of her first sleep in the world, to the little prepared bed a nurse had carried her to after she had left her mother's body and been washed and clothed. Later, she thought, as if it were a project, she might select other memories, separated from one another by the passage of years, and cling to them for the comfort they contained. Now she was hardly herself, despite Nurse Rosemary's confidence, she would look for the best she had been. How she had been that best remained a mystery; her part in it might have been small. And in the things she regretted and now had no time to examine the same tolerance might apply.

Kit was bending over her, stroking her hair back from her forehead. Nurse Rosemary had a towel in her hand. 'Don't,' she wanted to say to Kit, for it was no longer soothing. Then sleep came and she was back in her crib with its calico sides and baseboard and the mattress her mother had aired so religiously for months it smelled of the sun.

Isobel woke and there was a figure sitting in the visitor's chair beside the bed. How quickly the eye knew a shape was unfamiliar, a posture foreign. Sylvie was in the doorway, a guard waiting for her to wake.

It was Cora Taverner, her hands folded in her lap. Isobel saw she had taken pains, that her face was powdered; a scent drifted towards her like a chemical intimation of spring.

Isobel had the advantage of opening her eyes first. An enemy is a complete package, she thought, for she was refreshed by sleep, her injection had not yet worn off. And she had the advantage of being able to close her eyes at any time, severing the contact by a blink. At the same time she felt something more than pity: that this proud self-important delusional woman should have come to her for a last passage of arms. Under the sheets Isobel felt her weapons: her arms, pinioned by her side, might deflect an embrace. She might command more pillows, which Nurse Rosemary could bring. Any imperious gesture she would apologise for later. Surreptitiously—but Sylvie noticed—she stretched her legs and moved her toes. Wasted, she thought. How many they might have kicked or tripped, how salutary that might have been. Seat Isobel at a table again with a cascading white cloth and how many stumbles there might have been from a slender shod-foot shot forward. But only one talent had been perfected and employed: her intimate but faintly distant glance as she raised her wine glass to her lips to absolve herself of guilt.

Now Sylvie came forward and Isobel could see the relationship with her mother-in-law had changed. There was a pact between them, new minted, a novelty to both. This was to be concealed from her until the little scene was over. Swiftly Isobel closed her eyes to overcome a moment of panic and hurt. She bent over the child, Sylvie, again, and pressed against her not her own failing body but some kind of essence stronger even than the stiff watchful figure on the chair. It must be enough, she told herself before, after the deepest breaths she could manage, she opened her eyes for the scene.

'You're awake,' Sylvie said.

'Yes, darling. I'm awake.'

She seemed suddenly to be aware of everything, as if a shaft of light had appeared, like the criss-crossing searchlights of Twentieth Century Fox or Metro-Goldwyn-Mayer's roaring lion that had enchanted her and her brother when they sat, swinging their legs, in the worn-down seats in the cinema where mice scuttled across the stage.

Then there was a great deal of rustling; she drew her foot back under the table while behind her back chaos had broken out and a waiter was running; someone had gone down and a circle was forming which perfectly matched the round table.

But Isobel, while the voices floated overhead, remained calm.

'Do you think she saw me?' came a voice.

'I'm sure you were recognised,' came another.

'There'll be another opportunity. Now the ice is broken.'

It wasn't icy at all where Isobel was, which was odd because she was closing down. It was warm. So was Kit's hand when finally, like a heavy bird, it landed on hers.

Madeleine was found in a coffee shop, the morning paper open in front of her. When Kit appeared in the doorway her hand brushed her cup and the dregs fell on the face of a politician. She rose to her feet and followed her father into the street.

'Am I too late?' she asked.

'Yes,' he replied. 'But only if you think it is the end.'

She ran to keep up with him, attempted to draw him back by linking her arm through his. The arm that had supported hers was loose; she could feel the bone inside the sleeve.

'What painting will do for this?' she asked. 'What sculpture?'

The tears began to run down her face. A few puzzled looks were directed at them.

It's the least I can do, Madeleine thought. The very least.

They were caught in a machine. Why not draw the curtains and seal the doors? Sylvie drew up a timetable—all the tutorials she had organised made her surprisingly adept—and while Isobel stayed, and when she returned, no hour was passed alone in the room that was soon crowded with vases. A procession of vases filled the hall, the kitchen table and benches. Reaching up, Madeleine, still not meeting Sylvie's eyes or making a gesture, placed a wreath on top of the refrigerator.

Sylvie, with downcast eyes in case they thought she had done the baking, delivered food to a night shelter. She pressed a box of lamingtons on a bearded man. Kit thought the library should be a retiring room, and sobs were occasionally heard coming from it and once a crash as if books were being thrown.

Kit's biggest resentment was that others touched Isobel's forehead with their lips, that their stale or scented breath floated over a surface that was cleared, winnowed of all motion. Or that her makeup was commented on, her hair.

In her house Cora Taverner waited like a spider for the day of the funeral. She bought a new black hat, drycleaned her black woollen suit. Then she expected she would be drawn, like the last-minute arrival of an aristocrat, to the pew reserved for the family. This gesture would fall to Madeleine whose air of vagueness would prove useful.

A little army, Kit thought, looking across the row they made. Sylvie defiantly in red, everyone else in black. A line of archers could dispatch them; he saw the arrows rising and quivering in the dust-strobed light of the ancient church. And then Isobel's hand seemed to slip into his and they were walking again around the outdoor stage on the university lawn, on their first date when his hand had taken advantage of the darkness. Titania and Oberon and the ludicrous Bottom: all present and at the same time lost under the night sky. He would watch the funeral like a play, for Isobel had arranged it, in the same way she had arranged letters to each of them in thick creamy envelopes. There was even one for Nurse Rosemary. None of the contents were to be shared. His was still unopened.

Isobel had chosen the baroque music she loved, the music she had tried to explain to him: its bareness, like a visible heart pumping, unadorned, naked, as true as expression could be. If a string broke you would hear it; you would see it fluttering in the air while the music went on.

Among the tombstones Freddy was walking. He would appear on the steps as the coffin was borne down. The music floated towards him as he read a few inscriptions, compared the lifespan of a husband to a wife. The wife was usually at the bottom, the children crammed into the space that remained.

Madeleine, coming out into the sudden sunlight, blinking, fighting the urge to regard the light as an omen, was alarmed by the bulky figure that appeared at her side. Then she realised it was a customary gesture: he liked to appear silently in a doorway or disturb a dinner party with a provocative remark.

Some people have no sense of timing, Isobel had said to her once. Their lives are short of music.

Still she took the fool's lines from *Twelfth Night*, 'Come away, come away, death', and walked with him between the tilting headstones. They must have stood straight once; the rearing came later. Isobel had insisted on a tombstone, so singly or together there was a place to visit.

Sylvie's red and Cora's black made a painterly contrast in the dining room. Cora's manner was restrained, deferential. Side by side they poured cups of strong tea after whisky, brandy and port had been passed. A black forest of bodies.

'Are you Red Riding Hood?' someone, inebriated, asked. A little red lipstick was smeared on Sylvie's eye tooth where she had bitten her lip.

When the last visitor had gone Sylvie, Madeleine and Cora stood at the sink, washing glasses. Someone had poured too much detergent in and Sylvie scooped the foam in her hands like a votive offering. Then she plunged her hands back into the clear water and brought out a gold-rimmed shot glass. When they were finished, Madeleine reached out and untied the knot in Sylvie's apron.

Freddy, lying back in the bergère chair in the den, his feet on an embroidered ottoman, tipped the last golden drops of a Bushmills single malt down his throat. He had already been informed he was useless, but he knew it was simply a warning. He thought of all that might be required of him before the day ended. The reconciliatory lovemaking, in which, if it were permitted, he must hold back the slightest sign of his own need for comfort. He would remember Isobel who had looked at him like a judge.

For Ben there was a surprise in store. He had seen his mother home, reassuring her they were reconciled, that her presence—an exaggeration—had been well received. He wanted to caution her against haste, but given her nature he doubted she would listen.

Sylvie was still in the red dress when he let himself in. She was in the middle of the round carpet, turning slowly in a circle, the way a dervish might begin, though he had no experience of dervishes. She was bound to fall after so many brandies and then so many mixed dregs before washing up. From the doorway he had seen her head tipped back and a glass in each hand. He moved alongside her and caught her as she spun and then lost her footing and staggered towards their best easy chair. He fell into it first, thanking its good springs, catching her as she fell against his hip.

When, eventually, he stood, like one half of a water carrier with a shoulder yoke, and guided her towards the bed—tugging back the covers with his free hand—the twirling began again but with an embellishment, for clothes were discarded. Shoes first, earrings, necklace, the little fascinator with red feathers that had completed her outfit—even her head had stood out. The dress presented a problem: its zip descended further than Sylvie's hand could reach, however much she craned and twisted her back. Ben held her still, and the red dress slid from her or she slid from the red dress. And then Isobel was enfolded in it, a whole life of joys and disappointments, loss and longing, that could hardly be contained in a human frame. In one as frail as Sylvie Lehmann it was impossible. But to compensate she seemed to take something from the air around her, immediate things, like an aura, that her body touched. An exchange was taking place. She drew the energy she needed into her and bestowed it, so the process could continue, with him. He hesitated at first and then, whatever the cause—he knew he should not enquire—he joined her. He crushed her to him as if she were a boy—he had just enough control to spare her a little. His palm touched the sheet and he was amazed to find it was not grass and his hand came away clean.

·•⟩ ⟨•·

The others might go to the grave site but Kit went alone to the Pah homestead. He was first outside the vast doors studded with bolts to which countless layers of paint had been applied. Two years earlier they had been sanded and painted black. A few people joined him, greeted him in a slightly abashed way, as if art was a drug or they had come to secure a parking space. Early birds, Kit thought. They would have the rooms to themselves; they could have coffee while the queues were forming.

He sat in front of just one painting: *Garden Study* by Pat Hanly. There was a settle opposite, backless. He thought he could sit for half an hour. It would take a reverie for him to forget his aching muscles. The heart was a muscle, whichever way you looked at it. It began its clenching in the womb, and on the lungs' first breath it was allied until death. But none of this seemed real in the serene room with its long white walls and the dome over his head which someone had raised slightly so a breeze came through. He looked at the painting through blurred eyes. How had it been conceived? On what sort of day? It had the feeling of strong sunlight. Had there been a sketch first? It was entirely about nature and yet the artist was there. He doubted his own self would ever come together now: it would be particles and perceptions, and there would need to be a frame around them. Something baroque and heavy with geometric corner shapes and a thin coating of gilt.

Almost thirty minutes had passed when Kit rose, feeling his back clench. No more Isobel to lie against, no more other spine. He ordered coffee and sat on the veranda overlooking the sculpture garden. Children were running and touching bronze shapes; a docent had gathered a small crowd around her; phrases floated towards him. He thought he heard a date, a propitious year. If he had had the energy he could have stood on the outskirts, like an unwelcome visitor, and protested. As if a year in a human life could float clear of the dross, the dark moods, the near-failure even of a work that would later be considered seminal. What about the flu, he wanted to ask, the weeks shivering and sweating in a bed? But the docent was already leading her band along the path, her bright cap of hair gleaming in the sunlight; all that was missing was a jaunty umbrella.

The coffee took half an hour too: Kit had time to fill. He crumbled his lemon drizzle cake for a sparrow, scouting under his chair. Then, placing his hand on his back again, making a fist and rubbing it against his lowest vertebrae, he got up and walked towards the entrance.

Madeleine, walking between the soldiers' and settlers' graves with Freddy, had given him the answer that might have caused Madame Récamier to place her hand over her mouth as if in shock. It was an old feminine gesture of hers when someone bought a pile of novels, like the American who had taken ten Philip Roths, emptying half a shelf and leaving only the duplicates. Madame Récamier had glided to the till so she could receive him, hand over her mouth, for she was already making calculations. 'I'm being greedy,' the man said in an accent that sounded Texan. Long live greed, Madeleine thought to herself, quickly moving Thomas Pynchon and Wallace Stegner closer to cover the gap. And when the man had left with two carrier bags, after Madeleine's cheek had been kissed and brushed by his Texan moustache, Madame had kissed Madeleine too, two dry powdery kisses like stale madeleines.

'I will stay with my father,' Madeleine was saying. 'For now. I can't say for how long. Make any arrangement you like.'

She was looking down at the grave of a young boy called Edward. *Edward Fitzwilliam (Foxy) Beauchamp, 23 May 1911 – 1 April 1921. Our beloved Fox.*

Sylvie waited for the first cemetery visit to be over before she opened her envelope. She looked long and hard at the handwriting, trying to gauge its strength, its flow. Isobel would have parcelled out her energy, written on a series of good afternoons.

It was just a brief paragraph, followed by the flowing signature and a huge X.

Why, it read, *was the genuine tenderness of a loving grandmother any less satisfying than the tenderness of a mother?*

Isobel X

At the very bottom, in a smaller hand, since Isobel was a stickler for sources, Sylvie could just make out

*Philip Roth: *Nemesis*. Houghton Mifflin Harcourt, 2010.

Author photograph by Jane Dove Juneau

Elizabeth Smither has published eighteen collections of poetry and was New Zealand's poet laureate from 2001 to 2003. In 2004 she was awarded an honorary Doctorate of Literature from the University of Auckland, and in 2008 she received the Prime Minister's Award for Literary Achievement in Poetry. She has also published five novels and five short story collections, as well as journals and memoirs. Her poetry collection *Night Horse* won the Ockham New Zealand Book Award for Poetry in 2018.